THE LONDON TRILO

autumn
INFERNO

THE LONDON TRILOGY: BOOK II

autumn
INFERNO

DAVID MOODY

Author's note:
Although many of the locations featured in this
novel are real, I have taken fictional liberties with them.
This is a work of fiction, not a travel guide.
Please also note - 'The Highway' is the full name
of a street in London and should be capitalised as such.

First published in 2022 by Infected Books

A CIP catalogue record for this book
is available from the British Library

ISBN 978-1-7397535-1-1

Cover design by Craig Paton
www.craigpaton.com

www.davidmoody.net

www.lastoftheliving.net

www.infectedbooks.co.uk

DAY SEVENTY-TWO
MONUMENT BASE
TOWER PLACE – 7:00am

In the four weeks since the chaotic day that had brought this group together, the dead had advanced and blocked them in tight. There were thousands upon thousands of them, crammed up against each other and against the barricades that protected the living, and the pressure of their numbers had wedged them into position. Decaying flesh had seeped into wrinkles, folds, tears and open wounds like wet putty.

On the other side of the towering boundary walls, the group had had to shore-up their defences to protect the scrap of land they'd managed to hold onto around the Monument and the Tower of London. Once the perimeter had been sealed, the violence and bloodshed had, thankfully, stopped.

Until today.

The group was now a victim of its own success.

At more than three hundred and fifty strong, they were the biggest group of survivors for many miles, if not in the whole country. Those numbers meant they had relative strength and security but, Christ, that was a lot of mouths to feed. They hadn't had time to stockpile before locking down; the base had almost fallen as the last eighty or so folks had arrived. And though they'd done what they could to eke out their supplies for as long as possible, they'd known all along that this day was going to come. If it hadn't been today, it would inevitably have been tomorrow.

Having lost substantial swathes of land in those battles a month ago, they were now living on a sliver of space about half a square mile in area, a fraction of the size the bosses had originally envisaged. Claustrophobic and unsanitary, it was little better than the wastelands beyond the walls.

For now, the bulk of the dead were being held back by the barriers to the west and by an elevated and fortified section of railway line stretching from Fenchurch Street to Limehouse to the north. With the Thames to their south, that left only one logical direction in which the group could advance.

More than eighty volunteers gathered on the lawn in front of the Tower Hill Memorial in Trinity Square Gardens. The once well-tended grass was churned up and muddy, the memorial defaced with graffiti – poignantly scrawled outpourings of anger and grief. The volunteers were a motley bunch. Survival these days seemed random, arbitrary; the only thing these folks had in common was that they still had a pulse. They huddled close to each other because of the cold and listened as Dominic Grove addressed them.

'This is a big day. A *monumental* day. The work we're going to start this morning will make life much more comfortable for all of us. It's going to be hard, there's no disputing that, and dangerous too, but we all know that nothing we do from hereon in is going to be easy. Today we're taking our first steps towards carving out a safe future for ourselves.'

He paused, waiting for a reaction that didn't come.

'It's almost a month now since David, Marianne, and the others joined us, and we've all benefited from our increased numbers. Until now we've been focused on protecting this place and keeping it secure and on getting everyone settled in, but the time's come to start reclaiming some of what we've lost. We've already achieved a lot, but there's much more we need. Today, that work begins in earnest.

'I know this is a huge ask of all of you, but there really is no alternative. With increased numbers comes an increased need for food, water, clothing, medicines, and space. We're surrounded by a vast number of resources, and every scrap of it is ours for the taking. We just have to go and get it.

'Fighting's not in our nature, and I wish there was another way of doing this, but clearing the dead from Wapping and reclaiming the streets is our only option. We must take a stand against them. We have to forget who they used to be and focus on what they are now and the threat they present. We cannot allow the dead to dictate the way we spend the rest of our lives.

'Before we go out there today, I want you all to take a moment to think about how strong we are, both individually and collectively. Our ability to coordinate and communicate puts us at a clear advantage over our enemy. Sure, there are many thousands of them and only a few hundred of us, but we have the upper hand. We can do this, I know we can. It's going to be tough and it's going to take time, but we're going to take small steps every day beginning today to take back what's rightfully ours. Soon, all those small steps will add up to colossal strides.

'The place where we're gathered this morning is a monument to some of those who lost their lives in the first and second world wars. Take a moment to remember the sacrifices countless generations made to give us our freedoms. Although our world has changed beyond recognition, and the danger we're now having to deal with is very different from the threats that anyone before us had to face, but there's just as much at stake, perhaps more. For though they fought for Human liberty, we battle now for the very survival of our race. And we're not just doing this for the people who are here with us today, we're doing it for all those who will come after us. We do this for our children; we do this for our children's children. It's no exaggeration to say that groups like ours may be all that's left of Humanity; ensuring our future is an unparalleled responsibility that all of us here must now share.

'Our group includes people from all walks of life. We represent many cultures and many beliefs. We have an enormous range of abilities and capabilities, skills both honed and yet undiscovered. Collectively, we represent an inexhaustible store of knowledge and experience, all of which is going to be vital to rebuilding our world from the ashes of what's been lost.

'So, I want you to look out for each other today. Like I said, we may have many differences, but there's one thing that every single one of us has in common... we're *survivors*.'

Dominic paused, almost overcome by the gravity of his own words. Sanjay leant across and whispered to David Shires. 'Bloke's a fucking twat. Do you think he actually believes any of that horseshit?'

David laughed. 'If he does, he's the only one.'

If Dominic was disappointed by the reaction of the crowd, he didn't let it show. 'I'm going to hand over now to Piotr who will talk us through the detail of this morning's operation.'

Dominic stood down; Piotr stepped up. The difference in their styles was notable. Where Dominic took his time and waxed lyrical, Piotr didn't.

'We secured almost a mile of Cable Street at the beginning of all of this, when we blocked the gaps under the train line.' He pointed towards the main roads as he spoke. 'Over there is East Smithfield. It runs parallel with Cable Street and is clear as far as the junction with Vaughan Way, Dock Street, and The Highway. The buildings in the area north of East Smithfield have already been stripped. Today we continue east along The Highway and clear another half mile, as far as Cannon Street Road. North of that is a valuable area that we'll then focus on clearing.'

Dominic couldn't help himself butting in. 'Piotr's right, it'll give us access to some prime real estate. There are several tower blocks that we think will be easier to clear out than the lower-level buildings we're used to, and there's a lot of green space that we can use for recreation, and, in due course, farming. There's a school, hundreds of individual residences... it'll take some time for us to secure the area completely, but the potential rewards make all that effort worthwhile.'

His enthusiasm wasn't matched by any of the faces looking back at him. Piotr, too, appeared unimpressed and he turned back towards the crowd. 'Listen up. This is important.'

Everyone was already quiet, but now the group became pin-drop silent.

'These are the rules. First, every one of you is a fighter, and everybody goes out there with a weapon. Second, you follow instructions, because if any of you go rogue, it puts *everyone* at risk. Third, you forget that those things out there used to be like us. If they remind you of your mother or your mate or your missus or your kid, or, God help us they are your kid, it still doesn't matter. They're not human. They are our enemy. If we don't destroy them, they will destroy us.'

THE BATTLE OF WAPPING

They may have looked like an army as they marched along Tower Hill together, but most of them felt woefully underprepared. David Shires was near the back, cursing himself for volunteering but knowing he'd had no alternative. It just wasn't in his nature to sit back and let others take the risks on his behalf. Also, he'd wanted to see for himself how bad things were out there. But now his nerves were clanging, and he wished he could trade places with someone who'd stayed behind. He was a reluctant combatant at the best of times, and today was far from the best of times. They came to a halt a short distance from the junction of East Smithfield and The Highway. David was sandwiched between Gary Welch on one side and Sanjay on the other, bracing himself against the crisp, icy-cold wind of the dry, mid-November morning. He didn't think he'd ever felt more out of place in his life.

'You're shivering,' Gary said. 'Nerves or cold?'

'Both. You?'

'Shitting bricks. I don't know about you, Dave, but when I come up against those dead fuckers and I'm not expecting it, I can cope. It's the anticipation that gets to me, all this waiting around. Puts the fear of god into me, it really does.'

'I'm the same,' Sanjay said. 'It amplifies the nerves, makes everything feel a thousand times worse. Reacting is one thing, thinking about how you're going to have to react is something else altogether.'

'Still, we'll let that lot take the brunt of it, eh? They're the pros, apparently.' Gary gestured towards the large pack of fighters ahead of them, closer to the frontline. Some of them appeared disturbingly keen, chomping at the bit to release weeks of pent-up tension by battering the dead. There was nothing professional about them; many of them just looked the part because they'd taken the initiative and helped themselves to armour and weapons from the relics on display in the Tower of London.

'They've definitely got the kit for it,' David said, looking down at his own gear. His makeshift protection had been fashioned from reclaimed scrap metal, fastened in position with wire and rope. Gary was wearing a breastplate cut from the bonnet of a green Toyota, held in place by gaffer tape wrapped around the arms of his jacket. Most people wore PPE; everyone was ordered to wear at least one item of fluorescent clothing to distinguish themselves from the decrepit masses they were about to wade into. Some people had hardhats taken from the corpses they'd found near construction sites, but most were going into battle wearing only goggles or safety glasses and facemasks to protect them from the inevitable noxious splashbacks. They were armed with crude but effective weapons. David had a metal railing from a fence, sharpened to a point; Sanjay carried a claw hammer in one hand and a dustbin lid shield in the other.

'You wouldn't think it, looking at me now,' Gary said, 'but I used to do a lot of running, back in the day. Three London Marathons, I did.'

David was impressed. 'I watched it on TV, and that was tiring enough. So, what are you saying? You going to make a run for it?'

He laughed. 'Not at all. I was just gonna say that I feel like I used to on the start line, waiting for the off. Frigging horrible, it was. No matter how much training you'd done, you never felt ready. You knew you had hours of pain ahead of you.'

'And that's what you think we've got coming?'

'No, mate, not hours. We've got days of pain ahead. Weeks. Months, even. The races I used to do had a finish line, but I can't see where this one ends.'

Sanjay butted in. 'And in marathons you didn't have thousands of people coming the other way, all trying to kill you.'

'Correct. Anyway, all I'm saying is that once that barrier's opened, this is gonna hurt.'

'Great. You're a real inspiration, Gary,' David grumbled.

'I aim to please.'

Marie Hannish, who worked in PR before the world had fallen apart, was standing on the other side of Gary, wearing tin-can armour and wielding a hockey stick. She just looked at him. 'Have you ever thought about becoming a motivational speaker?' she asked, deadpan.

'No.'

'Good. Don't.'

In front of David, Holly Wilkins appeared to laugh nervously. She'd been billeted on the same floor of the hotel as he had, and they'd left the building together this morning. When she looked around, he saw that she was crying. 'It'll be alright, Hol,' he told her, resting a hand on her shoulder.

'You think?'

'Oh, sure,' he said, and he pulled her close and squeezed. 'We'll look out for each other, okay?'

She just nodded, far from convinced.

Paul Duggan, one of Piotr's chiefs, climbed onto the roof of one of the two trucks they'd parked back-to-back across the street, blocking the full width of The Highway. The nervous chatter in the ranks was silenced because everyone knew the time had finally come. The floodgates were about to open.

Paul kept his back to the others and looked out over the dead hordes. Directly below, a couple of them lifted their ravaged faces and glared up at him with rheumy eyes. Most remained slumped forward against those in front, an immobile plug of diseased flesh, just waiting. The brightness of the morning allowed him to see everything in detail. He thought a little autumn fog might have made the view a bit more palatable. As it was, the queue of death stretched so far into the distance that he couldn't see the end. The most disconcerting thing was the movement. Whereas they frequently wandered the desolate streets, today they were all moving in this direction, filling in the gaps.

The sound of approaching engines.

The crowd of fighters on the street parted to allow the well-used backhoe loader through. It had proved equally adept at moving rot as rubble. It rumbled into position, flanked by a tractor and a pick-up truck, both of which had seen better days.

David kept hold of Holly, but he found himself on the opposite side of the road to Gary and Sanjay now. He watched them across the gap and wondered if they felt as absolutely fucking terrified as he did. It was the uncertainty, as well as the apprehension, he decided. What were they about to face? How aggressive would the dead be after all this time? This was going to be their first direct confrontation since... well, since forever. He realised this was the first time he'd gone out into the wilds with the sole aim of wiping out as many of those diseased fuckers as possible. Individually, he knew they were nothing, but collectively... well, that was a different matter altogether. He started doing a few pointless back-of-a-fag-packet calculations in his head as a distraction. *If we can get rid of an average of fifty each, and if the backhoe loader can wipe out several hundred, then maybe we have half a chance.* It was only ever going to be half a chance because he knew that even if they hacked down around a thousand of them today, the same number would be lining up to take them on tomorrow. He tried every tactic he could think of to remain positive. *Don't think about them in individual numbers. Think about it in terms of ground gained. Reclaim a few metres every day, that's all it's going to take. Step by step by small, incremental step.*

The moment had arrived.

Alfonso Morterero was an HGV driver from Bilbao who'd found himself stuck in central London on the day the world ended. His English was limited (but rapidly improving), but Alf, as he'd inevitably become known, didn't shy away from taking responsibility. Any opportunity to drive and he was there, volunteering before most people had even heard the call. He climbed up into the cab of one of the blocking trucks then hung out of the open door, looking up at Paul and waiting for the signal.

Thumbs up.

Alfonso had kept the truck well maintained; he'd always known it would need to be moved at some point. The engine started first time, and he glanced across and saw the corpses immediately reacting to the noise. A wave of excited movement rippled through the mindless swarm. Alfonso turned the wheel sharp and drove along Dock Street, opening up The Highway.

For a moment that seemed to last an eternity, nothing happened. The first few rows of dead creatures, for so long pressed up against the side of the truck and compacted in place by the ceaseless weight of thousands more behind, initially remained rigid. They were stuck in place, brittle bones interlocked, glued together with dried out decay. From his position, David noticed signs of movement along the fleshy dam. A few slight wobbles and vibrations, then parts of it began to rock back and forth, the pressure increasing. A couple of seconds longer and it gave way, sending a lumpy tide of once human slurry gushing across the street. The fighters who were furthest forward scrambled back. Still on top of the other truck, Paul Duggan yelled at them to hold their positions.

After the initial flood had subsided, the dead began to advance.

The first of them appeared barely human, deformed by the pressures being exerted on the front of the pack. Everything was wrong about the horrific, dripping monsters that lurched forward. One was a barrel shaped torso on spindly legs, both arms torn off, long gone. The next appeared to have its head on sideways; its neck was broken, but decapitation had been averted by the few stubborn sinews that had refused to tear. Another one had originally been two. With a pair of ribcages intertwined like latticework, the combined monstrosity walked crablike with two heads, four arms, four legs, and a single intent.

A guy standing behind David ripped off his facemask and

vomited over his boots. The acidic smell was barely perceptible over the stench of everything else.

Paul signalled for the backhoe loader to move up. Kevin Greatrex was the only one who ever drove the machine. He'd got hold of the keys when they'd first found it and had refused to let them go. Now he carried them with him everywhere, even slept with them in his hand because the digger was his protection, his suit of armour. It enabled him to exact long overdue revenge on the dead without too much personal risk. He usually found the destruction therapeutic, but right now he'd have happily given up his seat to anyone who asked.

Here goes everything.

Kevin accelerated and dropped the digger scoop. It scraped along the road, filling the air with ugly noise, making him the focus of everything. He levelled off his speed slightly, aiming for the sweet spot between control and carnage, then ploughed into the hordes head-on.

The tractor and pick-up truck followed in the wake of the powerful digger, veering off in either direction to obliterate even more of the dead on either side. Between them, they covered almost the entire width of the road and drove forward in a line, substantially reducing the flow of corpses that might otherwise have broken through.

Behind the three vehicles, the first of the troops were dispatched into the chaos. The undead proved frustratingly difficult to deal with because of their unpredictability and miserable physical state. Hardly any of this first wave had enough strength to stay standing. Similarly, it was hard for many of the fighters to remain upright as they waded through the semi-liquid filth. It was slippery as a slick out there, and they had only the remains of corpses and each other to hold onto for support.

David was holding back, watching the madness unfold. Christ, all they'd done was open one side of a road junction, but from where he was standing, it was as if they'd prised open the gates of Hell.

Standing above them, Paul was far from impressed. 'Fight, you fuckers!' he yelled, as if there was an alternative.

As the people all around him began to move, David too started to run forward. The first body came at him and he skewered it with his railing, effortlessly driving the spike into its chest then flipping it over and slamming it down onto the road. He stamped hard on its upturned face then yanked free his spear. It had been weeks since he'd seen the dead up close like this, and the degree to which they'd deteriorated was astonishing. The creature under his boot was unrecognisable. He couldn't tell if it had been male or female, young or old... hell, he was having trouble believing the damn thing had ever been human.

No time to waste. Straight onto the next.

David lunged at the next cadaver but slipped in the mire and went over. He struggled to get back up, the treads of his boots already clogged with filth. Someone smacked the corpse he'd been aiming for over the head with a baseball bat, then grabbed his arm and hauled him upright. It was Holly.

'You're not allowed to get hurt; you've got my back, remember?' she said, managing half a smile.

'Got it. Thanks, Hol.'

They both selected their next targets and lashed out. Holly split another skull with a hollow-sounding thunk while David forced the tip of his railing up through the chin of another ghoul and scrambled what was left of its brain.

Then the next.

And the next.

And the next.

The backhoe loader and its entourage continued to roll forward, their speed now substantially reduced. Agile dead were crawling all over the machines, others were crushed under wheels and caterpillar tracks, ground into the tarmac. David and Holly fought as a pair behind the tractor, back-to-back, defending the bubble of space around them. David tried to concentrate on each individual corpse that stumbled into range, but it was hard not to be distracted by the madness unfolding in his periphery. The brutality of what he was witnessing, what he was a part of, was sobering. Beheadings. Disembowelments. Amputations. The slicing, hacking, ripping, tearing, shredding of flesh. As deserving as the dead surely were of all of this, the savagery of the fighters was astonishing. He remembered what Piotr had said about these undead monsters being no longer human, but from where he was standing, no one on the battlefield appeared civilised today.

He sensed that Holly was struggling. Poor kid. He booted away a half-height corpse that was crawling towards him then turned to check if she was okay. She'd been wearing a hardhat and glasses but had discarded both. Her eyes were wide and filled with fear, her pale face streaked with grubby blood. 'Can't do this,' she said.

'You can,' he told her. 'We have to.'

She shook her head. She was breathing too fast. Panic attack. David held her upright when her legs threatened to buckle and locked his eyes on hers. 'You've got this, Hol. Breathe slowly.'

'I'm okay,' she said, but she wasn't.

'You will be. Just take your time. It's the sudden start that's done it. Weeks of doing nothing, now everything's gone batshit crazy.'

She nodded.

'Keep fighting!' Paul Duggan yelled. David looked back and saw he was still up on the roof of the truck.

'Hark at him, telling us what to do. Here's us up to our necks in shite, and he hasn't even got his boots dirty yet. Cheeky fucker.'

Holly smiled. That was progress.

As the fighting continued, so the first attacking wave moved deeper into the dead. Consequently, the area around David and Holly was now relatively clear, though the ground remained covered with body parts and oily gore. A second tranche of people had arrived to mop up the remains. These folks were equally keen to do their bit, but generally older or carrying an injury or otherwise less physically able. They scoured the filth on their hands and knees and used kitchen knives, garden trowels, screwdrivers, and all manner of other implements to put the twitching dead out of their misery. A swift stab to the temple usually did it; enough trauma to inflict sufficient damage on what was left of the creatures' mushy brains and stop them functioning. Their arrival was a welcome distraction. It gave Holly time to compose herself.

'You good now?' David asked, and he could see that she was.

'I'm good.'

'Sure?'

'Yep.'

'Ready for more?'

'I'm ready,' she said, and they marched on together.

It felt like they'd walked miles, but the backhoe loader had only managed to advance some fifty metres from the junction with East Smithfield, where the battle had begun. David found the gruff noise it made strangely cathartic, a huge *fuck you* to the undead. He could hear another sound now, yet more vehicles were approaching, blasting their horns to alert those clearing the streets. David and Holly shifted out of the way as two industrial-sized lawnmowers drove forward. They'd been cannibalised and modified by the petrolheads and mechanics in the group's makeshift chop shop. Mowing blades were replaced with sheets of metal that acted as rudimentary ploughs, churning up tonnes of flesh and offal and dumping the resultant gunk into the gutters.

The frontages of buildings, metal railings, and the hoardings around never-to-be-completed construction sites had largely kept the bulk of the dead channelled forward, but there were junctions being uncovered now which needed to be blocked. More cars were driven out along The Highway – expendable, battered old wrecks that barely limped along but which were useful as mobile blockades. The driver of a wrecked Ford Focus overtook one of the lawnmower-ploughs then accelerated into the writhing chaos at the mouth of Virginia Street. He abandoned his car at an angle, straddling the gap, then scrambled out with hardly a second to spare before another Ford drove into the back of his, completely blocking the side-street. As the way ahead was secured, the trucks that had originally been used to block the width of The Highway were moved up, ready to take up new positions further east.

After a month of enforced inactivity, the frantic movement all around was overwhelming. David was also struggling to take it all in, and now it was Holly keeping him moving in the right direction. It was the intense physicality of battle that had caught him so off-guard. He was sweating profusely under many protective layers, and his arms felt heavy as lead. He couldn't stop fighting, not even for a second, because, despite destroying a swathe of corpses already, they hadn't made the slightest dent in their numbers. The dead were uniform in both their grotesqueness and their limitless aggression. There was barely anything left of some of them – hardly any meat left on their bones – and yet they continued to attack as if the battle had only just begun.

David swung around and skewered one through the eye then drove the metal spike through the throat of another that Holly had tackled to the ground. He twisted the spike, moving it back and forth, back and forth, until he'd separated the dead thing's skull from its spinal cord with a sickening pop. He looked around, trying to orientate himself, but didn't have time to focus before yet another staggering, stick-man cadaver came straight at him, arms outstretched. He lanced it on the tip of his spike, hefted it up, then smashed it against a building site hoarding.

Then, finally, another few seconds of space. Holly caught up with him and they leant against each other, exhausted. The fighting continued up ahead. 'Look at them, Dave,' she said. 'They're actually enjoying this.'

She was right. There were cheers, shouts of encouragement, and whoops of delight as bodies were battered and broken. Two men were keeping score against each other, racing first to fifty. David watched Lisa Kaur and her partner Richard Finnegan fighting ferociously alongside each other. They were both in their mid-twenties and in good shape. He often saw them exercising together around the grounds of the Tower, and he envied their physicality. The lack of food and the group's desperate situation apart, they were otherwise at their peak, and they made the killing look effortless. It made him feel double his age. It also made him wonder what kind of a future these people had. Christ, at their age he'd still been spending much of his time in the pub, avoiding any responsibility for as long he could get away with it. The contrast with these kids was sobering.

His thoughts were interrupted by more movement. A third wave of people had been sent out from the base. These folks were cleaning up, trying to make each metre of reclaimed land useable again. Wrapped up in many layers of protective gear, they shovelled slurry from the surface of the road and loaded body parts into barrows. The remains of the dead were piled up in immense, foul-smelling heaps, where they would be left to dry out then incinerated. It was a technique that had proved useful previously: mass cremation on an industrial scale. The bodies were so much easier to deal with once they'd been reduced to ash. Less bulk. Less risk of disease.

David was conscious that he and Holly were the only ones standing still in a sea of movement. 'We should get back to it,' he told her.

'I guess so.'

'Are you sure you're okay?'

'I'm not sure any of us are okay anymore.'

'Fair point,' he agreed, and they waded back into battle.

3

Several hours in now, and the stop-start reclamation of The Highway had continued at a decent pace. Cannon Street Road, the street they needed to take between The Highway and Cable Street, was finally in sight. Equally important was the discovery of a half-full fuel tanker in the frozen traffic queue on the approach to a petrol station. This unexpected haul of fuel was a heck of a bonus, and a couple of mechanics had already been summoned from base to try and get the behemoth vehicle started and driven back. Piotr had sent Chapman, another trusted aide, to coordinate efforts, such was the importance of the find.

The clearance operation continued while the logistics of moving the tanker were explored. The backhoe loader and its companion vehicles, along with a pack of some thirty fighters, continued to push back the dead tide. The road-blocking trucks were parked up a way back to provide additional cover.

Running parallel with Cannon Street Road was Crowder Street. It was accessed from Cable Street, and a dead-end meant that, while it didn't fully reach The Highway, it served a similar purpose. Gary had found himself waiting for orders a short distance back from the frontline, and it occurred to him that they could save time and effort if they stopped sooner and used Crowder Street as the eastern boundary of their reclamation efforts today. He hunted out Paul Duggan and put his proposal to him. 'Look, Paul, we're better off just stopping here. It'll save us a load more effort for very little gain.'

'What do you mean?'

He gestured for Paul to follow him through to the end of Crowder Street. 'If we stop and firm up the blockade across The Highway here, we'll have access to the frontages of all the buildings that Dominic wanted. If we keep going to Cannon Street Road, it's going to take a shedload more effort and all we'll gain is access to the backs of the same buildings and a bit of grassland behind them. I really think we should stop here for today.'

Paul took a moment to weigh up their options. 'I see what you're saying. It makes sense.'

'Good. We can get the trucks parked up across the road here, and that'll be job done for today.'

'I'll need to check first.'

And before Gary could object, Paul called Chapman over and explained. Chapman shook his head. 'No way. Piotr says we keep going.' He gestured towards a formidable looking block of flats and maisonettes that appeared to stretch along nearly the entire length of Crowder Street, a brutalist concrete wedge. 'That's Brockmer House. Piotr told me he wants it secured, front and back. It's strategically important, he said.'

Gary couldn't help himself. 'Strategically important? Are you fucking serious?'

'According to Dominic there's about seventy apartments in there. There will be food and supplies in each one of them. So yes, it's strategically important. Get it done.'

No negotiation. Conversation over. Chapman walked back towards the tanker, pausing only when a lone corpse slipped through the defensive line and came towards him. He floored it with a single punch to what was left of its face.

Paul slapped the side of the nearest truck and woke Alfonso who, incredibly, had been napping. 'Move up,' he shouted. 'Final push for the day.'

David and Holly were fighting near the back of the group again, dealing with the stragglers that had escaped the backhoe loader and other vehicles that were continuing to nudge through the crowds up ahead, inching towards the finishing line at Cannon Street Road. It reminded David of another running analogy Gary had shared earlier. He'd been talking about how, when he'd been racing, no matter how hard he'd run or how knackered he was, when the home straight appeared he always managed to get a second wind. David wasn't feeling it. Just a few more metres left to claw back from the dead today, but he was struggling to keep going. They'd discovered a branch of McDonald's adjacent to the petrol station. 'Come and hide in there with me, Hol! I'll treat us both to a burger,' he shouted.

'Twenty chicken nuggets please,' she shouted back. 'Used to love my nuggets after a night on the lash.'

David swung his railing around and almost lopped the head off another dripping, scarecrow-like monster. He looked up at the grime-covered golden arches and felt an aching sadness, bordering on disbelief. Sadness because it reminded him of everything he'd lost, of tea-time treats for the kids back home in Ireland; disbelief because it was becoming increasingly hard to hold onto memories of the world before all of this had happened. It was hard to imagine there'd ever been a time when they'd been able to move around without fear, a time when food and drink and anything else they needed had been available, close at hand, and with the minimum of effort.

The backhoe loader had finally reached Cannon Street Road. Kevin turned right and accelerated up towards Cable Street, heading home. Alfonso and the driver of the other truck moved their vehicles up to block The Highway on the other side of Cannon Street Road. The bastardised lawnmowers continued to churn through the hacked-up remains of the rotting population of this part of London, and David turned away as they drove past him in parallel, spraying him with blood and filling the air with their abrasive twin noise. Once they'd passed and followed the backhoe loader up Cannon Street Road, it became much quieter, but not quiet enough. Not as quiet as it should have been. David could hear something else, and he crossed the road to investigate.

'Problem?' Marie Hannish asked, concerned. He hadn't seen her since first thing, and it took a couple of seconds for him to recognise her through the gore.

'Maybe. I'm not sure.'

He could hear a dull banging noise, a constant patter of thumps and thuds coming from somewhere around the petrol station forecourt and the McDonald's drive thru lane. Other people heard it too.

'Did they send someone over there to clear those buildings out?' Holly asked.

David shook his head. The noise they could hear had nothing to do with the living. The tall wooden fence to the rear of McDonald's and the petrol station was being battered by a glut of furious corpses trapped behind. The panels were beginning to sag and separate, and he could see the dead crowding forward. It looked like an unfortunate coincidence; dumb fuckers had been trying to get to the source of all the noise and had got themselves trapped. They'd been whipped into a frenzy by the activity along The Highway and were stuck, those at the front unable to go anywhere because of the mob that had followed. David was only watching for a second, but it was long enough to realise that a substantial part of the fence had been weakened by the combined weight of the dead pressed against it. It wasn't going to take much more for them to bring it down.

The mechanics got the engine of the fuel tanker started at the worst possible moment. The driver revved the motor hard, keen to keep it running after weeks of inactivity, then blasted the horn to get people out of the way. He swung the nose of the tanker around in a tight arc, crossing the forecourt, abandoned the foot soldiers, and drove back down The Highway towards home.

It was like a slow-motion nightmare, inevitable and unstoppable. The sudden crescendo of noise caused an equally sudden swell of movement, and the weakened section of the fence collapsed with staggering ease. A swarm of newly freed corpses tripped into the open, gravitating towards exhausted fighters who'd thought their day's work was done.

'*Seriously?*' Marie said.

'Keep fighting,' Paul Duggan shouted. 'Let those fuckers through now and we'll lose everything we've fought for today.'

He was right. It had only been a couple of seconds since the fence had gone down, but already there was a wall of angry dead flesh coming at them. David watched his co-fighters wearily pick up their weapons and ready themselves for more conflict. Everything about their demeanour had changed since their first encounters with the enemy this morning. Back then, they'd been raring to go, eager to start battling. Now, though, many people were simply too tired to keep going. They were holding back, waiting for the dead to come to them instead of taking the initiative. In shocking contrast, these corpses were moving with just as much speed and unnatural intent as ever. They never got tired, never gave up. There were scores of them coming, and through a gap in the chaos David could see thousands more filling the streets behind, ready to pour through.

'Stop them!' Paul screamed, and he launched himself at the nearest rancid creature. More people forced themselves to move, but many others remained frozen to the spot, unable to keep going.

Holly stood her ground. 'There are too many. We'll never clear all of them. We're trying to fight a war with bits of fence and baseball bats, for crying out loud.'

Someone shoved her forward and David lost sight of her in the unfolding madness. It was like a medieval conflict, and what was left of their relatively small army was now hopelessly outnumbered. Everywhere he looked he could see more of the dead being hacked down, but there were endless others waiting to join the fray. David thought they'd been lucky so far. It was good fortune that only part of the fence had toppled, leaving the bulk of the dumb dead stuck in a bottleneck of their own making. He heard someone yell for runners to get a message to base and get more drivers out here to plug the hole, but they couldn't afford to wait. Everyone was fighting now. Even those folks who'd just been out here to clean up the mess had been dragged into the hand-to-hand, everyone doing whatever they could to hold back the dead tide.

Except they weren't, were they?

They weren't thinking, they were just reacting.

All around him, David saw people attacking individual corpses. Their reactions were understandable and instinctive, adrenalin-fuelled responses, but it wasn't the solution. They didn't need to wipe out all the thousands of corpses being drawn here by the noise, they just needed to block the fucking hole in the fence and stop more of them getting through. And they couldn't afford to wait for reinforcements, because other fence panels were beginning to tip forward.

There were cars on the forecourt of the garage that were being ignored. They'd not moved for months, but that didn't matter because they didn't need to drive them, just shift them. David ran across the street, shoving shambling corpses away as they came at him, ducking and weaving through the individual scraps unfolding all around. He dove for the nearest car – didn't even pause to check what it was – and smashed through the driver's window with the tip of his fence spike. He reached in and opened the door, shoved the rags and bones of the long dead driver out of the way, then released the handbrake. He paused for an instant, startled by the sudden fury of two thrashing dead kids strapped in on the backseat, then started to push. The car's steering was stiff, the wheel locked, but it was pointing in the right general direction, and even if he didn't fully block the hole in the fence, he'd at least make it harder for some of the dead to get through.

It was a start.

'Get out of the way!' he yelled as the car finally began to gain momentum, and, despite the chaos everywhere, people reacted to his voice and jumped clear. Marie Hannish cursed him in surprise then thanked him once she saw what he was doing.

Others began to follow his lead, and by the time David had found another car to move, he could see six more vehicles being steered towards the breach. A knackered old van brushed past him with four people pushing and a woman behind the wheel, steering a path through the confusion. She tried the ignition on a whim, and it caught. She blasted the horn repeatedly, then accelerated and thumped the van's snub nose into the glut of advancing dead flesh. She scrambled clear just before another car collided with the side of the van, wedging it in place.

Vehicles were coming from all angles now, rolling at various speeds from various directions, all converging on the same general area. They crushed scores of bodies. Others were trapped between the wrecks. Paul Duggan ordered another attack, invigorated by the success of their improvised defence. With renewed energy they dealt with any rogue cadavers that slipped through, but the battle was far from being won. The army of the dead had been slowed but not beaten. If anything, the battle unfolding around the fallen section of fence was whipping them up; the harder the people from the Monument pushed forward, the harder the dead fought back, their appetite for confrontation insatiable.

David was relieved when he heard more engines close behind. More vehicles were approaching from the base, and Kevin Greatrex was back with the backhoe loader.

A mechanic got another car started and raced it across the fuel station forecourt, swerving through the ongoing fighting and other wrecks, then drove through a newly opened gap and carried on out into the crowds of dead. He carved a clear line through the corpses as if he'd driven through a field of unharvested corn then scrambled out through the sunroof and set light to the interior before racing back to safety. By the time he'd reached the fuel station, the car was completely ablaze, dirty black smoke belching into the air. With the hordes temporarily distracted, Kevin began to shift some of the other wrecked vehicles into position, building up a makeshift wall in front of the fallen fence.

Paul relaxed. 'That should hold it.'

'For now,' David said.

'I saw what you did back there. That was quick thinking.

23

Thanks.'

'It's the only quick thing I've managed all day,' David replied, self-deprecating. 'That's the advantage of being old and unfit. Things look different when you're standing on the fringes, trying to get your breath back.'

'Just take the compliment; it was a smart move. We're safe, thanks to you.'

'You reckon? Did you see those bloody things out there? Doesn't matter what you do to them... there's never any hesitation, no emotion, never a thought for self-preservation... they just exist to attack, and the sooner we learn to deal with that, the better.'

He started walking back to base but stopped when he saw Sanjay crouching over a body. He gently rolled the corpse onto its back, and David saw that it was Marie. She had a puncture wound in her belly and her neck had been slashed. Her blood was vivid red, contrasting against the gallons of dark, stinking muck that covered the battlefield.

'We need to find out who did this,' Sanjay said, furious.

'It doesn't matter,' David sighed.

'How can you say that? It's Marie, for fuck's sake.'

'I know. It's the price of war I guess, Sanj, as shitty as that sounds.'

'Are you serious?'

'Sadly, yes. Whoever did this probably didn't even realise. This world makes no sense anymore. There's no rhyme or reason... It's shit and it hurts, but that's just how things are now. We're not soldiers, you and me, and we never will be. Everyone's just doing the best they can. Let's get Marie home. We'll show her a little respect and say a few words. That's the best we can do.'

4

People worked well into the night, scavenging through several of the smaller buildings that had been reclaimed during the day's operation and picking through the bones of the vehicles on the streets. The small army of folks transported their hauls back in carts and barrows, then dumped everything in the atrium of Tower Place. Mihai Ardelean coordinated the unpacking, sorting, grading, and storage of everything. Clothes, tools, medicines, food, drink... it was a promising start. It augured well for when the real work started tomorrow.

Most of the buildings that lined this stretch of road were apartment blocks, many of them were never occupied, their construction barely complete. There was another fuel station which had been overlooked during the height of the fighting, and Vicky, Ruth, and Selena had arrived to strip the kiosk of anything of value. The glass and chrome door had stuck in its frame, but Ruth managed to get it open with a couple of shoves. She disappeared inside to deal with the thrashing remains of a lone member of staff trapped in a room out back, ending its dogged resistance with a swift stab of a screwdriver through its temple. 'All yours,' she said, and Vicky and Selena disappeared inside. Ruth frisked the corpse for anything useful, found nothing, then dumped it on one of the bonfires burning along The Highway.

They propped the door of the kiosk stockroom open to let in some light and the three of them began emptying the shelves. Ruth heard the hiss of a bottle of Coke being opened and looked around. Selena was hiding behind the propped door, guzzling the drink. 'Are you stealing Mihai's stock?' she said with mock disapproval. 'I'll have to let Dominic know about this.'

'Spoils of war,' Selena said, laughing, and she crammed a bar of chocolate into her mouth.

Ruth carried another load out to Vicky. 'She's in there nicking food, little madam.'

'I know. I told her to. Have you seen her? Kid's like a stick insect. It's probably not doing her any good eating all that sugar and crap, but it's better than nothing.'

'Tell me about it. I'd kill for something fresh, you know? Can't remember the last time I ate a vegetable that wasn't canned. I'll be eating shoots and leaves at this rate. And I'm not even joking.'

Vicky was acutely aware of her own weight loss. She could count every rib. Her leggings were loose. Who the hell ever had baggy leggings, for crying out loud?

'Wish I could lose weight,' Ruth said, watching her. 'I hardly eat anything, but I'm still the size of a house.'

'Better than being scrawny as hell, like me.'

'I think you look good.'

'I'm wasting away,' Vicky said, and she went back to work.

The light was fading fast. Between them, they finished clearing the kiosk and piled everything up at the side of the road to be transported back to base. It was a good haul, one of the best of the day. Ruth checked the cars on the forecourt while they waited for someone to bring a cart across. Mark Desai, a strip of a lad who spent most of his days running between different folks and passing on messages, raced over to them, breathless. 'Mihai's sending one of the forklifts down for this lot,' he said, hands on his knees, gasping for breath. 'He says you're to wait with the stash, Ruth, so no one helps themselves.'

'Great.'

Selena was cold and walked back to base with Mark. Vicky stayed to keep Ruth company. They sat next to each other on the low brick wall bordering the forecourt and waited for the forklift.

As the sun sank below the horizon, the brightness of the body part bonfires appeared to intensify. It was as if they were sucking in the light, the rest of the world becoming darker around them. Vicky checked no one was watching, then opened a packet of cigarettes and lit up. She offered one to her friend. Ruth declined. 'No thanks. Bad for your health.'

Ruth watched Vicky as she took a long draw on the cigarette, held the smoke, then gently exhaled. 'You never told me you smoked.'

'I gave up years ago. Didn't realise how much I'd missed it.'

'Strange time to start again.'

'Best time, if you ask me.'

'It was awful out here today.'

'I heard. I stayed back at the hotel. I've got this cough I can't shift.'

'And you think starting smoking again is going to help?'

Vicky managed half a smile. 'I just thought that, as we're dealing with an enemy that reacts to sound, the last thing you need is some idiot on your side having a coughing fits every couple of minutes.'

Ruth laughed. 'Fair point. I'll take my chances, though. I'd want you on my side whatever. You can be vicious when you need to be.'

'I'll take that as a compliment.'

'You should.'

'So, why was today so bad?' Vicky asked.

'The dead were ferocious, and there were so many. The first few hundred were in such bad shape that they virtually fell apart. The others, though... some of them were crazy aggressive.' Ruth stared into the flames of the bonfire and thought for a moment.

'Tell me what you're thinking.'

'It's just that every time I look over the border wall, all I see is thousands and thousands and thousands of them, just lining up to get at us.'

'But they're not really, are they? It's nothing personal. They're here because there's nothing else going on in London to distract them.'

'If you say so.'

'So what's your point?'

27

'It just makes me realise how hard everything's getting, you know what I'm saying? A bloody horrific day fighting monsters in the street just to take back a little strip of road and a handful of buildings.'

'Is there an alternative?'

'I don't know. I don't think so. But it's depressing if this is all we've got to look forward to. Fight, rest, start again tomorrow. Rinse, dry, repeat.'

'Or just give up altogether?'

'I'm not going to do that,' Ruth said, defensive.

'I know you won't.'

'You bust your balls all day and feel like you've made some progress, then you come back next morning and you're right back to square one again.' She pointed at the building across the way, a prison-like grey block. 'Freaks me out to think that most of the time, buildings like that are all that's separating us from them. That's nothing. Remember when they used to say you're never more than six feet from a rat in London? Just swap rats for walking corpses.'

'We've got rats *and* walking corpses. Have you seen the number of them around the food stores? It's ridiculous. The frigging vermin eat better than we do.'

Ruth laughed. 'I'm just waiting for someone to start catching them and cooking them. I bet Phillipa could do a wicked rat curry, don't you think?'

'Gross.'

'I can see it happening! Rats, disease, insects... nothing surprises me anymore. So, when you start one of your regular arguments with Dominic Grove about getting out of London, just remember, I'm behind you one hundred per cent.'

'Good. Because I still reckon that's our best option. I'm going to get me and Selena out of this place if it's the last thing I do. At this rate it probably will be.'

'She's properly bought into the Ledsey Cross dream, you know.'

'Good. She needs something to hold on to. I made a promise to

Kath to get her there. Even if it's just me and Selena, we're going.'

'I'll come along if I'm invited.'

Vicky smiled, a rare event.

The forklift was approaching, its flashing orange hazard light blinking in the gloom. It made a hell of a noise as it rattled down the rubbish-strewn street towards them. Nick Hubbard, the driver, was a grumpy bugger who clearly resented having been sent out. They helped him load the pallet on the front of the forklift then followed him back.

He'd only driven a couple of metres when the forklift stopped. Nick jumped out of his seat and kicked the side of the machine in anger.

'Problem?' Ruth asked.

'Out of gas. I knew this would happen.'

'Go get some more.'

Nick rapped his knuckles on the empty LPG cylinder. 'There isn't any more. That's the last one. Frigging Mihai sending me off here there and everywhere to get stuff. He never plans, he just reacts. Too scared of Dominic and Piotr to say no.'

'Great. So, what now?'

'Wait here. I'll go get some trolleys,' Nick grunted, and he wandered off.

'Good,' Ruth said once he was well out of earshot. 'I didn't want to go back just yet. I'd rather stay out here with you.'

They helped themselves to a little more from their haul and sat by the nearest funeral pyre to keep warm while they waited.

5

Dominic was lauding over the spoils of the day, watching everything being stashed away in the bowels of Tower Place. 'This is phenomenal,' he enthused, summoning up more energy than the other three hundred or so people in the base combined. 'Look at all this stuff.'

'It's really not all that, Dom,' Mihai tried to explain, but Dominic was having none of it.

'This is just one day's work. By the time we've cleared as much of the area as we plan to and we've collected everything of value, we should be well placed.'

'For a few weeks, maybe.'

Dominic looked stung. 'Why do you always have to be so bloody negative all the time?'

'I'm not being negative, I'm being realistic.'

'Pessimistic, more like. Just humour me, Mihai, what's the grand total? How much stuff did we actually bring back today?'

Mihai scanned his clipboard with a torch. He took his time, double-checking figures. 'Well, we've already got more clothes than we need. Not so much in the way of medicines. A little food and drink, but not a huge amount.'

Dominic's frustration was clear. 'You're missing the point. All of this came from a quick scavenge after a land-grab. The focus of today was clearing the street.'

'There's more furniture than anything.'

'It'll be different when we get to work on the residential buildings, like Brockmer House. Anyway, furniture will still be useful.'

Mihai shook his head. 'Dom, we've got about three hundred and seventy people here. There's a limit to the number of beds and chairs we're going to need.'

'You need to broaden your horizons, think big. I'm looking longer term. We can use it for fuel, burn it to keep people warm. I'm not looking to open a branch of Ikea.'

'A lot of furniture is fire resistant these days,' he said, and Dominic looked to the heavens.

'Now you're being deliberately difficult.'

A man appeared carrying a crate. 'Where do you want this, boss?' he asked.

'What's in it, Tony?'

'Tools, mostly.'

'I'll show you. Come with me,' Mihai said, and he walked away, keen to escape before Dominic could say anything else.

'Does he do your head in as much as he does mine?' Tony asked as they entered the stores.

'I shouldn't say this, but yes. Probably more so,' Mihai admitted. 'He makes me nervous. He's quite intimidating.'

'He's a jackass. I couldn't handle working so close with him. I just keep myself to myself.'

'I wish I had that luxury. He's always on at me, never lets up. Too busy talking to listen.'

'Keep your chin up, lad,' Tony said. Mihai showed him where the tools were kept, and he began unpacking the crate.

Gary Welch was already in the stores. 'You could tell him to sling his hook.'

Mihai was confused. 'Who, Scouse Tony?'

'No, Dominic. Jesus, Mihai, why the long face? I thought you'd be in your element with all this stuff to catalogue and sort away. Has Mr Grove been bending your ear about his vision of a utopian future again?'

'Something like that.'

'Thought as much. I could hear the bullshit flowing from down here.'

'I just don't think he gets it. He reckons we're gonna feed all these folks with the stuff we find stashed away in dead people's kitchen cupboards.'

'Has he told you about his farming plans yet?'

'Only about a thousand times.'

'He'll be even worse now we've actually got some grassland. I've tried to talk to him about it, but he doesn't want to listen. Even if we can grow our own food, we've still got to feed people between now and the first harvest. He's talking about production on an industrial scale. Where are we going to get the machinery and supplies for that in the middle of London, for Christ's sake?'

'I know. I get it. You don't have to convince me.'

Gary checked himself. He sat down heavily on a bale of clothing. 'Sorry, mate. I've had a gutful today, and it sounds like you have too. I shouldn't take it out on you. No offence.'

'None taken.'

'You know two more people died out there today?'

'Yes.'

'From a purely practical perspective, we can't afford to sustain that level of loss.'

'I know. That's eight people in the last month. Three of them died from pre-existing conditions. Six months ago, they could have been treated, but Liz and Dr Ahmad don't have the experience or resources to deal with them. At this rate, we'll solve the food shortage problem by having no one left alive to feed. I was out there on the frontline today, Mihai.'

'What was it like?'

'As bad as you'd imagine. Worse, maybe. Point is, I think we're close to the stage where the risks of going out looking for food are greater than the risks of us starving.'

6

Ruth had only just made it back when Piotr cornered her outside Tower Place. 'Lynette needs you,' he said.

'Can't it wait? I only just got here.'

'No. Go now.'

'Why me?'

'Because I said so. Go.'

She didn't have the energy to argue. There was no point. She climbed up to the first floor of the cavernous office building, keen to get this done then get to bed. She found Lynette sitting with Georgie, both struggling to complete paperwork by the fading light of a candle nub. Ruth's footsteps echoed on the marbled floor, announcing her arrival.

'I heard you were looking for me.'

Lynette nodded. 'Thanks for coming up, love. We need your services again, if you don't mind.'

'Shit. How many did we lose?'

'That's the problem. We know about Marie, but there are a couple more still missing.'

'It's Jay Morris and Amy Hooper,' Georgie said. 'I think we've accounted for everyone else who went out today.'

'Okay. Jay's flat was just down the hall from my old place. I'll go and check it out. Damn shame if he's gone; he was a nice guy. Straight-talking, you know?'

'He was,' Lynette agreed.

'I liked Amy, too. She was living in the hotel, wasn't she?'

Georgie checked a form. 'That's right.'

'Let us know if you find either of them,' Lynette said.

'Of course. I'll make sure their rooms are secure and I'll let you know.'

'Thanks.'

'Once we know for sure that they're not coming back, I'll talk to Mihai. He can go and see if they had anything useful worth recycling.'

'Okay,' Ruth said.

'It's a horrible job, I know. We're just glad we've got you to do it. There'd be a free-for-all for people's possessions and their digs if you didn't secure them for us. Horrible, really.'

Ruth shook her head. 'It's okay. I'm happy to do it.'

Georgie flicked through more paperwork. 'So, the confirmed death was Marie.'

She took Marie's form from her ring-binder, drew a diagonal line across the page, annotated it with the date and a few other details, then filed it away.

'Marie's apartment was just below mine,' Lynette said. She paused, then spoke again. 'Do you know what happened, Ruth?'

'An accident, I heard. Things got a bit hairy towards the end of the day and a fence came down. I heard someone saying they thought it might have been deliberate.'

'Deliberate? Seriously?'

'That's just pointless gossip,' Dominic said. He was standing in the doorway of the board room, his voice filling the first floor of the building, and taking them all by surprise. 'It's nonsense. Scaremongering.'

Ruth walked over to him and lowered her voice. 'So what do you think happened? Out there today... could it have been Taylor? Don't forget, I know what he's capable of. I saw him shoot Tayyab and Jonah in front of me, in cold blood. He did enough damage to the barricades to almost wipe all of us out.'

Dominic beckoned her to follow him into the boardroom. 'You shouldn't be talking like this. I hope you haven't said anything to anyone else.'

'I haven't.'

'Because you're just going to frighten people if you do, and they're scared enough already. Taylor's dead, remember. Piotr found his body after the explosions.'

'I know, but how do you know for sure it was him?'

'Are you calling Piotr a liar?'

'No.'

'Then what are you saying? You need to think very carefully. The last thing we need is to give people yet another reason to think the worst.'

'That's the thing you're worried about? We're very different, Dom. You were a politician; I was a debt collector. My job was the polar opposite to yours. It was about being direct and telling people how things were, not trying to win them over with what they wanted to hear.'

'That's not lost on me. It's why people trust you more than they trust me.'

'You sure? I think it's got more to do with the fact you spend most of your time up here, making plans and giving out orders. You should try getting your hands dirty from time to time. You'd have more credibility if people saw you actually doing something instead of just delegating.'

He thought for a moment. 'Then let's do a deal. I'll make myself more visible, you keep all talk of Taylor to yourself. He's dead.'

'Maybe if people had seen the body...'

'It wouldn't have made any difference. Like you said, I could have wheeled any corpse out – Christ knows we've had more than enough to choose from. Piotr found the body at the site of one of the blasts, on this side of the barrier, badly burned. I've told you all this before.'

'Fine.'

'You look exhausted. You should get some rest. We've got another busy day ahead of us tomorrow.'

'That's the absolute last thing I want to hear right now.'

'I understand that, I really do. Here, look at this.' He showed her a hand-drawn map that he'd hung on one wall. The distinctive shape of the river Thames made it easy to pinpoint the location. Tower Place and the Tower of London were at the centre of the map. All the land they'd lost to the west when Taylor had blown the barricades had been blacked out. The area to the east had been carved into sections. Ruth could see the area they'd managed to secure along The Highway outlined in red.

He gestured at the map like an overexcited schoolteacher. 'It feels less daunting when you break it down into chunks. We took back all this space from the dead today, and now we can spend some time exploiting the area so we can see exactly what we've got.'

'Then what?'

'We go south and clear another chunk down towards the Thames,' he explained, and he pointed out St Katharine's Docks Marina. 'We stopped halfway across the marina, if you remember.'

'How could I forget? The dead are still in spitting distance of my bedroom window.'

'I know. We thought the water would make the docks easy to defend, but it's not good enough. So, the next thing I want us to do is focus on clearing the rest of that area out to make the hotel accommodations more secure. Eventually this whole region will be ours, all the way down from the train lines to the river, and right across from Tower Place to the centre of Wapping. Most of that space is prime residential. There's more quality accommodations there than we could ever hope to need.'

He could tell by her expression that she wasn't convinced.

'One step at a time, Dom. You're doing it again. You've been sitting up here all day drawing pretty maps and plotting, while some of us have been literally up to our necks in dead flesh. You need to slow down. The last thing I want to be thinking about tonight is having to go out there and do it all over again tomorrow.'

'I get it. I'm sorry.' Dominic put a hand on her shoulder. She was too tired to shrug it off. 'Things are going to get better, Ruth. When the salvage teams go in tomorrow and start stripping the tower blocks, things will start feeling very different. It's been tough, but there are better days ahead.'

7

DAY SEVENTY-THREE

November had so far been brighter and drier than expected and, when the wind dropped, the morning was unseasonably mild. More than a hundred people walked down East Smithfield together, ready to start stripping the reclaimed land of anything of value. It was a different mix of folks out here today. The work ahead of them was less violent, hopefully less dangerous too. There were some here who hadn't been able to face the gruesome work of battling a vast horde of corpses yesterday, but who could just about cope with clearance work and the occasional one-on-one. Others had stayed behind today for the opposite reason; there were some who only wanted to fight, no interest in salvage work or other menial tasks. Many more remained shut away in their hotel rooms and apartments as they did every day. Nothing could persuade that core of frightened, broken people that there was anything to be gained from going out and facing the outside world ever again.

It was too early for Orla, but she made an effort to sound more positive and awake than she felt, more for the benefit of the folks around her than for herself. She spotted Selena's red hoodie just ahead. 'Morning, Selena. You sleep well?'

Selena grunted something unintelligible.

'Nice morning, though, don't you think? I mean, it's not raining and the sun's out, that's got to count for something, don't you think?'

Selena shrugged her shoulders and quickened her pace to avoid the awkwardness of prolonging the conversation.

'Bloody teenagers,' Vicky said. 'The end of the frigging world, and she's still got more problems than anyone else.'

Orla laughed. 'Ha! Tell me about it. But I was no better at her age, and at least she's got an excuse for being a grumpy arse.'

'You're right about the weather, though. The sun's out. Makes the prospect of turfing dead people out of their homes just that bit more palatable.'

'Smells better out here today as well, don't you think?'

'What, because of the bonfires?'

'Yeah. Really says something when you're glad of the smell of burnt bodies because it hides the usual stink.'

'It's marginally better, I suppose.'

'Hey, maybe we should just torch the whole lot of them?'

'Don't give Piotr ideas. Speaking of which, what the bloody hell is he doing?'

Orla and Vicky stopped when they reached the edge of the crowd that had gathered at the agreed meeting point. Piotr had got hold of a cherry picker – a bucket on a boom mounted on the back of a truck. It would likely have been used to maintain streetlights, but he was using it to tower over the crowd, giving actual altitude to his usual self-appointed height. Piotr had only elevated himself halfway, but it was enough to give him dominion over the workers; an angry street preacher with a height-adjustable pulpit.

'That guy has ideas way above his station' Orla whispered.

'We should cut the power and leave the fucker stuck up there,' Vicky replied, and, for a moment, she considered doing it.

The sermon according to Piotr was being delivered a short distance along The Highway. The crowd had been marshalled to a point about a quarter of the way along the section of road that had been cleared yesterday, overlooking an expanse of untended parkland. On the far side of the green there were three immense tower blocks with many smaller residential properties hiding in their shadows.

Piotr waited impatiently for the last few stragglers to catch up, then pointed across the park and began barking out orders. 'The tower on the left is Hatton House. Twenty-three storeys, about eighty flats. Today we are going to empty it from top to bottom.'

Vicky was already distracted. There were plenty of dead ex-residents who had taken more of an interest in what Piotr was saying than she had. They were shuffling across the grassland, some spread out and others in bunches, stopping abruptly when they reached the railings. Two men walked up and down the pavement, stabbing and slicing, keeping the numbers down. They worked in silence and with an unnerving nonchalance, hacking at the dead as if they were trimming an overgrown hedge.

Piotr continued. 'A clearance team has already carried out the initial removal of bodies from the stairwells and landings. You'll be divided into teams and allocated specific floors to clear. Bodies will be dumped over balconies; food and anything else useful is to be left on landings. Mihai's logistics team will be responsible for shifting stuff down to ground level, to minimise traffic on the stairs. There will be further clean-up teams working in and around the building to remove human remains. Is that clear?'

He paused. Mumbles from the crowd.

'You will be split into your teams shortly. For those of you who haven't scavenged in a while, remember that we take *everything* that isn't nailed down. Just because you think something is useless, doesn't mean that it is. A broken piece of equipment might seem like nothing to you, but there could be useful spare parts to repair something else. These days, everything has value, understand?'

Another muted ripple of acknowledgement.

'Some of the clearance teams will start at the top of the building, others lower down. Stay off the stairs so we don't have people getting in each other's way. One person from each group will carry paper and a pen. You shift the stuff you can, and you write down the details, location, and condition of everything you can't move because it's too big or too heavy. Furniture, for example. You will also record the details of any flats that are uninhabitable for whatever reason.'

Piotr paused to let his words sink in, then spoke again.

'You will find misery and decay throughout that building, and in every other building we take back from the dead. Deal with it. Remove all corpses quickly and efficiently. Human remains are to be treated the same as any other rubbish. There is no time for dignity and respect now. Just get the job done.'

Vicky made sure she ended up in the same group as Selena, much to Selena's annoyance. They were paired up with Darren Adams, the ex-Transport for London employee who'd looked after access to the Monument and Bank tube stations before they'd been destroyed in Taylor's attacks. He clearly still held a grudge. 'There wasn't a problem until you lot turned up,' he'd said to Vicky on more than one occasion before now. Times past, she might have tried to talk him around. Today, though, she really couldn't be bothered. He wasn't worth the effort.

Selena was arguing with the final member of their team. He was Sean Phelps, a grubby looking guy in a grubby looking tracksuit, a few years older than she was. 'He's a real dick,' Selena had said when they'd first been grouped together, 'never does nothing to help.' Vicky hadn't recognised him. Apparently, he'd been part of the Fleet Street hotel group and had travelled across town in the buses with her, Selena, and the others. He evidently hadn't made much of an impression.

There were four flats on each floor of Hatton House. They were dispatched up to floor nineteen. Darren forced the landing door open and immediately realised the corpse removal team had missed this level when a husk-like creature that had been trapped in the narrow space charged straight at him. Darren wrestled the thing to the ground and Vicky thrust the tip of her crowbar through its temple. He upended the cadaver over the bannister and watched it drop, wincing every time its head or some other body part ricocheted off the railings. He brushed himself down, self-conscious because the others were staring at him. 'What have I become?' he asked, sounding serious. 'This time last year I was dealing with train delays and platform alterations. Now look at me. I'm a fucking ninja.'

They laughed at his out of character outburst and the sound they made travelled the entire length of the vast, column-like building.

Vicky and Selena went into one flat, Darren and Sean another. Despite all Piotr's threats, and the endless lectures from Dominic about not hoarding food and considering the needs of those members of the group who weren't able to fend for themselves, there was plenty of petty pilfering going on. When they found that their flat was corpse-free, Vicky and Selena barricaded the kitchen door and demolished a whole packet of biscuits between them. They were a little stale, but heavenly.

They worked hard, and the first apartments were cleared with little incident. Each dwelling had its own private balcony, and most were easily accessible. Corpses plummeted past the windows with alarming regularity as the last remaining residents were evicted; heaved up and over and sent on their final one-way trips down to the ground floor. It was almost comical, and Vicky almost laughed. It must have looked bizarre from a distance, like a grotesque piece of performance art. She was just glad she hadn't been put on the clean-up team. The tangled mess of remains spattered around the base of the building was horrific.

For a while, she thought they might be onto something here, because the haul of supplies they'd accumulated from the first two flats on this floor alone looked truly impressive. Food, drink, drugs, tools, clothing, bedding... everything was useful. They'd found enough books to fill several libraries but had been instructed to leave them behind. Although people had plenty of time to read, most chose not to. Everything that had ever been written was history now, every word rooted in a world long gone. There was little enjoyment to be found immersing yourself in memories of everything you'd lost.

Back to work.

Selena signalled she was ready, and Vicky barged the door of the next flat open. They burst into a musty hallway space and waited, listening to the sounds of the apartment around them. They heard sudden scratching, shifting, thumping noises... there were dead residents in situ in the lounge. 'Stay close,' Vicky said, crowbar held ready. 'You get the door and I'll deal with whatever's in there.'

'Okay,' Selena said.

'Right. Do it.'

Selena threw the door open and Vicky rushed in.

Hit them hard, hit them fast. React first, think about it later.

It had sounded like a crowd, but there was only one corpse here, and, fortunately, it was that of an elderly woman, judging from the thing's shrunken frame and heavily stained clothes. She launched herself at Vicky with the venom and aggression of someone half her age and twice her size, but Vicky focused past her fury. She held her nerve, brushed away the woman's thrashing arms, grabbed her by the throat, and pinned the old crone up against the window. She realised, too late, that she'd dropped her crowbar in the scuffle. She reached across, but the door to the balcony was locked. 'Selena, get this bloody door open,' she yelled. Shouting made her start coughing and, once she'd started, she couldn't stop.

'Where are the keys?'

Struggling to keep her coughing fit under control, Vicky cracked the back of the dead woman's head against the glass, frustrated by the inanity of Selena's stereotypical teenager's delay tactic. '*How the hell should I know?* Granny's in the house, so her keys are going to be here somewhere. Just bloody find them!'

'Alright, alright,' Selena moaned.

Vicky's arm was getting tired. The spoiled flesh of the woman's neck was starting to ooze under her tightening grip, threatening to split. 'Hurry up,' she shouted, and she looked around in vain for something else with which she could end the corpse's struggling. This woman's home appeared frustratingly clear of tat.

'Can't find them,' Selena grumbled from elsewhere.

Vicky shifted her weight and swapped arms then gave up waiting and smashed the woman's head against the glass again. And again. And again, and again, until she felt the back of her skull crack like an egg and cave in. The corpse finally stopped fighting.

Selena turned up with the keys.

'Where were they?'

'Back of the front door,' she said. 'Obvious, really. Should have looked there first.'

She found the correct key, opened the balcony, and Vicky dropped the woman over the edge. 'Gross,' she said, and she found a dusty towel in the bathroom to wipe her bloody hands clean.

There was another dead woman in the kitchen, trapped in a corner between a table, the cooker, and the wall. She was bundled off the balcony with no fuss at all. 'Christ, I'm knackered,' Vicky moaned. 'This is exhausting. I hope they don't think any of us are going to move into this place. There's no way I'm climbing all those steps to get home every day. And what if there's a problem? It'll take half an hour to get out again, don't you think? Are you even listening to me, Selena?'

She wasn't. Selena was hanging over the balcony, looking at the bloody splat where the last body had hit the ground. 'I reckon it was her flat,' she said, pointing down. 'It was that one's flat, and the first one you chucked over was her mum.'

'Is that right?'

'Yep.'

'I try not to make this personal; you should do the same.'

'Jeez, you suck the fun out of everything.'

'It's bad enough that we're having to do this at all. We should show these people some respect.'

'Respect? Have you lost the plot, Vic? They're dead. Anyway, you're the one what smashed Granny's head up the window.'

'I know. I'm not proud.'

'So, what's the problem?'

'Nothing. Forget it. Suppose it doesn't matter.'

'So why you having a go at me if it doesn't matter? You're always having a go at me, you are.'

'I'm not; I'm just trying to look out for you because—'

'You're not my mum, you know.'

'I'm well aware of that, thank you very much. I just think it's unhealthy when you start trying to unpick these people's lives. What's gone is gone. We don't know how long any of us have left and—'

'You think I don't know that? You think you know better than me just because you're older? It don't work like that anymore. We've been living in this fucked up version of the world as long as each other, so stop patronising me and just let me get on with it.'

'Suit yourself,' Vicky said, because she just couldn't be bothered to argue, and she sat down to catch her breath.

Selena stormed off in the opposite direction. She'd stuck with Vicky because it was what Kath had wanted her to do, but the woman was seriously starting to piss her off. It had been obvious from the outset that Kath was the one who'd had the brains. She was the one who'd found out about Ledsey Cross, and she was the one who'd been trying to get them out of London. And what had happened since Kath died? Nothing. How much further had they got? Absolutely nowhere. Thanks to Vicky they'd ended up stuck in this hellhole with no obvious way out. Right now, alone in this bloody tower block, surrounded by death and filth, the chances of ever getting to Kath's friends at Ledsey Cross felt more remote than ever. Selena found a can of Red Bull in a kitchen cupboard and swigged from it as she checked out the rest of the flat.

There was another corpse in one of the bedrooms.

It caught her off-guard because it wasn't acting like most of the others she'd seen. It was a girl, a little shorter than she was, probably a similar age once, with shoulder-length hair and badly stained pyjamas. She had her back to Selena, standing uncharacteristically still, just staring out of the window, swaying slightly.

Is she alive?

That was the only explanation Selena could think of because the dead never stopped moving. In the moment of unexpected calm she looked around and noticed the girl had a poster on the wall that she'd had in her own room back home. 'Oh, man, I loved that band,' she said, not thinking, then she froze because she knew her voice had been too loud. The girl didn't immediately react, and Selena spoke again. 'Are you okay?'

Nothing.

Then, ever so slowly and awkwardly, the girl started to turn around, pivoting on stiff legs like a ballerina on crutches. Selena knew straightaway by the movement that she was dead, but seeing the kid's face ravaged by decay, was proof positive. Her profile was irregular and jagged, the end of her nose and one cheek completely devoured and crumbling, clacking yellow teeth visible through the hole. She kept shuffling on the spot, dragging her feet on the thin carpet, until she was looking directly at Selena.

Selena didn't know what to do. The stand-off didn't make sense. Automatically, she started to apologise for bursting into the dead girl's room, but she didn't manage more than an "I'm so—" before the girl launched herself, half-running, half-stumbling across the cluttered bedroom space.

Instinct took over.

Selena whipped out the kitchen knife she carried in her belt, caught the dead girl by the throat, and plunged the blade into her left eye socket, deep enough to do sufficient damage and end the attack as quickly as it had begun. The weight of the corpse took Selena by surprise, and she tripped back and smacked against the bedroom door, slamming it shut with a noise like a gunshot. Vicky was there in a heartbeat.

'Selena! *Selena!*'

Selena was on the floor with the dead girl on top of her, dripping. She rolled her off then picked herself back up and opened the door. 'Chill out. It's fine.'

46

'What happened?'

She took a step back so that Vicky could work it out for herself. 'Frigging thing was hiding in here.'

'What do you mean, hiding?'

Selena shrugged. She couldn't be bothered to elaborate, so she just gave her the minimum. 'What do you think I mean? It was standing in here, waiting for us to find it.'

She wiped her blade on the dead girl's pyjamas. She took the poster off the wall, rolled it up tightly, then started turfing through her things.

Later, when the work was done and most people had already returned to the main part of the compound, Vicky held back and climbed to the top floor of Hatton House. She was tired, her chest tight, but she lit another cigarette regardless. She'd found a bottle of Benylin in a bathroom cabinet which had helped keep the coughing under control as she went from flat to flat, room to room, soaking up the panoramic views of dead London.

Strange how beautiful the city looked from a distance tonight. The orange light of the sinking sun picked out endless familiarly shaped highlights across the iconic London skyline. By focusing on the horizon, she could kid herself that the street-level chaos didn't exist, that everything in the world was back how it should be. But, as so many times before, she couldn't stop herself looking down.

The tower block was close enough to enable her to see beyond their train track northern boundary. It was hard to discern any details, though. It wasn't that she was unfamiliar with the area, more that the number of dead bodies on the other side of the tracks made it hard to make out lines and boundaries. Out there, everything merged into a single, writhing mass of putrefaction. It was like an oozing scab that got bigger the more you picked at it. It reminded her of the mould that covered the months-old food they'd found in various cupboards and fridges today.

The view from the other side of the building was marginally

more palatable. From here she could see some signs of progress being made. There were more bonfires in the streets, ant-like figures scurrying through the spaces between them, transporting the spoils of the day's looting back to base. Beyond all that, the river. It was too far to see, but just knowing it was there was reassuring. The power of the water was a constant, separating them from the inevitable hell on the south bank.

From where she was watching, she could see the fuel station she and Ruth had cleared out yesterday evening. Something was happening in front of the imposing grey-fronted building opposite. People began racing towards it from all directions. A vehicle arrived, and in the flash of its headlamps everything was illuminated for a moment. Bodies had found their way inside the building, and someone had stupidly opened a door and let them walk out. The brief incursion was dealt with quickly and efficiently, but it was worrying. Yesterday, that building had appeared empty; now it was filled with monsters. No matter how close she thought the dead were, they were always closer.

The view to the east was the worst of all.

The position of Hatton House afforded her a clear, uninterrupted view over the parts of Wapping which had not yet been reclaimed from the dead and, Christ, even from a distance, it was a terrifying sight. The corpses immediately to the north had been there for months and had hardly moved in all that time, but she could see that swarms were closing on them from the east, drawn in by the man-made chaos of the last couple of days.

The vast ranks of the dead knew no fear. If they'd had any sense, or any degree of individual self-awareness, they'd have tried to get away from this place instead of moving towards it. All they'd find here was oblivion. But these vile creatures were riddled with impossibilities. No matter what physical dangers they faced, they just kept coming. She could see huge numbers of them queuing up to take the place of the thousands that had been culled during the recent fighting. They inched ever closer along every available route.

Vicky felt uneasy, horribly exposed up here at the top of the tower block on her own. She flicked her cigarette butt over the balcony then started back down, acutely aware of every noise she made. Tonight, more than ever, sound was the enemy. In this desolate ruin of a place, every unnecessary noise was a call to arms for the seemingly infinite hordes of the undead.

Yesterday had been nothing but noise, and today had been much the same. Tomorrow, it would start again, and if Dominic and Piotr got the results they were expecting, it would be the same the day after and then the day after that. Were they even aware of the effect their scurrying would have on the dead population of London? Did they care?

Tonight, the line between security and disaster felt thinner than ever.

8

There were steps outside the hotel that led up onto Tower Bridge. Lynette often took herself up there when she needed a break from everyone else. She'd always been alone there before, but tonight she found Selena sitting in the shadows, tucked away in a corner. The light was such that she'd have walked straight past had the girl not flinched and pulled her knees up out of the way. 'You scared the life out of me, love,' Lynette said, her heart pounding.

'Sorry,' Selena grunted, and she did what she could to make herself as small as possible so that Lynette could get past.

'What are you doing up here on your own?'

'I'm not on my own anymore, am I?' Selena replied shortly.

'Fair point. I take it you'd like me to leave you alone then? I don't know if I've mentioned it, but I'm fluent in teenager-speak.'

Selena almost laughed. Almost.

'I had twins, you know. A boy and a girl. Emily and Tom. Fifteen. A bit younger than you, they were.'

'You never said.'

That was true. It was the first time Lynette had spoken about them in long time. Their names felt alien on her lips. Selena knew better than to ask questions. What would it achieve?

'I come up here quite often,' Lynette said. 'Piotr would have kittens if he knew.'

'Isn't it risky?'

'I think it used to be, but not so much now.'

'How come?'

'I'll show you.'

Lynette beckoned for Selena to follow her up. On the road across the bridge, on the outermost edge of the cordon that had been erected to prevent the dead crossing from the south bank, she crouched down next to the wreck of a car. Selena peered through the grime and saw a mass of putrid features pressed against the glass on the other side of the vehicle. They'd seeped into each other as they'd deteriorated, now forming a single, repulsive mask with several gaping mouths and far too many eyes. 'That's gross,' Selena said, tasting bile.

'Isn't it just? Thing is, none of them have moved for weeks now. When I first started coming up here, it seemed there were different faces at the window every day. They've been stuck like that for ages. There's hardly any movement in the queue right across the bridge now. They've been there so long they've grown roots. Disgusting, really.'

Selena shrugged, indifferent. Lynette continued to talk, enjoying the novelty of having someone to chat to.

'I wish there'd been a lot less panic and a bit more foresight when we first set ourselves up here. Piotr didn't think it through when he blocked the traffic here. I tried to tell him, but you know what he's like. If I'd been in charge, I'd have pushed them another ten metres or so back across the bridge, beyond the first tower. Know why?'

Selena couldn't have sounded less interested if she'd tried. 'Why?'

Lynette pointed up. 'Because here's a walkway up there. We could have got all the way across - not that we'd have wanted to, I suppose. But from up there you can see for miles.'

'Not much to see now, though. Just the river. That and all the places we can't go.'

'Have you seen the fire?'

'What fire?'

She pointed. A portion of the sky over to the east was blood red, heavy cloud cover illuminated from below. Lynette started to sing. *'London's burning, London's burning, fetch the engines, fetch the engines, fire, fire...* Something's been burning over there for a couple of days now. Looks like it's around the Isle of Dogs,

Canary Wharf.'

'Might be a good thing,' Selena suggested. 'Might get rid of some of the bodies.'

Selena continued to stare into the distance. Lynette watched her with concern. 'What's on your mind, love? And don't forget, I told you I speak teenager. I'll know if you're not telling me the truth.'

Selena almost managed a smile. She continued looking east along the water. She had lots on her mind tonight, as it happened. For a start, there was the fact she was so desperate to get away from this place that she'd happily jump from the bridge right now and try swimming for freedom. Or maybe the fact she was sick and fucking tired of Vicky and Marianne and some of the others – particularly Vicky – mollycoddling her when there was no fucking need. Also, the fact she felt bad for re-killing that kid in her own bedroom earlier today. And the fact she was hungry. And cold. And the fact she felt scared, tired, hurt, hollow...

But there was nothing anyone could do about any of it, so there was no point talking about it.

'Nothing's wrong,' she said to Lynette, forcing a bit more of a smile. 'I'm good.'

It had taken several days longer than expected to recover all the loot from Hatton House. Vicky appreciated the slowdown in pace; she'd found the sudden exertion a struggle after weeks of inactivity. She'd had to drag herself out of her room on the second floor to find David and Marianne this morning, hoping to catch them before their meeting with Dominic and the others.

This place had been a four-star hotel, but the lack of heat, light, running water, and sanitation had stripped it of any sense of luxury. It was dark and damp, and, despite the protection of the waters of St Katharine's Docks immediately behind the building, the dead were closer to the living here than anywhere else in the compound. Vicky could see them from her window, inching closer, clawing against the barricades. The tall buildings that surrounded the water had felt like a defensive line when they'd first been billeted here. Now they looked more like prison walls.

'Christ, it stinks down here,' she said when she reached the lobby and found Marianne. There was no mistaking the smell; the entire ground floor of the building stank of sewerage.

'I know. Vile, isn't it?'

Vicky was puzzled. 'I don't understand... London stopped flushing its loos months ago, and as far as I know, everyone here's crapping in buckets and emptying it into the river. Where's it coming from?'

'David and Stan are trying to work it out. This is a side of post-apocalyptic life you never saw in the movies.'

Right on cue, Alec Stanley and David emerged from the bowels of the building. 'Jesus Christ, things must be bad if we've had to call in the dream team,' Vicky said.

'There's no need for sarcasm, Victoria,' Stan said, annoyed. 'I did some planning work on the sewers around here many years ago.'

'And?'

'And it's likely some kind of blockage somewhere.'

'No shit.'

'The opposite, actually,' David said. 'Too much shit.'

'Is there anything we can do about it?' Marianne asked.

Stan shook his head. 'The problem could be anywhere. We've checked all we can at this end, but there's nothing obvious. Who knows what's going on with the sewers these days? I mean, there are no toilets being flushed, but there's no running water and there's hardly been any rain recently. There are bodies in the gutters and I've no doubt a few buildings have been damaged or even collapsed by now... anything could have happened.'

'So, we're stuck with this shitty stink then?' Omar said. The kid had wormed his way into the middle of the conversation without anyone noticing.

'Yes.'

'And you can't do nuffink about it?'

Stan ignored him. 'We could try and find an outlet into the river and work our way back this way, maybe. Nasty, dangerous work though. Could be a job for you, Omar.'

'Screw you. I ain't crawling up no shit pipe.'

'I think we've just got to live with it until we can get ourselves into better digs,' David said. 'Even if there is a blockage or a leak, we've got bugger all chance of locating it, and even less chance of fixing it.

'You're right,' Marianne said, 'there's no point wasting time and effort trying to sort it. First decent downpour we get and it'll probably clear itself. We just need to get out of this building and into somewhere better as quickly as we can. We're going to talk to the council about it now, try and put a rocket up their arses.'

The days of the week were interchangeable now; things tending to happen whenever they happened rather than at predetermined times, yet Sunday mornings were still clearly Sunday mornings to some folks. Ten o'clock sharp every Sunday, Audrey Adebayo opened the doors of All Hallows by the Tower church for those who sought spiritual guidance. Despite everything that had happened, attendance numbers were up week on week. 'How anyone can still believe in gods, after all this, is beyond me,' David grumbled. 'Bloody skivers.'

'Give them a break,' Marianne said as they walked past the church doors en route to Tower Place. 'Though you are right. It's funny how Audrey draws the faithful like flies whenever there's work to be done.'

The council was already in session when they reached the boardroom. They were the last to take their places alongside Dominic, Piotr, Lynette, Orla, Liz, and Mihai.

'Morning, everyone, thanks for coming,' Dominic said, calling the meeting to order as if the end of the world had never happened. He passed around sheets of paper with a handwritten agenda. 'Okay, so the first thing we need to talk about this morning is—'

Marianne had her own ideas.

'The first thing we need to talk about is the stink of shit in the hotel,' she said, railroading the discussion. David sat back in his chair and watched, enjoying seeing all her old-world experience as a lawyer coming to the fore. 'I'm sorry to bulldoze my way to the top of the agenda like this, but there's a real and urgent issue here. The building we're staying in is unsanitary. It's dangerous to our health.'

'It's not that bad,' Piotr tried to say, but Marianne was having none of it.

'Have you been there recently? It fucking stinks.'

'Everywhere fucking stinks. We're surrounded by millions of dead bodies. London is a garbage heap. What do you expect?'

'But we're not all living next to millions of dead bodies, are we? The apartments most of you are living in are on the river, a decent distance from the boundary. We've literally got corpses at our back door.'

Dominic sighed. 'If you'd looked at the agenda first, Marianne, you'd have seen that clearance of the docks is high on our list of priorities. I'm sorry if things aren't perfect at the hotel. You and I have already talked about this at length.'

'Let's be honest, you talk about everything at length.'

He ignored her barb. He was used to it. 'The hotel was only ever a stop-gap measure. It was the safest, most suitable building we could get ready at short notice when we knew you were coming. We used it to expedite things. We'd not made provisions for a group of your size turning up unexpectedly, remember?'

'We understand that, and we appreciate what we've got here,' David said, trying to take some of the sting out of Marianne's abruptness. She was right, of course, but whilst seasoned bullshitters like Dominic could see through her, it was a red rag to a bull to a one-dimensional brute like Piotr.

'So, what's the problem?' Piotr asked. His tone of voice left David in no doubt that, from where Piotr was sitting, there was no problem at all.

Marianne sighed. 'Your group this, our group that; we've been pulling our weight trying to stay alive, same as you. It's all getting a bit us and them, don't you think, fellas? A bit tribal?'

'I don't see that at all,' Dominic said, defensive.

'You sure? Stan's managed to worm his way in over to your side, and you managed to find a nice room for Damien McAdams just because a couple of you used to be Arsenal fans and he played for your team, but other than that, all of the people who came here with us have remained segregated. Oh, and you demoted Ruth, sent her over to the dark side.'

'That's a strange way of putting it,' he said, focusing on Ruth to avoid admitting he'd supported the Gunners and had arranged Damien's accommodations upgrade. 'Ruth's doing us a favour. She's very capable, and she knows the ropes. She was more than happy to move across and help out settle you all in.'

'I can imagine the kind of offer you made to her,' Marianne said.

He shook his head. 'Look, I know where you're coming from, Marianne, and I understand why you feel the way you do, but you know the plan is to get you all out of the hotel and into somewhere larger and cleaner as quickly as possible.'

'Somewhere like that tower block monstrosity you've had folks clearing out this week?'

'Somewhere like Hatton House, yes. Listen, I know you've had a bum deal in the hotel, but like I said, it was only ever temporary. Look at the agenda for this meeting again. I listed the items for discussion in that order for a reason. Our number one priority right now must be to get enough supplies together to see us through the winter, so that's what we're focusing on first. Getting people moved is the next job on the list. There's no point us putting people in better accommodations if they're going to starve when they get there. It should only take a couple of weeks.'

'I think that's a bit optimistic,' Mihai said.

'How are the stores looking?' Dominic asked.

'Well, Hatton House has been completely cleared, and I'll be honest, we haven't got anywhere near as much stuff as I'd hoped. There's plenty of clothing and bedding, more than we need, but so far we've found next to no food and barely any medical supplies.'

'We need to talk about drugs,' Liz said, interrupting. 'I need loads more.'

'What kind of stuff?'

'All the usual basics, and probably all the anti-depressants left in London.'

'These people just need to get a grip and get on with life,' Piotr said. 'All the fucking tranquilizers in the world won't sort this mess out.'

Liz held her head in her hands. 'Just when I think you couldn't be more blinkered, Piotr, you go and prove me wrong yet again. Just about the only thing left I can rely on with any certainty is you getting on my tits.'

'People just need to face facts and get on with it,' he continued, oblivious. 'We spend too much time talking about these bloody people who are depressed. Fuck's sake, we're all fucking depressed.'

'But that's the thing, you don't spend any time talking about it, do you? Every time we're sat around this table I tell you there's an issue, and you tell me people need to man up and stop crying about everything, and that's where the conversation ends. But that should only be the beginning of the conversation.'

Orla agreed. 'Liz is right. A bit of care and consideration now will save lives in the long term. We have to invest in these people, not write them off.'

'We don't have time,' Piotr snapped.

'Time is the only thing we do have.'

'We're fighting a fucking war out there to keep these people fed.'

'Why does it have to be a war all the time? And, anyway, there won't be any point if there's no one left to feed. Do you seriously think the mental health of every one of us isn't going to be an issue at some point? Is there one person around this table who hasn't lost everyone they loved? Is there any one of us here who hasn't cried themselves to sleep, night after night? I know I have. And I bet most of your best fighters who lined up this week to take potshots at the dead feel the exact same way. I've spoken to more than a few of them who are struggling to make sense of it all. They go and start hacking away at the bodies because they think it'll make them feel better but, newsflash: slashing, stabbing and burning just makes them feel a hundred times worse.'

'Exactly,' Liz said. 'You'd be surprised at some of the people I see in my surgery. Some of the folks you think are best at dealing with all of this are the ones who are struggling most. You might think they're hard as nails, but they're just putting on a brave face. Some of your biggest hitters have sat across the table from me and cried their bloody eyes out, Piotr.'

'Who?' he demanded.

'As if I'm going to tell you that. Pretty much everyone left alive has PTSD, and I know we're all getting hardened to the things we see and the things we have to do every day, but at this rate, we'll end up shells of people - if we make it through the winter.'

Dominic tried to assert control again. 'I acknowledge it's an issue, Liz, but I'm not sure it's quite as bad as you're saying.'

'No disrespect, but how the fuck would you know?'

'I was speaking to Dr Ahmad this morning, actually. He said he's barely seen anyone for the last few weeks.'

'Again, no disrespect, but that's because Dr Ahmad is a miserable cunt. People don't like him. They avoid him. That's why I'm so bloody swamped all the time. The fucker only comes out of his room for dinner or to take a piss.'

No one argued, not even Dominic.

'I've only seen him a handful of times,' Marianne said. 'And even then it was from a distance. I tried to get an appointment with him, and he shut the bloody door in my face.'

Mihai spoke again. 'I know what medicines you need, Liz, and I'm focussed on trying to get them.'

'Thank you, Mihai.'

'But like I said, we hardly found anything today.'

'That's what we expected,' Piotr said, dismissive. 'There are hundreds more buildings for us to clear yet. We'll get enough.'

'I don't think we will,' Lynette said. She'd been quiet so far, and the other people around the table turned to look. Dominic glared at her, and she took exception. 'Why are you looking at me like that? I'm just being honest. I'm getting tired of all the bullshit, Dom.'

'Bullshit? What's got into you, Lyn? We all agreed on the approach we were going to take. No one ever said it was going to be easy, but we've still got the whole of Wapping to work our way through. There will be enough food there to keep us going all winter.'

'And are you certain about that?'

'Yes.'

'Are you, Mihai?'

Mihai shifted uncomfortably in his seat. 'I don't know. There *should* be, but if I'm honest, I can't say I'm completely comfortable, not after this week's haul.'

'But I was with you just a short time ago. The stores seemed better stocked than they have been in weeks.'

'They are. I'm not disputing that.' He paused, choosing his words carefully. 'We've got more than three hundred people here, Dominic. Phillipa and Steven run the kitchen like a military operation. They waste nothing. They make the little we give them go a long way, and they generally make it so that it's relatively palatable.'

'I'm not asking you to be a food critic, Mihai, I just need to know if we've got enough of the damn stuff.'

'What I'm trying to say, Dom, is that we are doing the best we can with what we have, but it takes an enormous amount of supplies to keep three hundred plus people fed day after day. We've done really well so far, and what we collected this week will keep us going a little while longer, but in my honest opinion, if the plan is to stay hunkered down here until the end of February or into March, we're not going to have anywhere near enough.'

'There's another factor you're not considering,' David said. 'Look, I've been out there this week. I helped seal off The Highway, and I did a couple of shifts in Hatton House. I think you may be right, there may well be enough food across the whole of Wapping to see us through, but what's it going to cost us to get it? It's exhausting. Dangerous. The dead are more of a threat than we anticipated. There's nothing much left of some of them, but there are others that are frigging ferocious.'

Piotr interrupted. 'They're more aggressive, sure, but they're no stronger. Most of the ones around the perimeter have been worn down to nothing. They're like soup.'

'That's true, but once we clear them, they're replaced by the more tenacious ones. And the more we fight, the more violent they seem to become, and the more we have to fight, the more effort it takes to keep going. Jesus, a couple of days of this and I'm done in. I don't know how long I'll be able to keep it up for. People are exhausted. Like Liz says, many of us are broken or are barely holding ourselves together.'

'David's right,' Lynette said. 'I was trying to say this very thing before you got all shitty with me, Dominic. Breaking into hundreds of individual houses to take a few cans of beans from each one doesn't seem like the most sensible way of going about it. It's hardly efficient.'

'What's the alternative?' Piotr asked, already out of patience. 'And before anyone starts, it's too dangerous to try getting out of London, too much of a risk. Don't give me any of your Ledsey Cross bullshit.'

'Despite the fact we know there are people waiting for us up there?' Marianne said.

'It's too dangerous,' he said again. 'Remember the shit-show when you lot tried to get a few miles across London? Unless you've got access to a fleet of helicopters complete with pilots, I don't see how anyone's getting out of here until the end of winter.'

'I don't think we have any option,' Dominic said. 'We need to continue clearing as much of Wapping as we can, no matter how long it takes or how hard it is. We have to strip the bones of the place clean. There's no other way.'

'There is, actually,' Marianne said. 'Lynette and I have been talking about an alternative. If you'd all be quiet for a minute and wind your necks in, we'd happily tell you.'

All eyes were on her now.

'We've been talking about this for a while,' she explained, 'but we didn't think there was any point sharing. The problem is that even though much of the world has changed, it's still testosterone that's doing all the talking, certainly around this table, anyway. Also, we didn't want to say anything at first, because we were both hoping things were going to work out and we'd find everything we needed without having to look elsewhere.'

'Were you not listening?' Piotr interrupted, furious. 'We're not looking elsewhere. It's. Too. Dangerous.'

Marianne glared at him. 'There really are far too many chiefs here. You're very good at telling everyone else what they can and can't do, Piotr, but you're incapable of shutting up long enough to listen. Please, do me a favour, dear, and keep your mouth closed for a couple of minutes so I can explain.'

For once, he did.

'We've all come to accept that central London has proved to be the absolute worst place in the world to be stuck, not just because of the lack of facilities in this area, but also because of the sheer number of dead bodies we've got on almost all sides.'

'*Almost* all sides?' Mihai said. Marianne seized on his interruption.

'You see! Good, lad, Mihai. Someone's paying attention! We've got the river. We're camped on the Thames, but the only thing we're using it for is dumping our shit and keeping a few bodies at bay.'

Marianne's dislike of Dominic Grove was mutual. He made no effort to hide his contempt. 'Jesus Christ, Marianne, tell me you're not going to suggest we start fishing, are you?' he groaned.

'Are you volunteering to be used as bait?' she asked, immediately silencing him. 'No, you silly little man, we're talking about travelling on the river. We're talking about Surrey Quays.'

'Where's that?' David asked. 'And what is it? I'm not local, don't forget.'

'It's a shopping centre,' Lynette said.

'But it's on the south bank,' Piotr added. 'Are you insane? Jesus Christ, why are we wasting our time listening to this crap?'

Unfazed, Marianne waited for him to stop ranting, then continued. 'You lot look at things from such a bloody limited perspective. Lynette and I aren't idiots. We know which bank of the Thames Surrey Quays is on, thank you very much. The clue is in the name, Surrey *Quays*. It's not quite on the water, but it's not far off. I think we're causing enough of a distraction to keep most corpses looking this way, even those on the other side of the river. If we can get a boat, there's a chance we can go right around the back of them.'

'And what's there?' David asked.

'It's a shopping centre,' Lynette explained. 'There's a massive branch of Tesco for starters. Our thinking is that as risky as it will inevitably be, a day spent emptying that place could keep us all fed for months, maybe even right the way through the winter if we're lucky.'

'But how are we supposed to get it all back here?' Mihai asked. 'We'd need a bloody big boat by the sounds of it.'

'Then we'll find a bloody big boat. For goodness's sake, enough of them used to go up and down the Thames every day.'

'And who's going to sail it for us?'

'Why don't you stop looking for problems and start trying to find solutions?' Marianne said. 'I'm amazed anything ever gets done here.'

Lynette got up.

'Where do you think you're going?' Dominic asked.

'To find Georgie. She'll know if we've got anyone suitable.'

'Are we seriously considering this?' said Piotr, making no attempt to hide his disdain.

'*We* are,' David said. 'You do what you want.'

'This is insane.'

'Is it? Let me tell you, mate, as someone who stood on the frontline of the fighting the other day, going a few miles down the Thames in a boat looking for food sounds like a pleasant day out.'

'And you don't think there will be corpses around Surrey Quays?'

'There are corpses *everywhere*. Thing is, they're queuing up to get at us here. We've seen them lining the south bank and trying to get across the bridges, but Marianne's plan sounds sensible. It sounds like it'll take us right around the back of the bulk of them.'

Dominic had been uncharacteristically quiet, listening to the back-and-forth. 'I know Surrey Quays. Maybe you're onto something.'

'*Seriously?*' Piotr said, appalled.

'Why not? Marianne makes a good point. It's not like we'd be able to empty the supermarket straight into a boat, but we'd have a better chance of bringing back a good haul by river than any other method I can think of.'

'It's got to be worth a try,' Mihai agreed.

Marianne wasn't finished. 'The other advantage, of course, going back to my earlier point, is that if we can sort out the food problems in one fell swoop, then we can focus our energies here on improving our accommodations and making this a better place to live for everyone.'

Piotr said, 'I don't like it.'

'You don't like anything. What's your objection, exactly?'

'The risk is shared here. You're suggesting sending a few people out on their own.'

'Let's just dissect that. All we're suggesting at this stage is sending people out to take a look. If they can bring a load of food back without too much of a risk, then so much the better. And as for the risk being fairly shared here, I don't know how you can say that when, by all accounts, you've spent most of the week up in a bloody crane, watching everyone else doing your dirty work from a safe distance.'

'I was coordinating.'

'Is that what you call it?'

The meeting was poised to devolve into another pointless slanging match when Lynette returned. Georgie was behind her, looking petrified, clutching her thick ring-binder full of papers to her chest.

'No need to be nervous, Georgie,' Dominic said.

She relaxed – slightly – then sat down next to Lynette. Georgie had done an exceptional job for the group, keeping manual records up to date, recording relevant information, and maintaining calendars and clocks to make sure they followed the old-world date and time. She was at home with her forms and her paperwork; the boardroom was most definitely not her happy place. Marianne sensed her unease and moved swiftly to put her out of her misery. 'We've been talking about Surrey Quays,' she said, and Georgie's face lit up.

'I used to live by there. I know it well.' Then she froze again. 'Wait... I'm not going. I'm not leaving this place without—'

Lynette put a reassuring hand on her arm. 'You're not going anywhere, love, *we* are. Some of us, anyway. We just want you to consult your records and see if there's anyone who you think might be able to help.'

'Help? How?'

'We'd like to go by river. We need to know if there's anyone who could help us with a boat... anyone who used to be involved in commercial shipping or fishing, anything like that...'

'Give me a sec,' Georgie said, and she turned to the back of her heavy paper file and ran her finger down the columns on a form. She found what she was looking for then turned to another part of the file, screwed up her face, flicked back, then tried again.

'We don't have all day,' Piotr grumbled.

'We do, actually,' Marianne corrected him. 'And all day tomorrow and the next day too if we need it. Take your time, Georgie, love.'

And she did. She kept them waiting another couple of minutes, then looked up. 'Allison Woodhouse.'

'I know Allison,' Liz said. 'Lovely girl.'

'She used to be the captain of a Thames Clipper,' Georgie explained. 'Water taxis.'

Dominic didn't sound convinced. 'Seriously? That little blonde girl?'

Marianne held her head in her hands. 'Did we suddenly all get transported back to the 1970s when the world ended? Tell me, Dominic, what is it about Allison that makes you think she couldn't be captain of a Thames Clipper?'

'I didn't say that, I just...'

'Was it that she's not particularly tall, or do you have a problem with blondes operating heavy machinery? Hang on, it couldn't possibly be because she's a girl, could it?'

Dominic tried to bluff his way out of trouble but failed spectacularly. 'Not at all. It's just that she's the last person I expected you to say.'

'You've made your point, Marianne. Georgie, do you know where we can find Allison?' David asked.

Georgie checked another section of her file. 'She's in the apartments. Give me a minute and I'll tell you the number.'

'No fucking way.'

Allison slammed the door in Lynette's face. Lynette knocked again.

'Come on, love. Let's at least talk about it.'

She could hear Allison's muffled voice on the other side, but the door remained shut. 'There's nothing to talk about. No way. I'm not doing it.'

'You're our best chance. All we want you to do is to get us over there so we can have a look. After that you can just sit tight on the boat.'

Lynette waited with her ear pressed against the door. She could hear pacing inside the room. She waited for a moment longer, then knocked again.

'I said no,' Allison shouted.

'I know you did, and I know you can still hear me in there, so do me a favour and just listen, don't bite my head off.' She paused. The pacing stopped. 'You're the only one who can do this, Ali. I wouldn't be asking if it wasn't important. If you don't help, life's probably going to get much, much harder for everyone here, you and me included. And I'm sorry if you think I'm deliberately sending you on a guilt trip, but it's all true, no exaggeration. If we can get enough food from that supermarket, we'll be set up for the winter. We can sit tight and wait it out, and by the time next spring comes round, the dead won't be anywhere near the kind of threat they are today. You helping us do this now could save everyone a lot of hurt in the long run. I'm not kidding, love, it could literally be the difference between life and death.'

She paused. Nothing. Was that a good sign?

'Let's face facts, if we don't do this, we're going to have to keep fighting. And the way things are going, we could all end up on the frontline before long. There's no easy options for any of us anymore.'

Lynette waited for Allison's response, knowing that as honest as she'd been, she was running out of things to say. She hoped she sounded more convincing than she felt, because if she was in Allison's shoes, she didn't know if she'd be able to do it. But how else could she have put it? Dominic was the king of spin, not her. Christ, what she'd have given for a fraction of his bullshitting skills right now.

She was about to knock again and give it one more try when the door opened inwards. Allison was standing in front of Lynette with tears streaming down her face. 'I'm scared. I've been trying to come up with a good reason to turn you down, but I can't.'

All out of words, Lynette just hugged her.

There'd been a couple of little boats moored near Tower Bridge Quay since the group had first established its presence around the Monument to the Great Fire of London. They'd use one of those to sail downriver with the hope of finding something bigger while they were away. Depending how things went, this would either be a quick reconnaissance mission or a full-on supply run. One day away or several.

Finding a skipper was only half the battle. Picking the rest of the crew was the next challenge. The call went out for volunteers.

Allison had been drafted, and though her opinion was sought, she usually kept herself to herself and didn't have anyone specific in mind. Chapman, the ex-copper who'd worked closely with Piotr previously, offered to lead the crew. 'Can we afford to spare him?' Dominic had asked.

'Paul Duggan and Harjinder are leading the reclamation work,' Piotr told him. 'Chapman can go. He needs to prove himself.'

Lisa Kaur and Richard Finnegan also put themselves forward. The two of them were close, frequently bickering like an old married couple, and had proved themselves to be valuable out in the field. Lisa had been a personal trainer at a gym near Surrey Quays, so her inclusion in the crew was a no-brainer. Richard put up his hand as soon as Lisa agreed to go, and that itself triggered another argument. 'I don't need you looking after me,' she told him, but, in the absence of many other volunteers, they were both co-opted.

Ruth offered to go, as did Gary Welch. When the council reconvened to confirm final numbers, Marianne also raised her hand. 'I'll go,' she said.

David Shires turned on her. 'Don't be stupid, Marianne, you're not well. You can't go.'

'Yes, I can. I'm no freeloader. I want to do my bit. More to the point, I can't expect everyone else to risk their lives if I'm not prepared to do the same myself. And anyway, this whole thing was my idea.'

'Thank you, Marianne,' Dominic said, too keen. 'I think we're almost there. One more person, perhaps. Like I keep saying, I know there's a real element of risk, but if we pull this off, the next few months will be much easier for all of us.'

There was a moment of silence before Marianne spoke again. 'I think you should come with us, Dom. You can keep me company.'

Normally quick and silver-tongued, he now struggled to speak. Marianne spoke for him.

'It's just that, since we arrived here, your voice has been the only real constant. You're always ready to tell everybody how things are going to be and to let us all know what we need to do to make things work, but I can't remember ever having seen you lift a finger.'

The others in the room remained quiet, but Marianne still had more to say.

'I mean, you've taken great pains to tell us all how you're not a leader and how you're no longer a politician, so why not step up and get your hands dirty? If I can volunteer, there's no reason you can't.'

Whilst there were no mumbles of agreement from around the

table, no one jumped to Dominic's defence either. He looked around at the faces staring back at him and realised there was only one way of getting out of the situation with his credibility intact.

'Okay.'

Still no one else spoke. Dominic cleared his throat and did everything he could to make himself appear more confident than he was suddenly feeling. Once the initial shock had faded, his brain and his tongue clicked back into gear.

'Absolutely. Of course. You're right as usual, Marianne. I can't stand here expecting everyone else to take risks without taking any risks myself. I'll go. It'll be an honour.'

It had taken until the early hours, but eventually Marianne had bowed to pressure and accepted she wasn't the right person to go. She was overweight and unused to fighting; in truth, she had only volunteered herself to force Dominic's hand, though she'd been prepared to go. Unfortunately, her physical constraints meant she'd have contributed little and may even have presented a risk to the scavenging group. Vicky volunteered to take her place; another slanging match with Selena last night had sealed the deal. She didn't know how to get through to the stupid kid; didn't even know if she could be bothered to keep trying. It had been an argument over nothing, but it had been enough to make the prospect of heading out into the unchartered landscape of death-filled Rotherhithe seem preferable to another day of picking through the rubble of what was left of Wapping in the company of an angsty teen.

The focus was elsewhere when the group left. Another incursion of corpses along St Katharine's Way, to the rear of the hotel, occupied most folks. The dead hordes had been herded south and east by the clearance work along The Highway and had been agitated by so much unfettered noise after weeks of relative silence. A pressure point had built near the St Katharine's Docks drawbridge, behind the hotel, and the dead had eventually burst through. With the power down, the narrow bridge couldn't be raised, and the number of corpses being held back on the other side had grown and grown until the furthest forward cadavers had spurted over the insufficient, makeshift barrier like toothpaste squeezed from a tube.

The others could hear the frantic recovery work from down on the water; the chugging of machinery, mixed with Piotr's frequently yelled orders, carried on the wind. They could see him towering over everything in his cherry picker, gesticulating wildly like he was conducting an orchestra that had forgotten how to play. It almost made her glad to be down here on the river.

In places, the Thames seemed to flow with as much flesh and bone as water. Huge rafts of floating corpses had to be pushed out of the way with poles so that Allison could get one of the little boats out from its makeshift mooring, around the back of Tower Bridge Quay, a little downriver from Tower Millennium Pier. Vicky had first moored here with Sam, David, and the others, what felt like a lifetime ago. Vicky looked back along the Thames in the direction of Fleet Street and considered how much had happened in a relatively short period of time. The things she'd seen and done, the people she'd met and those they'd lost. She looked beyond Tower Bridge towards London Bridge and, even today, more than a month since Sam had sacrificed himself and blocked the crossing, she could still see the flesh-covered mound where he'd crashed the bus. He may have been an opinionated, self-obsessed, gobby lefty, but that had been a bloody horrible way to go by anyone's standards. Buried alive under all that putrid flesh, no way out, just waiting to die... it made her go cold just thinking about it.

'Vicky, get with it. It's time to go,' Chapman yelled. She was the last to board the boat. The group was largely silent, all no doubt feeling as apprehensive as she was. Dominic was alongside Allison at the helm – of course – wearing a fresh set of clothes that clearly hadn't seen a day's work. He reminded Vicky of a particularly useless lord of the manor, heading out with the plebs in his best bib and tucker to see what those in the lower ranks got up to. He tried telling Allison what to do but then shut up fast when Chapman said if he was that much of an expert, he could have captained the frigging boat himself and saved Allison the bother. She was clearly relieved when he shut up, but Vicky could see the poor kid was overwhelmed. It came as no surprise. One minute she'd been hiding away in her apartment, doing all she could to avoid the reality of what was happening everywhere else, the next she was shoved out into the thick of it, under extreme pressure, and with the intolerable weight of everyone's expectations on her shoulders.

The jury was out on Chapman. He was too pally with Piotr and Dominic for her liking. He'd let Dominic do all the talking so far this morning, but she got the impression he wasn't going to take any crap. By contrast, Gary, who was with her at the back of the boat, was a stalwart. Not a particularly likeable bloke at times, but there was no side to him, and he was always at the front of the queue when anything needed doing for the benefit of the group. 'You're always one of the first to put your hand up, Gary. Why is that?'

'Just need to keep myself busy. The more you're doing stuff these days, the less time you have to think.'

'Fair point.'

'Don't go thinking I'm some kind of good Samaritan,' he explained. 'It's about keeping myself distracted, that's all.'

'I'm not so sure,' Vicky said. Gary shrugged his shoulders and shuffled a little further up the boat. Ruth was keen to take his space.

'How you doing?' she asked. Vicky nodded and managed a flicker of a smile, doing what she could to hold in a cough. Allison opened the engine slightly. Ruth nudged Vicky and nodded at Richard and Lisa who held onto each other tight as the little boat bobbed through the rubbish-strewn tide. They were hardly star-crossed lovers, but it was clear they both took much comfort and support from being around each other. 'Ain't love grand, eh?' Ruth whispered, and she put her arm around Vicky and pulled her closer, reducing the space between them as the distance between the boat and everything else rapidly increased.

12

'It's even colder out here on the water, don't you think?' Dominic asked the others, finally finding his sea legs. His teeth were chattering, and he rubbed his hands together. The waterproof jacket he was wearing was a couple of sizes too big; it looked like he'd stolen it from one of the bigger boys. He watched the sky, following the clouds as they drifted overhead, dark greys against lighter greys, pockets of blue appearing between them. Vicky could see what he was doing. Looking up instead of down, talking non-stop about inarguable certainties like the temperature and the weather, focusing on inconsequential trivialities... it all helped him avoid having to face the reality of the emaciated world through which they were travelling.

Bloated bodies buffeted against the sides of the boat almost constantly, but Dominic ignored them. He looked away as seagulls pecked at the innards of some of the floaters. Equally, he paid no attention to scores more of the gangrenous things that tumbled and scrambled down the banks of the river and ended up in the polluted water. When ranks of foetid ex-humans were revealed in the gaps between buildings on either side, he paid them no heed. It was particularly noticeable on the north bank, where the entire dead population seemed to be herding towards the Tower of London in a slow-motion migration towards the living, as predictable as it was terrifying. Still, Dominic chose not to look.

'When did you last leave the base?' Vicky asked. He blew into his hands and rubbed them together to keep warm.

'I'm sorry, what?'

'I asked when you last left the base,' she said again, a little louder. She knew he'd heard her perfectly well.

'Honest answer, this is the first time,' he admitted, before ladling on a load of sugar-coated spin. 'It seemed more sensible for me to stay put once people started arriving and we'd put the first wall around the place, you know? I'm not going to lie to you, I had no desire to go outside, but I always knew I'd be of more use getting things organised inside the base.'

Vicky just nodded, not needing to prolong the conversation. Dominic, on the other hand, never knew when to stop.

'It's very different now I'm actually out here, though. I hadn't bargained on it. I know we're on the river and you probably get a false sense of security, but it's nowhere near as bad as I'd built it up in my head.'

Chapman just looked at him. 'You wait, mate. Don't reckon you'll be so cocky once we're back on dry land.'

As it was, within a few more minutes they'd all been stunned into silence. As they navigated the gentle curve of the Thames, the Isle of Dogs came into view. The tightly packed towers of Canary Wharf were burning. For so long a symbol of this remarkable city's power and prosperity, they were now being devoured by flames. It was impossible to tell how much or how little of each building was affected by the blaze that had spread unchecked through the area, but it didn't matter. With no one there to put out the fires, it would likely just burn until nothing was left standing.

It was some consolation that they could see snaking lines of miserable, shambling figures walking towards the inferno. Vicky hoped the flames would keep burning long enough to reduce every one of the fuckers to ash.

Surrey Quays.

'This is it,' Allison said, slowing the engine and steering towards the south bank. 'And look what I can see.'

There was a Thames Clipper moored at Greenland Surrey Quays Pier. It looked in relatively good condition. Its hull was clean in comparison to everything else, the paintwork bright white with flashes of deep purple. As their little boat drifted gently towards it, the sun appeared through a gap in the clouds, drenching everything with unexpected light and warmth, making the world look over-exposed. Dominic couldn't help himself. 'There you go. A sign. Someone's looking out for us.'

'Get a grip,' Gary muttered under his breath. 'The only things looking out for us today are several million corpses.'

Allison kept the boat at a safe distance and sailed parallel with the clipper. She gave the engine a short burst to take them around the bow of the larger vessel, and many of the corpses that had been trapped onboard reacted to the noise. They slammed up against the windows along the length of the boat, slapping at the safety glass with slippery palms. They looked remarkably well-preserved.

'Do they all look like that over here?' Dominic asked. 'They look in better shape than most of the horrible things crammed around the base.'

Vicky explained. 'I've seen a few like this recently. If they've been stuck indoors, they decay differently. It's because they're more sheltered, I think.' She gestured at the clipper. 'Those stuck in there, they've been protected from the wind and the rain and from the bulk of the crowds.'

'They all look the same to me.'

Vicky shook her head. 'Believe me, they're not. You need to be more careful when they're like this. There's little difference in terms of aggression and ferocity, but because they're less decayed, more complete, they're always going to be stronger and more coordinated. More dangerous.'

'Jeez, I'm glad you're here,' Lisa said.

'Are you? I'm not.'

Allison manoeuvred the boat around the pier. Chapman climbed out and tied them up. As the others disembarked, he crept along the seating area inside the pier where commuters would have waited for river taxis. A lone cadaver lurched off the clipper and ambled towards him. He shoved it back onto the boat then pulled the gate shut to stop more of them following.

A sloped, covered walkway connected the pier to the rest of south London. They grouped at the bottom of it to plan their next course of action. 'Might as well use this clipper. Can you get it going, Allison?' Dominic asked.

'I guess...'

She didn't sound convinced.

'I'll stay here and help with the bodies and the mechanics,' Chapman said. 'I suggest the rest of you go and do a recce.' He looked at Lisa and Rich. 'You both know the area well, don't you?'

'Yep,' Lisa said, though she too sounded less confident than she had previously.

'Good. You lead the way.'

Dominic looked lost, deposed from his usual position of authority. But he still couldn't stop himself trying to stamp his mark. 'Sounds like a sensible plan. Thank you. Is everyone alright with everything?'

But the others were already off.

Ruth held back. She caught Dominic's arm before he could walk away. 'There's something very important you need to remember while we're out here, Dom.'

'What's that?'

'Keep your fucking mouth shut.'

The pedestrian gate at the other end of the sloped walkway was unlocked and open. They paused again before stepping out onto dry land. There were many bodies nearby, but in far fewer numbers, more diffuse than they were used to on the north bank.

'Which way?' Vicky asked, her voice just a whisper.

'This is Surrey Quays,' Lisa replied, equally quietly, gesturing towards the water on their right. 'The shopping centre is on the other side. Our best bet is to go straight ahead here. We'll come to some residential buildings first, bit of a rabbit warren. I say we stop there and get our bearings.'

'Sounds like a plan,' Gary said.

'If we can get onto the top floor, we should be able to get a better idea of what we're gonna be dealing with.'

They took out their weapons, anticipating trouble. Vicky had her crowbar, most of the others carried knives. Gary had managed to get hold of a machete. Dominic was emptyhanded. Ruth glared at him. 'You're kidding? You've seriously come here without a weapon?'

'Sorry... I wasn't thinking.'

'Too busy talking,' Gary said, and the others might have laughed had their situation not felt quite so precarious. Inquisitive corpses had already started shuffling towards them. Ruth took a spare knife from a sheath on her belt and handed it to Dominic. 'You use the pointy end, yeah?'

'Look, just leave it out. I know I don't have anywhere near as much experience as the rest of you, but I'm not a complete idiot.'

'I don't think for a second that you're an idiot, but I do think you're a liability. What you've spent your time doing until now and what we've come out here to do today are very, very different things.'

'And that's why I knew it was important I came along.'

'Really? I heard it was because Marianne forced your hand.'

'Are we going to spend all day talking shite?' Vicky asked, frustrated by the bickering.

'No,' Gary said, annoyed, 'but Ruth does have a point. This matters.' He pointed the tip of his machete towards Dominic. 'If we get into trouble out here, we're going to have to rely on each other to all play our part. I don't want to have to rely on you, only for you to bottle it.'

'Give me a bloody chance, for Christ's sake. We've only just stepped off the boat.'

Ruth took a couple of steps away from the others, her sudden movement attracting the attention of a shambling corpse. Far faster than the dead man, she side-stepped him, grabbed him by the scruff of the neck, then pushed him towards the pier. She let go of the cadaver right in front of Dominic, and when he recoiled, the foul aberration came at him with almost predatory speed. Dominic panicked and pushed him away.

'Deal with it,' Ruth ordered.

'This is crazy,' he said, and the decaying man sped up. Dominic instinctively put out a hand to stop him getting too close, locking his arm and grabbing a fistful of wet flesh or wet clothing, he wasn't sure which. He looked around for help, but the others had all stepped back.

'I'm serious,' Ruth told him. 'This is important. We need to know you can do this. Now finish him.'

Dominic pushed the corpse back again and raised the knife, but instead of going on the offensive, he hesitated.

'Do it,' she hissed.

'With a grunt of effort, he finally lunged forward and slit his would-be-attacker's midsection with a poorly aimed swipe of the borrowed blade. The noxious contents of the dead man's belly gushed out, and he gagged. Ruth pulled the corpse away, then let it go. It immediately zeroed in on Dominic again.

'You need to do this, Dom. We're not going anywhere until we've seen what you can do.'

Dominic glanced around anxiously. He could see more of the dead beginning to show an interest in the group now, and it scared him. He swung the blade wildly again, slicing through parchment skin with little resistance, but it made no difference.

'You have to remember, they're not what they used to be,' Gary told him. 'They're not human anymore. They don't think or feel. Tell yourself you're doing them a favour ending their miserable existence because, honestly, you are.'

Another flash of the knife, and this time Dominic finally did enough damage to slow his persistent attacker down. By chance, not design, he'd sliced through muscles and tendons at the top of the dead man's right thigh. The monstrous creature collapsed in front of him. Dominic dropped down onto its hollow chest, pushed its face into the ground, then looked up once more for reassurance before stabbing it through the ear.

Shaking and sweating profusely, he picked himself up again and started wiping away the glutenous blood and other discharges with which he'd been covered, though all he succeeded in doing was smearing it over himself further. Another seven bodies were nearing. Lisa, Rich, Gary, Chapman, and Vicky made short work of them without breaking a sweat.

'We're not messing around here,' Ruth warned him. 'Fuck up, and you could end up dead. Worse than that, one of us might end up copping it.'

'At least you look like the rest of us now,' Richard said, looking him up and down.

13

There were bodies everywhere. It was nothing like the chaos they'd left on the north bank where the dead had mashed themselves into a paste, but their numbers here were still daunting. They were quicker, more in control of their movements, and it was terrifying in a different way. They roamed with relative freedom here, not drawn to any specific place as they had been around the Monument and the Tower of London. Sure, there were spots where something had attracted their limited attention and they'd gathered, but they were few and far between, and the crowds of them soon dispersed. For now, they drifted rather than herded, and that was reassuring. It made Ruth watch Dominic like a hawk. She was worried he'd get cocky and not lose sight of the danger, and the fragility of the quiet here was deceptive. She felt like they were tiptoeing through a minefield, and Dom wore particularly heavy boots. One slip, just one wrong step or unexpected noise, and they could trigger a chain reaction that might bring about the end of all of them. They could cope with hundreds, maybe thousands of them, if they stayed spread out like this, but similar numbers would pose an insurmountable threat in closer confines.

This had been an affluent area back in the day, and if they looked up instead of down, it still didn't look too shabby. It was similar in appearance to St Katharine's Docks – buildings of a comparable style and age, no doubt redeveloped around the same time – and yet it felt spacious and open in comparison. The layer of filth that seemed to coat everything on the north bank wasn't as obvious here and, in welcome contrast with what they'd left behind, many of the residential roads remained almost clear. Thousands of people used to undertake a daily mass migration from here to the other side of the river for work, and it showed. Even now, the streets for miles around the Monument base were clogged with the congested remnants of that final morning rush hour, almost eighty days ago.

The diffusion of the bodies made this side of the river feel vast and empty; Vicky reminded herself it was an illusion. They needed to take care moving through these spaces because the lack of other distractions left their small group even more exposed. Thankfully there were enough gaps between buildings, recessed doorways, and tucked away passageways to enable them to duck and cover whenever the need arose. For the most part, though, their tried and tested approach of mimicking the slothful gait of the lethargic dead seemed to work. The group dragged their feet, staying close but doing what they could to make it not look like they were moving together, spacing themselves out at a reasonable distance, seemingly aimless, moving along with empty, sullen expressions.

Shadowing Lisa, they'd walked a relatively straight route along Rope Street and into Cunard Walk. Indicating her direction with barely perceptible hand signals, she marshalled them along, taking them across the end of Greenland Dock in a ragged line towards an apartment block. Another subtle signal: this time, up.

The weather-beaten remains of a corpse had propped the door of the building ahead of them open, its bony ankle trapped in the gap. Other meandering bodies began to show a little interest as the group filed inside, but Richard dealt with them quickly and quietly before following. They regrouped in a small, musty vestibule and listened carefully to the sounds of the building.

'What do we do now?' Dominic asked. Gary glared at him.

'We shut our fucking mouths and we wait. We listen.'

And they did. The noise they'd made entering the block, along with Dominic's naïve chatter, had caused a reaction elsewhere. They could hear movement in one of the flats upstairs, though it sounded sufficiently muffled and distant to indicate it was away from the staircase.

'What do we reckon?' Ruth whispered.

Vicky looked up and around. 'Stuck in their apartments, it sounds like. We should be okay.'

She nodded, then started to climb.

The windows on the top floor all faced the wrong way, looking out over the docks and the area through which they'd already walked. It still looked relatively quiet, and that was a relief. Their arrival on the south bank hadn't yet caused the chaos it so easily might have.

'Sorry,' Lisa said. 'I thought we might be able to see better from up here.'

Vicky prised open a maintenance door opposite with her crowbar. She cringed when the wooden frame splintered with a loud crack, causing the dead trapped in their tomb-like flats to react again. She leant into the dark space beyond the door and saw more steps leading up. When she forced another second door open at the top, light flooded into the building, and she walked out onto the roof.

The wind was bracing up there, and it felt much colder too, but at least they were able to talk freely. They stayed back from the very edge. 'It's not just for safety,' Gary explained to Dominic. 'If they see us up here, they might start crowding and block our way out. We don't want to end up stuck on the roof.' Dominic just nodded. For once he was all out of words.

This high vantage point afforded them a half-decent view over the Surrey Quays shopping centre, just a couple of hundred metres further inland. One side of the complex and part of its frontage was visible over the tops of leaf-stripped trees. There were small crowds of corpses around parts of the building, but it was difficult to draw any useful conclusions from this distance.

'No obvious signs of activity,' Vicky said. 'Doesn't look like anything much has happened here recently.'

'How can you tell?' Dominic asked, completely out of his depth. 'There are loads of them out there.'

She scoffed. 'That's not loads. That's the size of crowd I'd expect to see when the dead are just drifting. Just my gut reaction, but I think we're good here. You've seen how the dead behave back near the Monument... if there were other people here, we'd see residual signs in the activity of the crowds, I'm sure we would.'

'There'd be thousands of the fuckers,' Gary agreed. 'Don't forget, Dom, there's barely anything left to attract their attention now. We're the hottest show in town.'

Lisa edged forward and pointed out parts of the shopping centre. 'So, that's the main part, dead ahead, no pun intended. You've got Tesco on this side, and the loading bays and service yards and whatever beyond, over there, to our right.'

'What's the best way of trying to get inside, d'you think?' Ruth asked. 'I'm guessing the front door's out of the question.'

'The gym I used to work at isn't far from here. Sometimes I'd get the overground train to work, and I'd get off at Surrey Quays station. I'd walk down that road in front of us to get to work. You see those black railings?'

'Yes.'

'Well, they run parallel with the fence around the back of Tesco. I reckon we can either try and get over there, or we can keep following it around and see if we can get access through the service entrances.'

Ruth nodded. She looked at Vicky for confirmation. 'Sounds sensible,' Vicky said. 'I can't see any better alternatives.'

They trooped back inside. At the bottom of the stairs, Dominic pulled Gary back. 'Wait, that's it? That's the plan?'

'Pretty much. We'll split and cause a distraction. It'll be easier to get inside if the creeps are looking the other way.'

'Blow something up, something like that?'

'You really have got a lot to learn, Dom. We don't want anything too dramatic, else we'll end up with thousands of the fuckers trooping down here to see what's going on. We don't want them all bringing their mates, do we?'

'I'll try and trigger a car alarm,' Vicky said. 'That was Sam's trick. Usually worked for him.'

'Cool,' Ruth said. 'Want a hand?'

'No, I'm good. I'll be quicker on my own. Just make sure you leave the door open for me.'

Vicky enjoyed being on her own again, despite the obvious discomfort of being alone among the dead. It was strangely liberating walking alongside them, mimicking their miserable, shuffling pace, taking her time. There was a kind of freedom to be found pretending to be one of the masses, an unexpected and welcome anonymity, and not without a certain thrill of the risk of being exposed, like a pre-apocalypse celebrity in sunglasses and wig, walking into a crowed event. Hey, she thought, maybe there were other living people like her out here, mixing with the undead, similarly camouflaged? The air was dry, and she swigged from the bottle of cough medicine she was carrying. A coughing fit out here would do the trick and get their attention, though it would also be suicidal.

She crept around the outer edge of the shopping centre carpark, moving painfully slowly, doing what she could to ensure her very definite changes in direction looked random and uncontrolled. It was hard not to be distracted by her surroundings, because this small part of London appeared to have been spared much of the devastation that had consumed the other side of the river. This carpark was almost completely fenced-off, cars still parked in orderly lines for the most part. And, if she squinted, those corpses that meandered lazily between the lines of stationary traffic looked a lot like weary shoppers. It was surreal, and she tried not to think about it. She needed to stay focused.

Confident that none of the dead could see her, she ducked down behind a small Fiat parked on its own and tugged at the door handle. It was locked, of course. Instead, she took a breath, braced herself for the impact of the noise, and smashed the window with her crowbar.

Nothing happened.

No alarm.

Months of inactivity had left the battery of this car – and most likely all the others in this carpark, maybe even the entire city – completely flat. She'd have to improvise, and the obvious solution was to just batter her crowbar against the chassis until the nearest bodies accepted her invitation, then slip away unnoticed.

It didn't take a lot to get the reaction she wanted.

She rattled the crowbar around the broken window frame like a cowboy dinner bell, and it was as if she'd flicked a switch. Every corpse she could see immediately stopped moving, pivoted to face the direction of the noise, then started towards her. It was sobering – no, horrifying – how quickly they stopped acting as individuals and coalesced into a mob. There was no conscious thought and zero communication between them, but the way they all did the exact same thing gave the impression they were all in on some secret, whispered plan.

Vicky continued hitting the side of the car for as long as she dared, then scooped up the closest cadaver and forced it in through the broken window. It immediately began thrashing around, trapped in the close confines of the little dead Fiat. It fought tirelessly, unable to escape, spreading its leaking, oily innards around the car's interior. It was more than enough to continue to attract the attention of every nearby corpse.

She started back towards the road and collided with a hideously ravaged figure coming the other way. They both ended up on the ground, limbs tangled together, but when the dead body ignored her and crawled past to get to the Fiat, Vicky knew she'd done enough. She picked herself up again and followed the footpath around the outside of the carpark. The road climbed, and when she looked back and saw the full impact of her actions, she was satisfied but unnerved. There was a decent swarm centred on the Fiat now, an ink blot that continued to grow. It had taken hardly any effort at all to elicit a disproportionately large response from the south bank hordes.

Ruth was waiting for her in the gap between the footpath

railings and the tall security fence that protected the back of the supermarket. She signalled for Vicky to keep walking around. More corpses staggered past her the other way, all but ignoring her as she clung to the shadows and worked her way around to reach the rest of the group.

The security fence around the back of the supermarket boxed in the rear of the building entirely, separating it from the rest of the shopping centre, and there appeared to be no obvious way through. It was too high to climb over and was topped with brutal-looking anti-theft spikes. The rest of the centre was not quite so well protected. The railings around the back of the other stores were a good metre or so lower than the Tesco fence. There was also a gate which was slightly lower still. Gary had already helped Lisa and Rich climb over to investigate.

The couple explored the service yard behind the centre while the rest of the group loitered behind a wall on the other side of the fence, hiding from the dead in the shadows of overhanging trees, glad to be out of the wind.

Richard was following the side wall of the supermarket. He found a padlocked fire door they could use to gain access once the others were over safely. He went to tell Lisa, who was lugging an aluminium ladder she'd found around the back of another store. It had been lying alongside the remains of a skeletal figure wearing maintenance overalls that had become glued to the floor with decay. She passed the ladder to Gary and Dominic, seesawing them on top of the gate. The two men got in each other's way and dropped the ladder to the ground with an awful metallic clatter and crash.

'Sorry,' Gary hissed, immediately assuming responsibility.

A handful of corpses was already closing in. Within seconds, at least twenty more had dragged themselves out from the shadows, following the pack. Vicky and Ruth held them off as Dominic scrambled to get the ladder secure and get over, Gary keeping it steady.

After weeks of relative inactivity, their recent battles on the streets of Wapping and in the corridors of Hatton House and other buildings had returned them to a good level of match fitness. With Dominic safely over, Gary began to hack feverishly at the creatures nearest to him. He'd developed a vicious but effective technique: grab a handful of lank hair, yank the head hard over to one side to stretch out the neck, then chop down on the spine like a butcher slicing meat on a block.

Ruth had her own tried and tested technique: a single stab into a high, soft spot – the eyes, the temples, the base of the skull – was almost always enough to stop even the most aggressive of undead attackers. She made far less noise, too. 'Gary, your turn, get over,' Ruth ordered. He did as he was told, but he was carrying post-apocalypse injuries, exacerbated by pre-apocalypse health problems, and when he jumped down from the top of the gate, he landed heavily on his ankle. His cry of pain, impossible to keep swallowed down, alerted the dead.

The ladder almost toppled over. Lisa shot an arm through the railings and grabbed a rung to steady it as Vicky climbed. 'Come on!' she screamed, forgetting about staying quiet and undetected now.

Vicky was up and over, quick and easy. Ruth followed close behind and had just scrambled over when a mass of corpses collided with the gate. Vicky reached back for the ladder, but it was too late. In the confusion it was knocked to the ground, out of reach.

'Doesn't matter,' Ruth said. 'We're in now. We'll worry later about how we're getting out again.'

14

'Why would you lock a fire door?' Dominic asked, peering over Vicky's shoulder as she prised the padlock with her crowbar. 'They were supposed to be left open during trading hours, and places like this hardly ever closed.'

'It might not be a fire door,' Gary said.

'Looks like one to me.'

'Whatever kind of door it is, we need to be careful,' Ruth said. 'Stay back. Depending on what the entrance arrangements were here, the whole building could be crawling with them.'

'That might explain why there are so few outside,' Lisa suggested.

Gary was more upbeat. 'I reckon we'll be okay. Think about it... none of them moved for the first couple of days. The power would probably have been down by the time they were mobile enough to trigger the sensors on the automatic doors.'

'Would they have even triggered the sensors?' Dominic asked.

'Good question. The corpses reflect the ambient temperature, so maybe not if they were heat sensors, but if it was movement or pressure that triggered them...' He shrugged.

Dominic was getting flustered again. 'Does anybody know? This is important, because if we're going to be facing hundreds of them in there then we need to make sure we're prepared, and we—'

'Dominic, just shut up,' Ruth interrupted. 'It doesn't matter. We'll find what we find when we open this door, and we'll have to deal with it whatever. End of.'

Before he could protest further, Vicky snapped the lock and Lisa pulled the door open.

The cavernous building was silent. Empty.

They paused before going inside.

'I don't like this. It's too quiet,' Rich said, and he was right. They might not have been anticipating quite the same levels of flesh-filled pandemonium as Dominic clearly feared, but there should have been *something*.

Vicky shared his concern. 'Weird. Even if the store was closed – which it would never have been on a Tuesday morning – there should have been a few folks wandering around here at least... security, staff...?' She walked out onto the shop floor with her crowbar ready.

The supermarket stank to high heaven. There were endless aisles of produce that had gone bad months earlier, now swarming with insects. Bread, fresh meat, vegetables – row upon row of spoiled food that invariably had either begun to resemble the walking corpses outside or had crumbled into mounds of blue-tinged dust. The contents of defrosted freezers had reduced to mush. The noxious, cloying smell was hard to stomach. Living alongside the decaying population of London, they'd grown accustomed to a certain level of stench, but this was something else. It was inescapable, suffocating. Gary handed around facemasks that he'd taken from a display near the clothing section. 'We need to get a few windows open,' he said, and his words rattled around Vicky's head. It did feel as if the building had been mothballed.

'This place is in better nick than most buildings I've been in recently. Either we've really struck lucky, or there's something odd going on here.'

'For once I'm going with good luck,' Ruth said, walking back from the front of the store. 'The main shutters are down. Something must have triggered them. Might have been automatic when everything went to hell that morning.'

'Good news for us,' Dominic said.

'Yeah, helpful. Means we can loot a lot more easily, take our time.'

Lisa and Gary were already helping themselves to food. Richard looked around, trying to take it all in. 'Don't want to tempt fate, but it looks like we've hit the motherlode.'

Dominic agreed. 'There should be enough food in this place to last us months if we're careful.'

'Just the small matter of getting it all back to base,' Gary reminded them, gulping down biscuits, 'but yeah,' he nodded, 'this is good.'

'Where do we start?' Lisa asked, looking around like a kid on Christmas morning. 'Christ, I can't believe I'm this excited to be standing in the middle of a bloody Tesco superstore.'

'Gary's right, we need to think logically,' Dominic said. 'I know we said this was just going to be a looksee, but now we're here I think we need to make this trip count.'

'I think we should just go back and get the others, bring everyone over here,' Ruth suggested. She threw a bottle of water over to Vicky who caught it and downed half of it in one go.

'I don't think that would be as straightforward as you make it sound,' Dominic said.

'It's not impossible, though.'

'Not at all, but we can't just assume. We need to put the idea to the rest of the group first. There's plenty of food here, sure, but we need more than that, don't we? I'd rather we try and fill the clipper to the rafters and take back everything we need, then consider our options in slower time.'

'Do clippers even have rafters?' Gary asked, semi-serious. 'Anyway, all this is academic if they haven't got the boat started. We need to check back with them before we make any decisions.'

'We also need to limit our trips back and forth out there. We can't keep coming and going; we're sure to be noticed.'

'How else did you think we were going to do this, Dom?'

'I don't know... get a truck or something?'

'Have you learnt nothing so far today? What effect do you think the noise of a truck is going to have on the crowds? You saw how much trouble we got into when we dropped a bloody ladder just now. Starting an engine would be like sounding an air raid siren.'

'So, you're saying we're going to have to cart everything from here to the boat by hand?' Dominic asked.

'Potentially, yes.'

'That'll mean hundreds of trips.'

'Look, I don't know if you missed the memo, Dom, but nothing's straightforward these days,' Vicky said. 'We did say this would likely end up just a scouting trip. It might make sense to head back and bring back an army of people over to help us.'

'But that's going to reduce the space we have to carry back supplies,' Dominic said.

'Like I said, nothing's straightforward anymore.'

'Well, whatever we decide, we need to be sensible about what we take. We should draw up a list of essentials.'

'Food,' Gary said quickly. 'And then more food.'

'And more food after that,' Rich added.

'Dominic's right,' Vicky said. 'We need to concentrate on what we need, not what we want. There will be oceans of booze in here, but we're going to have to show some self-control and leave it behind. And we shouldn't just grab whatever food we can get hold of that hasn't gone off. We need to look at the nutritional value, maximise the benefits.'

'Well, we need to get a move on,' Lisa said, sounding a little nervous. 'It's November, don't forget. It gets dark early these days.'

'With the best will in the world, however we decide to do it, I don't think we're going to get everything done this afternoon. I think we need to make a start, check in with Allison and Chapman as Gary suggested, then agree our next move.'

'Maybe start moving stuff over to the clipper in the morning?' Ruth suggested. 'That way, Chapman and Allison can help. We could do with two more pairs of hands.'

Lisa wasn't impressed. 'The morning? Fuck, you're definitely planning an overnighter then?'

'I don't think we have much of a choice. It was always on the cards.'

'Ruth's right,' Dominic agreed. 'We can sleep on the boat, even if it's a wreck. Whatever we end up doing longer term, we've landed on our feet here. This is way bigger than I thought it was going to be. We need to keep our heads, make sure we do it right.'

15

There was frantic activity on the other side of the river.

It had been like this all day. What had begun as a quick patch-up operation to prevent the dead advancing any further along St Katharine's Way had morphed into something else entirely. The ease with which the encroaching bodies had initially been repelled had instilled Piotr with confidence, and the repair job had turned into another land-grab. Harjinder, who jostled with Paul Duggan and Chapman for the unadvertised position of his deputy, had convinced him to do it. He'd been studying the area and had explained that, by continuing further along St Katharine's Way then clearing a similar length stretch of Mews Street to the north, as far as Thomas More Street to the east, a whole swathe of prime real estate could be snatched back from the dead with relatively little effort. It was a no-brainer.

But what sounded simple in principle, took an inordinate amount of effort in practice. The dead were despicably resilient, the living desperate and tired.

Harjinder led the troops along the first stretch of St Katharine's Way with ease, first thing. Heavy machinery did much of the work. They'd found a dumper truck near roadworks on The Highway a few days back, and the mechanics had been able to coax it back to life. It had been a squeeze getting it across the drawbridge, and they'd had to waste precious time removing road bollards, but it had been worth all the effort because, once it was through, the dumper made short work of the enemy. The driver kept it moving at a steady speed, and the dead had no answer to its power. A smaller van followed behind until the junction with Mews Street, then the two vehicles went their separate ways. The dumper truck continued slowly south along St Katharine's Way, clearing the gentle U-shaped curve of the road up towards Thomas More Street. The van went along Mews Street, a narrower, pedestrianised route. In places, it barely scraped through, but it had the desired effect. Those bodies that managed to get past, those that slipped and slid around the sides of the box-shaped vehicle as it trundled along, were dealt with easily by a pack of fighters following behind. There were gaps between buildings that opened straight out onto the docks through which tonnes of decaying flesh were flushed into the water.

Midway between the two cleared routes was a pedestrian cut-through that bisected the area Piotr was aiming to seize. It was rammed with death. David Shires was amongst those fighters sent out to clear it. There were hundreds of corpses trapped in the narrow strip of land. When they'd been battling to take back The Highway, they'd been fighting within a decent amount of space and had some room to manoeuvre. Here, the restrictive confines made everything twice as hard, and the crew suffered. The heat, the stench, having to be aware of the other people they were fighting alongside... it was a nightmare. David still carried his sharpened metal railing as a weapon, but there was hardly room to wield it properly. The prick fighting next to him – an inexperienced clown wrapped up in armour pinched from the Tower of London - was swinging a heavy broadsword around with zero skill and was in real danger of taking his bloody head off, or possibly even his own, which would have made things easier for David.

A surge of corpses came at the group of fighters from one side, squeezing through a random gap between trees and abandoned cars at the least opportune moment. David saw that Holly had been caught out in the open by three of them, and he charged over to help. He skewered one corpse through the eye, then swung the railing into the legs of another, hacking it down. He put his boot on its chest to keep it on the ground, while Holly caved in its skull with her baseball bat.

'I've had enough,' she said in a breathless moment between

attacks.

'We're nearly there, Hol,' he assured her. 'It's not going to be like this for much longer.'

'You said that last week,' she reminded him. 'I mean it. I can't keep going like this.'

He broke away to sort out another attack, this one coming from the half-height cadaver of a kid. He impaled it against a tree, then punched so hard that he caved in its face with his gloved fist. He hated having to deal with little ones; it made him think about his own children back home. After the last couple of months, he'd just about begun to accept that his family was lost, but what if there was someone like him fighting for survival back in Sixmilebridge, having to do what he'd just done to the reanimated remains of the people he'd loved more than anything else in the world?

Next, a woman wearing blood-stained surgical scrubs.

Then, another child.

A guy that had been about the same height and build as he.

A cumbersome giant of a corpse.

One wearing a high-vis jacket.

And one so badly disfigured he couldn't see any indication of who or even what it used to be.

Holly screamed again, this time with anger. He glanced across as she swung the baseball bat into the chest of a corpse with such force that she sent the damn thing flying into a wall. She was immediately onto the next one, which she felled by taking out its spindly legs with one swing then moved onto the next, which she battered against a wheelie bin, thumping it like a bass drum.

'Fuck me, look at her go!' Paul Duggan said, standing next to David in the sudden bubble of space created by Holly's frenzied attacks. 'Go on, girl! Christ, she's fucking amazing.'

'No, she's fucking terrified,' David said, because her expression reflected none of the glee and excitement that he'd seen plastered across other fighters' faces. She was traumatized, scared out of her mind. There'd been moments out here this morning when he'd felt the same, where the only thought he had was *keep killing them, keep killing them, keep killing them... before they can kill me...*

He wanted to get Holly as far as he could from here, but there was no time. He heard Paul curse next to him and when he looked up, he saw another tidal wave of filth rolling towards them. The other end of this alleyway was a jam of decay now, an inordinate number of writhing creatures wedged so tightly together that, as they advanced, they scraped against the walls on either side, leaving no room for escape. The only option the fighters had now was to try and batter their way through.

David waded in, but Holly was already ahead of him. He tried to keep her in his sights, but in seconds the world all around them had become a whirlwind of chaos and blood, and there was no making sense of anything. He fought for as long as he could, ready to lash out at any movement, holding back for just a fraction of a fraction of a second first to check if the next thing he was about to kill was still living or already dead. More fighters moved up around him, all attacking with every ounce of energy they had left, because they all knew that to stop now would be suicidal.

There were so many of the dead surging down this alleyway now... where were they coming from in such numbers, and how was it possible for them to move with such speed?

The answer was soon revealed.

The dumper truck was forcing them along this strip-like pathway from the opposite direction. Having cleared St Katharine's Way as far as they'd agreed, the driver had turned around and was now herding the remaining dead towards the fighters, trying to speed up their inevitable demise. Despite the sudden surge, there was much relief all round, because it meant the end of the battle was finally in sight. David summoned up a final burst of energy and struck out at the last of the dead around him, knowing now that each corpse he re-killed brought him one step closer to being able to stop and rest.

It took only a few more minutes before the final few corpses lay in pieces at their feet. For now, the fighting was done. There was relative calm around where David and the others stood, though they could still hear distant activity as the roads to the north and south were sealed and secured.

The only person left fighting was Holly. She was standing over what was left of a cadaver that had long since stopped moving, still battering it with her baseball bat.

David approached her carefully, worried she'd turn on him next. He caught the bat as she raised it again, ready for another strike, then gently prised it from her hands. There was fire in her wide, staring eyes. She looked ready to kill him. 'It's done, love,' he said softly. 'Come on. Time to stop now. Time to rest.'

'But there are more of them still out there,' she said. 'We can't stop yet.'

She was high on an adrenalin rush, not yet able to come down.

'Later,' he said. 'Come on, Hol, you need a break. We both do. Come back to base with me and we'll get you something to eat.'

He led her back towards the compound along roads that were quiet now but awash with blood. Workers were coming the other way, entering newly recovered buildings to strip them of anything of value.

Piotr stood at the drawbridge by the hotel, a distance back from the frontline. He blocked David's way. 'You're going in the wrong direction. There's still work to be done out there.'

'This kid's right on the edge and she needs a break,' he said, keeping his voice low so that Holly didn't hear more than she needed to.

'We all need a break. *I* need a break.'

'What, from ordering people about? Get a grip. I'm taking her back to get her some food.'

David started walking away.

'After that, you come back and you do your share,' Piotr yelled. David was on the verge of telling him to go fuck himself, but he didn't have the energy. Instead, he just kept walking.

16

It looked like Allison and Chapman had done it. As the rest of the group shuffled slowly back through the steadily encroaching early evening gloom, weighed down by bags filled with loot from the supermarket, they saw there were lights on inside the boat.

'Thank Christ for that,' Chapman said when they boarded. 'We were starting to think you weren't coming back.'

'I was getting worried,' Allison said as she counted them in, one by one. Vicky and Ruth brought up the rear.

'Not as worried as Chapman,' Vicky whispered to her. 'He's terrified of going back to his boss with an empty boat.'

'You reckon?'

'Absolutely. He's Piotr's bitch.'

Allison grinned. Vicky thought how nice her smile was. She hadn't seen it before.

'You think he'd have seen through the bullshit by now,' Ruth said. 'Mind you, it took me long enough.'

She closed the door, sealing them in from the cold outside. At the other end of the cabin, Chapman appeared more animated than at any point previously. 'Can't tell you how relieved I am. I wasn't sure what to do for the best. I didn't know whether to stay here or come looking for you. In the end we decided it was better if we just stayed put.'

'Good shout,' Gary said, and he collapsed into a seat, dripping with sweat and in pain.

'You hurt?' Allison asked, concerned.

'Dodgy ankle. It's been playing up for ages. I went over it again when we were trying to get into the supermarket. I'll be okay.'

'You'll need to rest it tomorrow, I think,' Ruth said. 'I'll strap it up for you later.'

'Now there's an offer,' he laughed.

Ruth ignored him. 'I'm not saying you're slow, Gaz, but I saw corpses out there just now outrunning you.'

'We're doing an overnighter, then?' Chapman asked. 'Figured as much.' He watched as the others unloaded food and drink from their bags, his eyes widening when he saw that Richard had brought beer. 'You found a decent amount of stash, by the looks of things.'

'Pretty good, yes,' Dominic said. He'd been quiet since they'd returned but was beginning to find his voice again now that they were safe from the dead. 'We could do very well for ourselves if we're sensible. But that's for tomorrow. Tonight, we relax and celebrate. We brought a few things back with us. I thought we could all do with a boost.'

'In moderation, remember?' Ruth warned, worried about the way people were already gravitating towards the booze. 'That's the deal. We don't want anyone getting pissed and making so much noise we can't get ashore again in the morning.'

Dominic looked around at the interior of the clipper. 'Are we all good here? I can see you cleaned it out and got the power on, but did you get the engine running?'

'Yep,' Allison said. 'We didn't leave it running for long because of the noise. Should be okay, though.'

'She showed me the ropes,' Chapman added. 'I'm obviously nowhere near as capable as Captain Ali here, but I reckon I could shift this thing if I needed to.'

'Good, good. Things are starting to come together.'

'Food,' Vicky said. She'd quickly laid out a spread on a table, and they descended like vultures. Dominic continued talking as he tucked in.

'It wasn't too bad out there today, you know, all things considered.'

'That's not what you said earlier,' she reminded him.

'I know, I know. That was just the nerves talking. I'm glad I came, though. I think it was important.'

'Think you've earned your spurs, then?' Chapman asked.

'I don't know about that, but it's given me a new perspective on things, that's for sure.'

Chapman turned to the others, more interested in facts than hyperbole. Vicky obliged. 'The supermarket was a genius suggestion by Lynette and Marianne. We really lucked out here. There's a huge amount of stuff, and the shutters are down at the front of the store, so the place is virtually corpse-free. There's more than enough food inside to see us through the winter, if we can load enough of it back. It has a decent pharmacy, too. Liz gave me a list of drugs and other stuff she wanted, but to be honest, we're pretty much just going to clear it out.'

'Do we not just haul everyone over here? Might be a better option.'

'It's something we need to think about,' Dominic quickly interrupted. 'On the face of it, it looks like a good idea.'

'I sense there's a but?'

'But it's not as straight forward as just shuttling everyone over here in this boat. We'd need to get accommodations arranged, make sure our defences are good enough. For now I think we need to report back to the others then look at our longer term options.'

'I agree,' Ruth said. 'And there's no sense us going back with a half-full boat, so getting as much as we can from the supermarket has to be our focus tomorrow.'

'And doing it in such a way that we can come back for more,' Gary added.

'The problem we've got is it's so quiet over here that it won't take much for us to attract thousands of them. And we can't risk making a decoy noise elsewhere, because we don't know how many of the dead might be waiting around the corner.'

'So what's the answer?' Allison asked.

'We've been giving it some thought, but I won't lie to you, it's not going to be easy.'

'That's a given,' Chapman grunted. 'Vehicles are out of the question, I assume.'

'Definitely. We went over a fence and got into the building through a fire door in a secured service yard. Rich loosened a few railings before we came back, so it should be a bit easier to get in and out tomorrow. We thought about trying to get hold of a truck but nixed that idea. We'd probably make enough noise getting the damn thing started, but then there's the noise we'd make around the supermarket...'

'Not to mention the impact a truck would have at this end,' Vicky added. 'We'd risk flooding the whole area.'

'So, it's the chain-gang?' Chapman said, resigned.

'Looks that way. It's going to take a lot more time doing it that way, but I guess that's the one thing we've got plenty of. Gary's going to mind the boat, the rest of us need to find a way to minimise the risk and get as much stuff over here as we can.'

'I told you, I'll be alright,' Gary protested.

'I know what you told me, and I also know that your ankle is fucked. Quit with the big man bullshit and just accept it. Your ankle is your weak spot, and I'm not prepared to let you become *our* weak spot. I'm sure there will be plenty of work for you to do at this end. You ever play Tetris, Gary?'

'Yeah, what's that got to do with anything?'

'We'll be bringing stuff back in dribs and drabs, so we'll need someone to stash it properly, maximise the space we have.'

He nodded, resigned to his fate. Vicky was right, but that didn't make him feel any better. He hated not being involved in the action, it made him feel like he was useless or worse, wasn't in control. But they were never really in control, any of them. It was just an illusion. And he reminded himself that when he was in the middle of a crisis, he hated that too. Best just to accept that he'd be stuck here tomorrow. 'So, it's a decent boat, is it?' he asked, looking around.

'Yep,' Allison replied. 'I like this one.'

'You seriously used to drive these things?'

'Yep, and I loved it. It's nice to be back onboard. This boat's in good nick, and it's got a decent amount of fuel. It should do us for a few trips to Tower Bridge and back.'

'Fantastic. And you didn't have any trouble clearing it out?'

'Well, we had about forty passengers, I think. That's right, isn't it, Chappers? A few of them were acting up, but to be honest, it's nothing I haven't seen before.'

'Pre- or post-apocalypse?'

'Yes,' she laughed, and she opened a can of lager and took a large swig, pleased with her own performance. She'd surprised herself with how she'd coped today. The fear of being outside the base, the responsibility of getting the boat ready, the emotion she'd kept swallowed down when they'd removed the uniformed corpses of people she'd likely once worked with... she'd dealt with all of it, and she deserved her first proper drink since the end of the world.

'Good work, team. Early night tonight, ready to graft in the morning,' Ruth said, raising her can and toasting the others. 'Hard day ahead of us tomorrow, eh, Dom?'

Dominic was miles away.

'What? Sorry, yes... tomorrow will make all the difference. Get this right, and the next few months will be a lot easier for everyone.'

'I'll drink to that,' Gary said, his busted leg resting on another seat. 'Drinking's about all I can manage right now.'

Unable to sleep, they talked well into the night, working out how best to transport supplies from the supermarket to the boat by hand. 'There's an underpass,' Lisa said. 'I've walked past it a million times, but I didn't think about it until now. I was too focused on trying to find a lookout point this morning. It goes under the road at the end of the docks, leads directly to the shops.'

'The front of the shops, I'm guessing? We need to get around the back,' Ruth said.

'Block access to the underpass with cars, go in the same way we did today, then cut a way out through the security fence around the supermarket,' Richard suggested.

'But we agreed no engines,' Dominic said.

Gary shook his head. 'Dave Shires played a blinder the other day when we found ourselves in a spot of bother. You heard about that didn't you, Chapman?'

'Yeah, he just took the handbrakes off and started rolling cars. Worked a treat.'

'So simple it's genius. There are enough cars around here to let us seal the docks off completely with no engine noise at all. We can block all the roads and alleys.'

'Sounds good, but that still leaves us the problem of lugging all that stuff a good half mile or so from there to here,' Dominic said. 'I suppose we could use trolleys?'

'They have the potential to be noisy as hell,' Ruth said. 'I guess if we pack them well and take our time, we might be okay.'

'Use another boat,' Allison suggested. 'If we can stop the bodies getting too close, we can risk sailing up and down the dock and reduce the trolley use. It doesn't have to be anything huge, just something big enough to help us with the heavy lifting.'

'I guess taking this thing up there is a no-go?' Dominic asked.

'Impossible. It's way too big. Anyway, there's no way of opening the locks and getting anything on or off the river. So even if we can use a boat, it's only going to help us get stuff closer. We'll still need to manually carry it all down the pier and onto the clipper.'

'It sounds doable, though,' Vicky said.

'Definitely sounds like a plan,' Ruth agreed, 'but we can't do anything else until first light, so, like I said several hours ago, let's rest.'

They eventually retired to separate parts of the clipper, but Vicky still wasn't ready to sleep. She went out onto the deck at the back of the boat and lit a cigarette. Ruth followed her, concerned.

'What's up?'

'Nothing,' Vicky said. 'I'm okay. Brain won't switch off, that's all. I'll be awake a few hours longer yet.'

'As long as you're alright?'

'I'm fine.'

Ruth managed half a smile. 'Okay. I'll leave you alone. I'm knackered.'

'I'll find you when I come in.'

Vicky liked Ruth more than she ever told her, but she was glad when she went inside and left her alone. She'd had too much stimulation for one day and needed headspace. She had a lot to unpack, more than any of them knew. She leant on the railings around the back of the clipper and smoked her cigarette while she watched the spectacle of Canary Wharf continuing to burn.

There was no moon visible tonight through the heavy cloud. With no light pollution, the world should have been inky black, all but invisible, and yet she could clearly make out the tightly packed skyscrapers across the river. Several were ablaze, the rest visible as silhouettes, their stark, brutalist outlines clear against a backdrop of ruddy oranges and reds.

Vicky's stomach was knotted with nerves, but it wasn't because of the devastation she could see in the near distance. What concerned her more was the ragged line of figures that stretched along the banks of this side of the river, pressed up against the safety rails in apparent awe of the fires across the water, their rotting faces lit up like disfigured kids around a bonfire on Guy Fawkes night. And it wasn't those at the front of the gathering that worried her most, it was a smattering of others she could see some way behind them. Their behaviour was unnerving. For a moment she wondered if they were alive; the way they were holding back and not being consumed by the crush indicated a level of control she'd rarely seen before. It reminded her of those corpses they'd come up against in Fenchurch Street station, protected from the elements and also some of those she'd come across inside Hatton House. By all accounts, every dead fucker should have been out of control, losing what was left of their minds to try and get closer to the pretty lights in the distance, but these creatures weren't doing that.

It scared her.

It made her think they were regaining a level of control she'd assumed they'd lost forever. And what frightened her more than anything was a nagging concern that she just couldn't shake: *If they're like this today, what are they going to be like tomorrow?*

17

On the north bank, the behaviour of the dead was also causing concern. On the fringes of the territory the group of survivors had recently reclaimed, the tens of thousands of desperate corpses had long since stopped acting as individuals and had seemingly become a bizarre cooperative organism, something akin to a basic hive-mind. But hive-mind wasn't right either; that phrase indicated an ability to understand, to plan and control. The dead didn't plan, they just *reacted*, driven by a shared instinct, perhaps, but without the ability to ever stop. Without an iota of consideration for what remained of their fragile physical selves, the interminable hordes reacted to the activities of the living in an unnaturally uniform way, surging ever closer. And that unspoken, slavish compliance, their mindless devotion to the collective cause, gave the endless tide of stinking flesh a monumental advantage.

During the fighting on the streets east of the Tower of London last week, more than two thousand dead creatures had been destroyed. Tens of thousands more had been displaced: beaten back and forced away in new directions. The irregular shifts and shoves within the ranks of the undead had triggered chain reactions, waves, shifts, and swells, which had caused problems like those seen around the St Katharine's Dock drawbridge this morning.

Out of sight, out of mind.

Clearing the corpses from around the drawbridge had solved the immediate problem, but there had been no consideration for the wider impacts, and Piotr's orders had caused chaos elsewhere. Those corpses that had been pushed away from the dock had collided with another swell of death sweeping towards the barricades, where thousands more of them fought to get closer to the people in the base, drawn here by the noise. The resultant writhing chaos had caused unseen pressures to build until the weight of dead flesh exposed a previously undetected weakness in the group's defences.

And the dam burst.

There were tall brick walls lining either side of the mouth of Thomas More Street where it opened out onto East Smithfield. Remnants of old London, the walls had so far proved sturdy enough to soak up the pressure and channel the undead moving away from St Katharine's docks. When the base here had first been established, the road here had been blocked with cars piled on top of each other to above head height, tall enough and strong enough to hold back the dead.

Until now.

Once the fighting around the docks to the south had died down, Piotr's focus returned to the recovery of larger items from Hatton House, things that had been too heavy or cumbersome to be shifted by hand. All afternoon and well into the evening, convoys of vehicles trundled back and forth along East Smithfield and The Highway. The constant engine noise, combined with the raised voices of workers who, spurred on by recent gains, had dropped their guard, acted as a trigger.

The corpses on the other side of the Thomas More Street blockade who had been there longest had been worn down to slurry and bone by the endless pressure of the masses behind. Their remains had become compacted and, eventually, cadavers that were less badly deteriorated had fought their way through to the front, where, given enough time, they, too, would become mash. The size of the flood of death coming up from the south today was unprecedented, so the strongest of the creatures were forced up and right over. One of the cars on the top of the makeshift wall (a small Fiat 500 which had been shoved up there precisely because of its size and weight) toppled over, and that proved to be the finger pulled from the dyke. With the height of the barrier unexpectedly reduced, the pressure behind the corpses increased and a flood of flesh tumbled right over the top with remarkable speed, spilling across East Smithfield like a lumpy slick.

The screams of panic were lost in the confusion of everything else. The dead reacted to the reactions of the living, and in the madness another part of the weakened barrier collapsed, releasing even more of them. Those corpses that remained sufficiently complete picked themselves up out of the noxious flood and staggered after the people running for cover. Other broken bodies dragged what was left of themselves along; less of a threat, but just as determined. The reaction of those people on the Tower side of the spill, across the street, was to race back to base to get under cover, but with the incursion now blocking the full width of the road, those on the other side were stranded.

David Shires was having one fucker of a day.

He'd been fighting all morning – against the dead first thing, and with Piotr since – and had ended up helping with clearance work all afternoon to take his mind off everything else. He'd been preoccupied thinking about the group who'd gone to Surrey Quays, and what was going to happen if they didn't come back. The prospect of Piotr being given free rein here just didn't bear thinking about. David hadn't been back to base for hours. He was physically and emotionally exhausted, and now he was stuck on the wrong side of the tracks, prevented from getting to safety by this sudden invasion of death.

Thomas More Street wasn't particularly long, but any distance with this level of decayed flesh was too far. A huge number of corpses had been trapped there, and it was only now they'd been released that the extent of their vast numbers was becoming apparent. They came in droves, dropping heavily through the gap in the half-height barrier, then picking themselves up to begin hunting out the living.

David was aware of there being other people with him on this side of the flood; he was equally aware of some of them disappearing back to shelter inside Hatton House. Others had started trying to loop around the trouble, running up the connecting side-streets to Cable Street and the train track boundary to the north. He saw Mark Desai about to go that way and grabbed him. Mark went to take a swing at David, thinking he was an attacking corpse, but lowered his fist just in time.

'Go and tell Piotr what's happened,' David ordered. 'Run like your fucking life depends on it, Mark, because it does. We have to get this blocked up quick.'

Mark nodded frantically then disappeared.

David felt as if what was left of the world was conspiring against him. This breach had occurred in an area where the reclamation work was well advanced, and anything that might have proved useful to help beat back the dead had already been taken back to Tower Place, put into storage. He saw that one of the trucks they'd been using to transport stuff was stranded in liquified gruel several inches deep, right in the middle of the chaos. Ghoulish figures were crowding around because its engine was still running, despite its driver having already run for cover. Ignoring the foul stink and the crunch of bone beneath his boots, David waded through the mire towards it, shoving corpses out of his way so he could get behind the wheel. Once safely in the cab, he reversed back as far as he could, the tyres struggling to gain traction on the slippery street. He put the truck into first and powered forward, ramming the part of the blockade through which the dead were continuing to pour, doing what he could to them back. Reverse then ram, reverse then ram; he did it again and again, compacting the decay and taking out another few spidery, scrambling cadavers with every hit. Only, there seemed to be an endless supply of them. Wave after wave were being forced up and over by the pressure of those on the other side of the barrier, desperate to be free.

A second vehicle approached at speed. The driver tried to follow David's lead but lost control on the glistening road surface and skidded into the side of his truck. More through luck than judgement, between the two of them they'd temporarily stemmed the tide, but their vehicles were wedged together, both going nowhere. David clambered out through his window and onto the roof, gesturing for the other driver to do the same. The flatbed behind David's cab was loaded up with furniture and she jumped across. Between them they began to lift the items they could manage and half-threw, half-dropped them to block the breach. Two more people climbed up to help but it was futile, like trying to soak up a reservoir with a sponge.

David didn't dare stop working, but this sudden incursion had made the futility of their situation clear. It was an impossible vicious circle: to hold back the dead, they needed to fight with remorseless ferocity, but in doing so they'd inevitably stoke the creatures' collective rage even more, and that would lead to more weaknesses in the group's makeshift defences, like this one, being exposed and exploited. All he could see ahead of them now was a long and bloody downward spiral of conflict. Against an enemy with endless numbers and an almost masochistic tenacity, he could only ever see this war ending one way. Right now, he was thinking he wouldn't even get off the back of this truck in one piece. From up here, isolated and vulnerable, he couldn't see any way out. Was this unexpected breach going to be the undoing of the entire group? If not this breach, would it be the next, or the next after that? He didn't think they'd be able to contain this level of pressure for long, certainly not forever.

The breach bell started tolling in the distance, and when David next looked up, he saw a line of vehicles approaching from the direction of the Tower. The light they provided was welcome; there was utter chaos everywhere, and it was getting harder to distinguish the living from the dead, to see who was who and what was what. It was impossible for some of the skittering things he could see to still be human; hideous half-creatures dragging themselves through the muck on broken bones. Yet their refusal to submit was absolute, no matter how much physical damage they endured.

Reinforcements ran alongside the oncoming vehicles, carrying brutal weapons and flaming torches, looking like a mob of angry villagers from long forgotten black-and-white horror films, pitchforks and death wishes. Even over all the noise, David could hear Piotr's voice.

'Do they even know we're up here?' the woman on the truck with David shouted, and they both panicked and jumped down just moments before the first of the approaching vehicles rammed the dilapidated barricade. On his hands and knees, crawling through what was left of the dead, David scrambled for cover as Piotr's fighters launched an onslaught.

When it was safe, he picked himself up and staggered away, drenched with putrescence, shivering with cold and with nerves. Avoiding everyone, he took the long route back, up towards the railway line. In this bedraggled, blood-soaked state, he doubted anyone would have been able to distinguish him from the dead. He wouldn't have had the energy to explain or even to deflect a blow. As it was, there was no one else around. They were all either mopping up the mess or sheltering in the Tower.

David's body felt heavy, weighed down with worry. How long would it be before Piotr realised his tactics weren't going to work? There was no reason to think what had happened tonight wouldn't happen again. Maybe it had already started somewhere; a chain-reaction triggered by the aftershocks of what had happened just now. At what point would Piotr understand that the more aggressive they were towards the dead, the stronger the enemy's reaction would inevitably be? How much more did they have to lose before he understood?

David walked through the base alone. He carried on past the hotel, past the entrance to the Tower, and went down to the river. He sat on the end of the jetty from which Vicky and the others had left this morning, and washed himself in the dirty, ice-cold water of the polluted River Thames.

18

DAY SEVENTY-EIGHT

The same sun rose over both banks of the Thames, but this morning, the scenes it illuminated on either side of the river were worlds apart.

The crew of the Thames Clipper were up and active at the crack of dawn, maximising the benefit of that brief sliver of day when the world was bright so they could see, but still dark enough so they could hide. The sky was icy blue, the sun untroubled by clouds, and yet the light remained hazy. Smoke from the fires around Canary Wharf drifted across the Thames, giving everything an ethereal blur.

Allison looked for a boat to transport supplies from one end of the dock to the other while the others worked their way inland from the river, blocking all the access points between buildings to leave themselves a clear and uninterrupted run from the supermarket back to the Thames. They worked with a silent determination, all of them very much aware how important the next few hours could prove to be. Get this right, and they'd be giving the group across the river the best possible chance of surviving the winter and making it through to spring when, as Dominic reminded them time and again, they'd be home and dry. The bulk of the dead would have decayed down to next to nothing, and those of the living who'd survived would be able to try to rebuild without having to live in silence, and without having to constantly look over their shoulders.

But if things didn't work out... well, that didn't bear thinking about. They were putting everything on the line over here today, but success would be well worth taking the risks.

*

On the other side of the river, the atmosphere couldn't have been more different. While the people at Surrey Quays had rediscovered some measure of positivity, many of those at the Monument base were on the verge of giving up.

The site of last night's incursion resembled a war zone: burnt-out wrecks and bonfires of body parts, streets stained with blood. East Smithfield had become a vital route for transporting loot from the reclamation area back to base, and a crew had laboured through the night to clear it so that work could continue today.

When dawn broke they looked out over the newly fortified blockade. The street beyond was packed with death again, the bodies remaining universally resolute and undeterred. Wipe out hundreds of them, and thousands more were queuing up to take their place.

Was it worth all the effort? All the risk? All the hurt?

That was the question Holly just couldn't shake.

She'd tried to find an answer, honest she had, but she couldn't see a way through it all. She'd reached her limit, and she just didn't want to fight anymore. It had taken too much out of her. She had nothing left. She should have gone out to help last night, but she'd ignored the call and now the guilt was gnawing at her too, as if she didn't have enough to worry about.

The thing that made all of this so hard to take was the injustice, how everything had been snatched away from her. None of it was her fault. She'd had so much to live for, so much she'd worked for, and it had all been snatched from her in a heartbeat. She'd given all she'd had, both before the world had gone to hell and since, but it had counted for nothing.

She and Andy had scrimped and saved for years to scrape enough cash together to put down a decent deposit on a house. They'd both worked so many hours they barely saw each other, but it was a sacrifice they'd been happy to make because they believed they'd have the rest of their lives together to enjoy the spoils. *Get the foundations right and we can do anything*, Andy always used to say to her. He'd believed it, and she'd believed him, but it had all come to nothing. They'd made an offer on a beautiful little house; it had been accepted the day before the apocalypse. For fuck's sake. How cruel was that? The fact it had all been so tantalisingly close was what made it so fucking hard to take.

Things had got worse and worse since then, never any better. These days Holly even had to fight for the space to think, and that just wasn't right.

Nothing was straightforward anymore.

Even finding a way of doing this had been frustratingly difficult, all her options reducing to nil. She couldn't get into a building tall enough to jump, and the chances of taking an overdose were zero when there was barely a single packet of paracetamol to share between more than three hundred folks. In the end, Marianne found her in the bathtub in her hotel room, wrists slashed with shards from the mirror she'd smashed.

19

Death never felt far away these days, but yesterday evening, standing on the back of that truck, surrounded by attacking corpses, David had felt it right at his shoulder. Even now, more than twelve hours later, he'd barely stopped shaking. When he heard about Holly, he wanted to nail his hotel room shut and lock himself away permanently.

Fortunately, Marianne had her foot in the door. 'If you think I'm leaving you up here on your own to wallow, you can think again,' she said, and she dragged him downstairs to get food.

The queue snaked away from the front of the restaurant on the edge of Trinity Square. It was a grand, formal-looking building with a formerly impressive frontage that was now mucky and unkempt, once-white columns smeared with dirt. The cobbles out front were a mass of grubby footprint trails, the endless back and forth of hungry souls. Inside, what had been a high-class restaurant serving food to an exclusive clientele at eye-watering prices, had been transformed through necessity into something more akin to a battlefield mess tent. The fancy tables and comfortable chairs had been removed and smashed up for firewood and replaced by repurposed office furniture arranged in rows like an overcrowded school dining hall.

The others hadn't yet returned from Surrey Quays, and though not wholly unexpected, their absence added to the feeling of general unease. Few people wanted the expedition to the south bank to be a success more than Phillipa Rochester and Steven Armitage and the army of volunteers that helped them cater for the group. Even with the provisions that had recently been harvested from Hatton House and other nearby buildings, they were struggling to scrape together enough food to keep everyone fed. Gone were the days of producing simple dishes in large volumes; today it was a case of handing out cans and packets of food. You ate whatever you were given, and woe betide anyone who complained. They were lucky to be getting anything at all.

Steven's background in army logistics helped keep the queues moving. He was stoic and resolute; Phillipa was not. She struggled to keep her temper in check. When a young kid dared ask if he could swap what she'd just given him, she snapped. The kid skulked off and swapped it anyway.

'It'll be different tonight once the others are back,' Marianne said to David, watching the chaos from midway along the queue. 'We'll have proper hot food again later. It'll be lovely.'

'Who are you trying to convince?'

Piotr burst through the restaurant doors with a pack of exhausted, blood-soaked workers in tow. He bypassed the queue and marched up to Phillipa. 'This lot needs feeding.'

'Then they need to join the line,' she said. 'There are other people waiting.'

'I don't give a shit. These people have been clearing up bodies all morning, and they're hungry. They need food.'

David had heard enough. He went to move, but Marianne pulled him back. 'Leave it,' she warned.

But he didn't. He shrugged her off and walked over to confront Piotr. 'What?' Piotr grunted at him.

'Wait your turn. We all need food.'

'If my lot don't get fed, no one is safe. They need strength to keep the dead under control.'

'And how's that working out? Not great from what I saw last night.'

'No one said it was going to be easy.'

'No, but what you're doing is making it unnecessarily hard. Don't you get it? The more noise you make, the more aggressive you are, the more the dead react. You're the cause, not the cure.'

'Do yourself a favour, Shires, shut your mouth and go and wait back in line.'

David didn't. 'I've had enough of your bullshit. I was out there last night. When your shitty defences failed and you and your pals were safely tucked away in your apartments, I was up to my neck in corpses, trying to stop this place from being overrun.'

'Everyone needs to play their part.'

'I agree. And everyone needs to eat, so join the back of the line.'

Piotr wasn't backing down. Neither was David. Everyone else in the restaurant had become silent, all eyes on the two men.

'You heard about Holly?' David asked. 'Slit her wrists this morning. Marianne found her. How does that make you feel?'

Piotr shrugged.

'That's about what I expected. One less person available to fight, I guess. One less worker to clear out whatever building you pick next. One less mouth to feed.'

'What's your point?'

Harjinder stepped up and tugged on Piotr's arm. 'Come on, boss, he's not worth it.'

Piotr stood his ground. 'Suicide is a coward's way out. Better she did it quietly and on her own than on the frontline where other people could have been hurt.'

David snapped. He went to swing for Piotr, but Piotr was taller, stronger, and faster. He jabbed David in the face, knocking him out cold. The crowds parted where he fell, leaving him sprawled out on the filthy floor. People stepped over him so they didn't lose their place in the queue. Only Marianne went to help. Omar had been elsewhere in the line. He squirmed through the crowd to get to Piotr. 'You're a piece of shit, you are.'

Piotr just laughed.

Marianne looked up at him. 'You can't carry on like this, Piotr. David's right, you're putting everyone in danger.'

'I'm keeping all of us safe.'

'When Dominic hears about this, he'll—'

'When Dominic hears about this, he'll do fuck-all, same as always. It's about time the pen-pushers like you and him got that through your heads. I'm the one holding this place together.'

'No, you're the one pushing us apart. Despite everything that's happened, Piotr, the reason we've managed to continue to function is because, until now, we've all been pulling in the same direction. We're a society in here. We're civilised.'

'You really believe that?'

'I have to.'

'Had a look over the wall recently?'

Marianne shook her head. She was nervous. Trembling.

'Do me a favour,' he continued. 'When this pointless conversation is done, go up onto the train tracks and have a look at the crowds out there. They're not a society. They're not civilised.'

'They're not *us*.'

'No, but they're what we have to deal with. Until they're gone, you need to forget about anything else.' He turned his back on her and returned his attention to Phillipa. 'Food for my lot. Now.'

She did as she was told, gesturing for them to help themselves. No one needed to be told twice. The fighters cleared the table of just about everything. Marianne remained standing in the middle of the scrum, protecting David, who was still on the deck. People moved around her as if she wasn't there. She did everything she could to hold herself together, tears of anger streaming down her cheeks.

Once Piotr and the others had left, she helped David up off the floor and held him steady. 'He okay?' Phillipa asked.

'Not sure,' she admitted, out of earshot.

'Go sit him down. I'll get you some food.'

'Thank you.'

Phillipa called over to Steven, who was watching the doors. 'We clear?'

'Yep, all gone.'

'Okay then, folks, breakfast is served,' she announced, and between her and a handful of helpers, they fetched more food from the sadly depleted stores and served up twice as much to the rest of the group.

20

Several hours of slow, stop-start work, and the group on the south bank were finally ready to begin the main task of the day. Although the docks were by no means impenetrable, they'd managed to wheel enough vehicles into place to block the most obvious access routes. Allison had also had success. She'd found a decent sized skiff she could paddle up and down the dock. It had an outboard motor which would have alerted the dead for miles; she decided she'd row instead. The activity felt calming and somehow strengthening. They'd so far mitigated the dangers this morning, though the peace around Surrey Quays felt fragile and misleading.

They divided into two groups. Vicky, Ruth, and Rich took the footpath under the road and started moving more cars to secure a route from the store to the water. The others, minus Gary, who'd remained on the clipper as ordered, headed back to the supermarket.

Lisa and Dominic retraced their steps in silence, Chapman and Allison taking in the sights for the first time. It was only when they'd made it safely into the service yard that they allowed themselves to speak, and only then in hushed whispers. Chapman was impressed. 'Looks like a good set-up here. I heard what you said last night, Dom, but maybe we should think again about moving people over here instead of taking all this stuff to them?'

'I'm not ruling it out. Like I said, I think it would be a mistake to rush into it. We'll talk about it, keep all our options open.'

'I guess Tesco Surrey Quays doesn't have the kudos of the Tower of London, does it? It's still a status thing with you, isn't it?'

Dominic just frowned at him, unsure if he was joking or serious.

When they reached the fire door through which they'd entered the building yesterday, they stopped. 'What the fuck?' Lisa said.

'What's the problem?' Chapman asked, immediately concerned. She stepped back to show him. There was another padlock and chain securing the door.

'We didn't do that.'

'Then who did?'

'Father bloody Christmas,' she answered, sarcastic. 'How the hell am I supposed to know?'

'Christ,' Dominic said, looking around anxiously. 'Just what we need, another bloody turf war.'

'That's what I was thinking. It's not that bloody Taylor bloke following us again, is it?' Chapman said, semi-seriously.

'Whoever we've annoyed was probably already here,' Lisa said. 'And for what it's worth, I don't think they want trouble any more than we do.'

'You reckon?'

'Yes. If they were that keen on keeping us out, they'd have warned us off while we were still here, not waited until we'd gone. My guess is it's just a handful of folks.'

'I agree,' Chapman said. 'And if there are people here, there's no reason why they can't come back with us. Safety in numbers, and all that; provided they're not going to be arseholes about it.'

'Who are the arseholes? We're the ones helping ourselves to their stuff.'

'Needs must,' Dominic said. 'We've got hundreds of folks counting on us, remember. Chapman's right, whoever's here can come back with us if they want to.'

Lisa began forcing the lock. 'It's all academic. We'll be leaving more stuff than we take. Let's just get on with it, get what we need, and get out.'

Everything was just as they'd left it inside. Allison, Dominic, and Lisa started shifting stuff into the service yard while Chapman removed a small section of fence at the side of the building that would allow them to access the carpark at the front. Ruth and Vicky spotted him and managed to snatch a quick, whispered word. 'They seem a bit more fractious out here today,' Vicky said, gesturing at the nearest corpses. 'We should be okay as long as we're careful.'

Chapman told them about the padlock on the fire door, warned them to be vigilant, then went back to work.

They'd moved sufficient cars to form a permanent, bubble-shaped traffic jam that protected both the mouth of the footpath under the road and the section of fence where Chapman was working. They worked well together, Ruth focusing on the final few vehicles, Vicky dealing with any stray corpses that wandered too close. She moved from kill to kill, barely breaking a sweat. When she looked back at the size of her cull, she was impressed and appalled in equal measure. The dead marching on the Monument base looked like an imperious invading army. Here, though, scattered around the carpark, they looked more like aimless shoppers. They were all just rotting meat but, more than ever, the bodies here reminded her of the people they used to be.

No matter how quiet or careful they were, in the absence of any other distractions around Surrey Quays, the dead were bound to react. Keeping out of sight was no longer an option for the scavenging group; being seen was a risk they had to take. Once they'd got everything onto the clipper at the pier, they'd set sail for home and be forgotten here, and by the time they were ready to come back and take more from the supermarket – if that was even necessary – today's noise and bluster would have long faded away to nothing and the south bank would again be desolate and silent. Still, there was no escaping the fact that the next couple of hours would be a test of nerves for everyone.

They'd felt uncomfortable about using trolleys to get the food from the back of the supermarket to the dock and found a better alternative. There were larger wheeled cages in the supermarket stores – high-sided, clattering units that would have been used by staff to replenish shelves, back in the day. They were rattletraps, but their haul capacity was undeniable and reduced the risk-to-noise ratio dramatically. Getting everything down to the skiff was a long, labour-intensive process. They worked quietly and cooperatively, picturing themselves loaded up and docking as returning heroes. 'I'll be glad when this is done,' Ruth whispered to Vicky as their paths crossed.

'Yeah, I know what you mean,' Vicky replied automatically, but then she thought about her words, and realised she wasn't so sure. It was a difficult one; would she trade the perceived safety of the base for the relative freedom they'd found here on the south bank? Standing out here today with a different perspective and a little more freedom to breathe, she almost dared to wonder if she might get Selena to Ledsey Cross one day after all.

There was a lot to get done first.

It had proved impossible to accurately gauge the volume of goods they'd collected at the supermarket, and what had appeared to be a substantial, almost greedy haul, only filled a fraction of the clipper. Half their total stash had been transported to the other end of the dock – three trips in the fully-loaded skiff – and they'd barely even filled the cabin. They just kept working and collected more, no need for debate, and no time for it. Every scrap of food they took back across the water today was precious; the more they had, the better their chances of survival. That was what it boiled down to: life or death. That was what kept them focused.

At the other end of the dock, Gary waited nervously for Allison to finish each short journey in the skiff. It was nerve-wracking just how slender the line between fragile calm and total turmoil felt this morning. Even though Allison had rowed across the water, the noise had been enough to pique the interest of the nearer sections of the dead crowds. Some of the corpses had even attempted to get over the cars and wheelie bins and other obstructions that had been left in their way. For now, though, the group's improvised defences appeared to be holding strong. Even when a gaggle of bodies managed to slip and squirm through a gap, Rich – who'd come down to help Gary and keep things moving at the clipper - had spotted it and acted swiftly. He blocked the way through then silently re-killed the over-achieving cadavers, quietly disposing of their remains in the dark water.

As soon as Allison reached the far end of the dock again, Gary forced himself to move. He limped along the same route for what felt like the thousandth time, from the pier into Princes Court, right into South Sea Street, then straight on to where Allison moored the boat. It was no distance at all, but his knackered ankle made everything feel twice as far. He cursed himself for having been so bloody clumsy yesterday.

Now Dominic was here too, sent down to this end to help because a bottleneck was forming. That was what they told him, anyway. Gary thought the others might have wanted rid of him. He was only marginally more useful than a corpse.

21

Spotters had been sent scrambling up to high vantage points in buildings near to the site of yesterday's late-night incursion. The news they reported back wasn't good. There was another build-up around Thomas More Street. The dead had spilled forward yet again, flooding the area immediately to the east. Piotr was in the boardroom now, poring over Dominic's maps with a handful of others, trying to work out why. Liz Hunter heard voices and went to investigate. When she found him with Mihai, Paul Duggan, and Harjinder, all hunched over the table, talking tactics, she demanded to know what they were doing.

'Keeping the rest of the group safe,' Piotr told her. 'Butt out.'

'There's a process for this. The council needs to be involved in any decisions.'

'The council's not here. Unless you've come to tell us they're back.'

'No. No sign yet. Anyway, it's only Dominic who's not here. Everyone else is. I'll go and get them.'

'Don't bother. Won't change anything.'

'What's that supposed to mean?'

'We're done here. We know what happened last night, and we know what we need to do to stop it happening again.' He nudged Paul. 'Show her.'

'It's all to do with water,' Paul explained, showing her one of the maps. 'Look... you've got the river and the docks here, and there's a canal goes right through Wapping to Shadwell Basin. That's the root cause of the problem.'

'I don't understand. How is that a problem?'

'Because it limits their options. It forces the dead to move in certain directions.'

'But surely they'd just walk into the water and get stuck?'

'Yeah, and we think plenty of them have. Thing is, you go near any stretch of open water in this country and there's going to be a fence around it or a wall... something to stop idiots from jumping in. But all that does now is channel more of the corpses in specific directions. There are only so many ways they can go.'

Liz thought for a moment. 'But it's not just that, is it? You noisy bastards have been driving up and down the streets you've cleared, fighting and scrapping and doing who the hell knows what else without thinking about the repercussions. It's nothing to do with canals, you're the main reason the dead keep coming for us. You've created this stampede.'

'It's hardly a stampede.'

'That's not the point.'

Harjinder was not impressed. 'What would you rather? You happy to go hungry?'

Liz pretended to give his question more consideration than it deserved. 'Let me think... would I rather be alive and hungry, or dead with a full belly? Tough choice, Harj.'

'You'd have no food at all if it wasn't for my people,' Piotr said.

'I disagree. Were any of you involved in clearing out Hatton House?'

'We were keeping the place secure,' Paul said.

'I'll take that as a no. That's pretty much what I thought. So, Piotr, it wasn't actually your people who gathered the food at all, was it? It was everyone *but* them.'

'You couldn't have got into the building without us clearing the way.'

'And if we hadn't gone inside and stripped it, all the food we scavenged would still be sitting there. And anyway, what is all this "your people" and "my people" crap? We're one team, don't you get it? We all need to play our part to make this work. Talking in terms of *us* and *them* is just a recipe for disaster.'

'Whatever.'

'But if you do want to go down that route, then as far as I can see, all your people have done so far is cause us a shedload of problems. I heard about your little performance in the mess hall this morning. Seems to me, all you need to do to stop the dead getting any closer is just shut the fuck up. Sit on your hands or go play with yourselves in your rooms, just stop antagonising those damn things.'

Piotr laughed at her.

'I give up with you lot,' she said. She was about to leave the boardroom, but she stopped herself. 'Wait, you're not planning to go out there again, are you?'

'We need to keep up the offensive,' Paul said.

'Jesus Christ. So, what's the great plan this time?'

'We keep moving east, away from the docks, to clear them out. With me so far? Then we block up the key routes along the way to stop them coming back. Simple, really.'

Liz smirked at his patronising. 'Let me get this straight, your plan didn't work yesterday, so today you're going to go back out and do the exact same thing again? That's the classic definition of madness, you know that, right?'

'Funny. Smaller chunks of land, a street at a time, this time,' Piotr said. 'It'll work.'

22

Nothing Liz or anyone else could have said would have made the slightest bit of difference. Piotr's decision was final. Hasty arrangements were made for another offensive to be launched and the word went out for volunteers, bribed with the promise of double rations. Liz told Lynette what she'd heard, and Lynette in turn went to the hotel to let Marianne, David, and the others know what was going on. She found most people gathered in a large, ground floor meeting room. The awful stench that had pervaded almost every part of the building was marginally more bearable there.

There was an ocean of empty space between the door and everyone else, and whoever crossed the void found their every step watched by many pairs of eyes. Lynette found the pressure intimidating. It was stupid, she knew it, but she kept her head lowered, eyes focused on the white and gold swirl patterns on the once smart, dark blue carpet. She followed a grubby line where people's muddy feet had traipsed back and forth. No one in the room spoke. She sensed that Holly's needless death had silenced all of them.

'What's up, love?' Marianne asked, anticipating more trouble.

Lynette sighed. It was an effort to have to explain. 'I just wanted to let you know, Piotr's on the warpath again. He wants to push on through Wapping. Double food if you go out and fight for him, apparently.'

'Piotr's a fucking headcase,' Sanjay said. 'How can he promise double food when there isn't any?'

'Twice nothing is nothing,' Marianne said.

'Tell him to stick it up his arse.'

'Tell him yourself, Sanj,' Lynette said. 'I'm just the messenger. I thought you needed to know.'

'Thank you, we appreciate it,' Marianne told her.

'That Piotr guy is a fucking dick,' Omar said, unhelpfully.

'What have I told you about your language?'

'Get over yourself, Marianne. Yous lot are always cursing.'

'You watch your lip, lad.'

The kid wasn't in the mood to be silenced. 'No, I won't. I'm sick of that frigging Piotr thinking he's boss. Don't he get it? Gonna get us all killed, he is. Frigging idiot.'

'You're absolutely right, Omar,' she said, doing her best to placate him, 'but we're stuck between a rock and a hard place here. A lot of people listen to Piotr—'

'Yeah, only coz they're scared of him. I seen him smack Dave up this morning, an' I bet it's coz of him that Holly done herself in.'

Marianne shook her head. 'The thing is, right now we don't have a lot of choice but to play ball and not wind him up. Hopefully things will change when Vicky and the others get back.'

'Don't be soft, they ain't coming back.'

'They *are*. You just need to have a little faith. We always knew it might take them a while.'

'They've been gone days.'

'They've been gone for *one* day.'

'You shut your mouth, Omar,' Selena said. 'They're coming back. You talking like this is just making things worse.'

'That prick Piotr's the one what's making things worse,' Omar snapped back, but Selena was right. Other people were becoming visibly nervous. They always did when voices were raised and the prospect of having to confront the dead once again reared its ugly head. Sanjay tried to calm Omar down.

'Look, I get why you're angry, mate, I really do. We all feel the same way. But it's like Marianne says, when the others get back with food everything will be different again. And if they've got enough, we won't have to fight anymore.'

He put his arms on Omar's shoulders, but Omar shrugged him off. 'You're just a bunch of pussies. We're always gonna be fighting, long as Piotr's around. He needs sorting out. You need to grow a pair of bollocks, Sanjay.'

'You can't talk to me like that, you little shit.'

'Fuck you,' Omar said, and he squirmed from Sanjay's grip and sprinted out of the hotel.

Marianne watched him race away. 'Bloody kid. Let him go. He just needs to get it out of his system.'

'He's a liability,' Sanjay said. 'I'll go stop him before he does anything stupid.'

By the time Sanjay got outside, there was no sign of Omar. The kid could run like lightning when he wanted to – usually when he'd been caught nicking food or when there was work to be done – and today he'd simply evaporated into the chaos of the open space between the Tower of London and the railway line perimeter of the base.

Sanjay stopped running when he hit the edge of the crowds. There was a considerable group moving from Tower Place towards Trinity Square Gardens, Piotr's favoured spot for making dramatic announcements ahead of leading the troops into battle. He skirted around the growing gathering, keen not to get dragged into another day of fighting. He agreed completely with Omar's assessment of the situation but was smart enough to keep his mouth shut. He hated the way Piotr railed against the dead as if he was some great military leader from the history books, when in reality, he was nothing but an ex-construction site manager ranting angrily at a couple of hundred tired, starving, and frightened men and women.

He caught a glimpse of half-height movement over on the far side of Trinity Square Gardens. He could only see the top of his head, but he was sure it was Omar. The kid was racing up along Tower Hill towards Minories, and he disappeared around the back of the fuel tanker they'd salvaged from The Highway. Sanjay tried to speed up, but the number of people gathered conspired to slow him down, everyone moving in the opposite direction. He dropped his shoulder and pushed through, but by the time he reached the space where Omar had been, the kid was long gone.

Sanjay used the welded steps to climb up onto the railway tracks, hoping to get a better view. He immediately regretted his decision because there were people up here already. Piotr and Harjinder were leaning over the wall, deep in conversation, not best pleased at having been disturbed. 'What?' Harjinder grunted.

'I'm looking for Omar.'

Piotr shrugged. 'No one up here but us. Haven't seen that little shit since this morning.'

Sanjay looked up and down the line then back over the crowds, but there was no sign of him. He went back down the steps. Harjinder stood up and stretched. 'I'll go get the troops rounded up, boss. See you down there.'

'Okay.'

Now alone, Piotr turned his attention to the dead on the other side of the rails. He looked down at them with absolute disdain. Dumb fucking things. He despised everything about them. There was no way these empty, mindless lumps were going to get the better of him, no matter how many of them there were. He hawked up a load of phlegm, spat, and watched it trickle down the face of an emotionless corpse. Fucking thing didn't even notice.

'You're a wanker,' Omar said.

Piotr turned around and laughed. Omar was directly behind him. 'Where have you been hiding? Your friend was just up here looking for you.'

'He ain't my friend. Anyway, I don't care about him. I was looking for you.'

'Now you've found me, and I'm very busy. What do you want?'

'You don't look busy. You look like a lazy fucker who does fuck all. Just shouts at other people and gets them to do stuff.'

'Is that right?'

'Yeah, you prick,' Omar said, edging closer.

Piotr laughed again. 'You're very rude, little boy.'

'And you're very stupid.'

Then, in a flash of movement that caught Omar completely off-guard, Piotr grabbed him by the throat and lifted him clean off the ground. Omar would have yelled out, but he could hardly breathe. He thrashed his arms and legs furiously, but it had no effect. Piotr smashed him double on the wall. 'I've really had enough of you and your friends,' he said. 'Give me one reason why I shouldn't get rid of you.'

Omar tried to prise Piotr's fingers from his neck, but his grip was vice-like. Piotr released the pressure just fractionally to give him enough air to answer. 'Fuck you,' Omar gasped.

Piotr shrugged, then heaved him up and over the wall. Omar dropped and immediately disappeared, swallowed up by the crowd.

23

The corpses broke his fall; he landed on top of several with a painful slap, face down, then slid through the gaps between them until he hit the gore-covered road below. Winded from the drop, his throat on fire, and his brain still playing catch-up, Omar lay curled up like a baby in a layer of semi-congealed remains. It swished and sloshed around him as dead feet shuffled; unable to ever get anywhere, but never stopping still. Occasionally there were more volatile waves of movement as individual cadavers collapsed under the pressure of others and were replaced by those pushing forward from behind. It was awful dark down here. The hole he'd punched through the corpses had immediately resealed above him, and it was unexpectedly quiet, too. The only noise was the irregular trickling of liquids from the decaying dead, like the sounds in a forest after a rainstorm, warm water dripping from branches and leaves.

Omar was frozen in uncertainty. He knew he had to move; he was on his own on the wrong side of the barrier, surrounded by what was left of tens of thousands of dead people. Staying put wasn't an option, but getting back to the others felt like an impossibility. He wasn't thinking straight, but he remained alert enough to know that if he made any noise or reacted in any way that the nearest bodies worked out that he was there... it was curtains.

Stuff like this should have made him sick, but he was used to it now. These days decay was all he knew. It wasn't the first time he'd been on his belly in human remains, and it likely wouldn't be the last, but it felt worse today. Maybe because he'd been thrown to the dead, completely alone, and with no way of getting help. He knew people would start looking for him once they realised he'd gone, but how were they ever going to find him buried in the middle of this lot? He couldn't alert them to where he was, couldn't scream or stand up and wave or do anything that would reveal his location. For now, it was Omar versus the undead. He had to get back, though. He had to make that fucker Piotr pay for what he'd done.

He was just about managing not to panic. He was the king of getting out of shitty situations like this. When Sam had first turned up at his estate that day, he'd have been screwed if it hadn't been for Omar throwing firebombs from the balcony. And the rest of the group he'd come here with would have probably died trapped in the ruins of Fenchurch Street station if he hadn't been smart enough to crawl away and raise the alarm. For a second, Omar thought about trying to get back to the station, but he didn't know where it was from here or how far. Instead, he decided he should just try and get into any building. If he could get to one tall enough, he might have half a chance of being seen. He could force a top floor window open, maybe, or climb onto the roof and start hollering and chucking stuff back into the compound until someone noticed and worked out where he was.

Maybe, he thought, feeling slightly more confident now, *he didn't need to go back at all*. There was no food at the base, and from what he could see, people were starting to fight with each other as much as they fought with the bodies outside, so what was the point? If he could find a building that hadn't been looted, maybe he could stay there on his own until things got better elsewhere? Set himself up with a mancave in a penthouse... he'd been happy enough on his own before, hadn't he?

It was all academic, of course, because so far, Omar hadn't moved. He was still lying face down in a sticky lake of cold flesh and rancid offal. He was going nowhere fast.

Another nearby cadaver collapsed under the weight of so many others pushing against it, and a whole load of them went down like dominoes. Omar thought he was going to be crushed; he scrambled a few metres to the right to get out of the way, unnoticed by the seething hordes. Everything looked exactly the same from his new vantage point. All he could see in every direction was *them*. In this hellish maze of dribbling rot, the only directions he was confident of were up and down, nothing else made sense. He carefully pulled his knees up to his chest and made himself into a tight ball. The crowd around him seemed to go on forever. The chances of finding his way back to the others felt slim to zero.

Over to one side, he was vaguely aware of something happening. It was another pressure shift, and though he didn't understand the physics (science had been his worst subject at school, apart from French), he knew he had to try and take advantage. He understood the difficulties of getting out of the crowd and inside any of the nearby buildings, hell, he wasn't even sure where the bloody doors were, *but*, Omar reminded himself, he was smaller, faster, and stronger than any of the rotting people crowded around him. At that, he very, very slowly picked himself up.

His mum used to say he'd got plenty of growing still to do, and he was glad of that now because when he stood up, he was only level with the chests of most of the dead, even the ones that were bent over, unable to stand upright. He didn't know how much they could see with their dark, cloudy eyes, but it felt like they were looking through him, not at him, and he thought that might give him half a chance. Maybe a quarter of a chance. Maybe ten percent. He was invisible for the moment, but he knew the second he moved, the dead all around would come to life. It was intense; he almost cried. Almost. *Grow up, you muppet,* he said to himself. *Sam never cried, did he?*

There was a groaning, popping noise as another corpse somewhere near gave way under the pressure of those around it. A great swathe of dead bodies collapsed in a chain reaction, and though Omar knew this was his chance to move, he still couldn't do it. At least he had a clearer view now, if only momentarily. He could see an inviting-looking door in the side of a building straight ahead, and he knew it was his best chance.

He didn't have time to talk himself out of it.

When another swathe of cadavers moved, displaced by the aftershocks of those that had just gone down, he ran through a narrow gap which immediately started closing around him like something out of a disaster movie. The faster he ran, the quicker the space around him disappeared, but he made it. He slammed against the door, which was locked, of course. *Frigging typical.* Omar was alongside a metal fence, and he started to work his way along, knowing there had to be a gate somewhere. Several of the nearest bodies had realised he was there now. Clinging onto the rails, Omar looked over his shoulder and saw dead expressions staring straight back at him. Three or four became five or six, became ten, became twenty, became all of them, it felt like. He jumped up and grabbed the top of the railings but couldn't get enough of a hold to pull himself over. And now he could feel them trying to grip, attempting to drag him back like they didn't want him to go. Dead hands snatched at his clothing, tugged at his hair. He felt sharp bones protruding from the tips of flesh-stripped fingers, raking lines across his skin.

Adrenaline kicked in with a vengeance.

He pulled himself up, planted the sole of a blood-splattered trainer onto the partially exposed ribcage of a cadaver that had a hold of him and shoved for all he was worth. The combination of his force and the dead body's surprisingly tenacious grip was sufficient to give him the little extra leverage he needed. He threw himself over the top of the fence and landed on his back on a hard, weed-covered pavement, winded for the second time in a matter of minutes.

He gazed up into the swirling clouds overhead, doing everything he could to ignore the infinite number of hands stretching through the railings to reach him.

Safe... ish. Just out of reach.

Omar didn't recognise the building he'd ended up in the grounds of. *Offices*, he thought, the structure stretching way up into the sky, towering over him. He walked over to the nearest dust-covered ground floor window and peered inside. It was hard to be certain, of course, but he didn't see any movement. He tapped his knuckles on the glass, and nothing inside reacted.

He circled until he found a door that was open. As soon as he entered the building, he knew for sure that it was empty. It hadn't just been cleared of bodies, though, it had been stripped of *everything*. There was nothing for him here – no food, no water, nothing to help him dry off and get warm... absolutely zip. The group had already emptied it out. Dejected, he climbed almost halfway up and worked his way around the perimeter of the block until he found a window that let him see into the base. He could only see as far as the train tracks, but he hoped that would be enough. There was no one up there now, but when he next saw someone, he'd bang on the glass and keep banging until they heard him.

In his heart, Omar knew it was a longshot. They'd probably never hear him. He thought about trying to write a message on the windows, but they hadn't left him anything to write with.

Omar pressed his face against the glass and looked down into the packed streets below. He must have made more noise than he thought getting in here because the dead had started crowding around this building now, leaving him trapped.

He was cut off from the others. No way out and no way back. More alone than he'd ever been before.

24

Gary had lost count of how many times he'd crossed paths with Rich and Dominic as they transferred supplies from the dock to the clipper, and the boat wasn't even a third full yet. He waited at the bottom of the pier for Rich to pass him with his next load of boxes then dragged himself up the slope again. They'd already emptied the skiff several times over, but the amount of empty space remaining in the clipper was daunting. Even if they stayed until this time tomorrow and worked straight through – and he sincerely hoped that wasn't going to be an option – there'd still be room for more. 'Come on, mate, don't look so glum,' Rich said. 'Almost there.'

Gary didn't deign his comment worthy of any response. He just huffed and headed back to the dock and a pile of supplies that seemed never to reduce in size. Christ, even Dominic was grumpy now and for once had stopped pontificating about the life saving properties of every salvaged packet of biscuits.

He watched the skiff heading back to the other end of the dock to fetch more. Through the haze of smoke drifting over from Canary Wharf, he could see Ruth and Vicky ready to start filling the little boat again. He wondered if they were as knackered as he was.

Allison was flagging too. It took more effort than the others realised to keep the boat moving. She sensed their frustration at her slow speed, but she couldn't row any faster. She eventually reached the other end of the water and threw the rope up for Ruth to moor the boat. Ruth handed her a can of Coke in return, and she knocked it back quickly.

Between them, Ruth and Vicky refilled the skiff quickly and

sent Allison on her way. 'My turn for a break,' Vicky said, exhausted. She leant against the wall of the underpass, trying to keep another coughing fit under control. Cigarettes helped. She lit up. Ruth watched her intently.

'I'm worried about you, Vic,' Ruth said. 'What's wrong?'

'Last time I checked, everything was wrong.'

'You know what I mean. What's wrong with you? Every day you're a bit more tired, a bit more angsty.'

'Par for the course these days.'

'Come on... it's more than that, isn't it?'

She could tell by Vicky's reaction – rather, the way she tried so hard not to react at all – that she was onto something. But Vicky was insistent. 'I'm fine.'

'Bollocks, love, none of us are fine. I keep catching you pulling faces.'

'I don't.'

'Stop denying it. You keep grimacing like you're in pain, then when you see me watching, you change your expression.'

'You're imagining things.'

'I'm not. You're always coughing, too.'

'Everybody's always coughing. The world stinks, Ruth. If it's not germs from the bodies then it's insects, and if it's not insects, it's smoke. Half the bloody city is on fire, in case you hadn't noticed.'

'No need to get so shitty with me. I know you better than you think I do, and I know something's not right.'

'I just feel a bit off today, that's all. I think I ate too much rich food yesterday. We gorged ourselves stupid last night. After living on thin air for weeks, it's given me a dodgy stomach.'

'I wish I could believe you. I wish you'd just be honest with me and—'

She was interrupted by a corpse falling from the road above the underpass. It faceplanted a short distance ahead with a dull thud and the sickening crack of bone.

'Bloody hell! They're dropping from the damned sky now!'

139

Vicky cried, edging forward and looking up. The emaciated figure writhed at her feet, trying to pick itself up on shattered arms. She inched out from under the cover of the tunnel, then ducked back fast when another one dropped. Its belly split when it hit the dirt, its contents splashing her boots. 'What the hell's going on?'

The section of road that passed overhead was congested, packed with bodies. Their numbers had been building all morning, and now they'd reached critical mass. The carriageway was rammed, the pressure forcing those nearest the side up and over the railings. Another glut of them dropped down, cushioned by the remains of those that had fallen before them. Vicky moved quickly to incapacitate them before they could cause any more problems.

When Chapman grabbed hold of her, she nearly put her crowbar through his skull. 'Jesus Christ! Don't creep up on me like that.'

'We've got a problem,' he said. 'There's a flood on the way.'

'A flood?'

'I thought it was weird that their numbers were so sparse over here. I don't know where they were all hiding, but the fuckers have found us out. Doesn't matter how quiet we try to be, we're always gonna be louder than everything else.'

Ruth ran back towards the apartment block they'd used as a lookout yesterday morning. Vicky followed her out onto the roof of the building. The streets had been empty when they'd been up here yesterday, but now they were teeming with putrid flesh.

'Why so many of them so suddenly? This must be something to do with whoever sealed the supermarket up again last night.'

'I reckon it's got *everything* to do with them,' Vicky said, and she pointed into the distance. 'Look over there... the bodies are filling the streets everywhere except directly around the shopping centre. I think this is deliberate. They're being herded this way.'

'Seriously?'

'Think about it, the people here on the south bank don't need the dock because they're already here. In fact, it's one area they could positively do without. They don't want to encourage more people like us turning up.'

Ruth moved to another part of the roof to try and get a better view. Jesus Christ, Vicky was right... it was as if a protective bubble had been drawn around the supermarket. Vast hordes were dragging themselves past on either side of the building, then continuing towards the river. There were thousands of them.

Chapman and Lisa had come to the same conclusion. When Ruth and Vicky returned to the docks, Chapman had already resealed their access point for getting into the supermarket, and he and Lisa were on their way down to the other end of the water, carrying as much as they could manage between them. Ruth followed their lead, scooping up boxes and heading for the river. Vicky was about to do the same when she remembered the large, wheeled cages they'd been using to transport stuff from the supermarket to the dock. Using one of them she could move ten times as much in a single trip. She dragged a cage around the still-growing mound of fallen bodies at the mouth of the underpass and began filling it.

At the far end of the dock, the others were unloading the last provisions from the skiff and transporting everything down onto the clipper. They moved at a frantic pace, as increased numbers of the dead had become visible, filling the gaps between the buildings along the water's edge. For now, the makeshift barriers they'd put in place first thing were holding, but it wouldn't take much to tip the balance.

The group was starting to get in each other's way, unhelpful bottlenecks forming. Ruth took charge, organising them into a human chain. Gary and Dominic were confined to the clipper while the others passed boxes, bags, and whatever else they could get hold of from person to person at speed. They hadn't even realised Vicky was still missing until they heard her coming. The wheels on the rattling, half-full cage made a din as she dragged it along the block-paved pathway of Brunswick Quay. For now, though, the dead appeared to be more interested by the activity around the clipper.

It was only a few hundred metres from the underpass to the pier, but the pressure of the moment made the distance appear several times as long. Wherever Vicky looked she could see loathsome figures dragging themselves along the streets parallel to the docks in massive numbers. Finland Street, the next road up from the water, was packed solid with decay. Ruth and Allison sprinted the other way to meet her and help. Soaked with sweat, Vicky willingly let them take the cage and they dragged it down towards the other end of the dock between them at twice her speed. She leant over the railings to catch her breath then followed them, too tired to keep running.

At the end of Greenland Dock was Lattice Footbridge, a narrow footpath over an inlet with a hefty step-up. Ruth hesitated for a second, looking for another route because there was no way they were going to get the cage up and over. It was too far to go around; they had no option but to unload the supplies and carry them across the bridge, handing them to Rich and Lisa who met them at the mid-point. In their haste to get the job done, the half-empty cage tipped over onto its side, filling the air with a godawful metallic clattering noise. The all-consuming, deliberately preserved silence amplified the din to a catastrophic volume, and the sudden reaction of scores of corpses was as terrifying as it was inevitable.

A sizeable throng changed direction and began flocking towards Greenland Dock and the footbridge. The group had blocked this part of the road earlier, and, though their barrier was strong enough to withstand the pressure of ten or twenty cadavers at a time, it was useless against a sudden surge like this. All that Ruth, Allison, Richard, and Lisa could do was grab whatever they could and scramble back across the bridge and over to the clipper. And all Vicky could do, stranded on the other side of the sudden incursion, was watch her chances of getting back to the Monument slip away. Directed by the shape of the road, by the buildings on one side and the safety rails along the water's edge on the other, the sudden glut of death had been steered away from the river and was now coming straight at her. She almost wished they'd move faster, because their miserable plodding gave her too much time to think about the inevitability of what was going to happen next. The food, medicine, and other supplies they'd loaded onto the clipper was an essential lifeline for the hundreds of people waiting back at base. Vicky knew that unless she could find another way through to the boat and fast, Ruth and the others would have no choice but to leave without her.

Her best path was to turn back on herself and run in the opposite direction, around the perimeter of the rectangular shaped dock. Vicky started back towards the underpass and the supermarket, easily outpacing the wave of death in pursuit, but she'd barely made it as far as the end of Greenland Dock when another weak point in their improvised blockades gave way under the pressure of the undead surge. A second swell of corpses was now coming towards her from the opposite direction.

She was just considering jumping into the filthy, cadaver filled water and swimming when she spotted a footpath immediately to her right that the dead were all but ignoring. It bisected a patch of grassland then disappeared under the road that the vast majority of corpses were continuing to lumber slowly along. She had no idea where it would lead, but she had no choice but to take it.

They were still working frantically at the other end of the dock. A sizeable pile of goods remained to be loaded onto the clipper, but time was running out. The dead hordes were pouring this way, too.

Gary was dragging himself along, barely able to lift his injured leg now, but he kept going just the same. 'What the fuck happened?' he asked as he was handed more boxes.

'We walked into a trap,' Dominic said, and he squeezed past Gary and down the ramp.

'Don't be so fucking melodramatic,' Lisa yelled, no point in keeping her voice down now. 'We strayed onto someone's patch, and they took objection. We'd have done the same if our positions were reversed.'

But she was shouting into the wind.

Ruth and Allison appeared. 'Where's Vicky?' Gary asked.

'On the other side of that lot,' Allison explained, gesturing into the expanding crowds behind them.

'I'm going back to find her,' Ruth said, dumping her stash at the end of the ramp. Gary grabbed her arm.

'No, you're not. She's tough as nails, Vicky is. She can look after herself.'

And much as she didn't want to accept it, Ruth knew he was right.

They continued working, all of them going at breakneck speed to get every scrap they could before the dock became impassable. They didn't have long, that much was clear. The nearest of the dead had passed the end of South Sea Street and were perilously close, moving towards the clipper together as an unstoppable, gelatinous mass. Richard tried to go back for one more box, but it was too late. 'Stop, it's not worth it,' Chapman yelled at him, and, though he almost did it anyway, he realised it was a risk too far and turned back. The thought of being buried under all that dead flesh was a fate too foul to even consider.

He slipped through the gap at the top of the pier, then Dominic and Chapman rolled a car across to block it. Allison started the clipper's engine, and the noise enraged the dead still further. The final few supplies were carried onboard from the pier – dumped now, rather than being carefully stacked as they had been previously – as corpses began to crowd around the car at the top of the ramp. Ruth was up there too, using a pair of binoculars she'd found on the bridge to scan the rapidly disappearing space on the dock for any sign of Vicky.

'We have to go, Ruth,' Chapman shouted.

'Just give her a couple more minutes.'

'We can't. There's no point. We need to leave.'

Everyone – Ruth included – knew that Vicky wasn't coming back. Even if she made it to this end of the dock, there was no way she'd be able to fight her way through this crowd of seething dead flesh. Regardless, Ruth continued to look for any sign of her friend. The drifting smoke from Canary Wharf made it even harder to make out details. Chapman took her arm and coaxed her back to the clipper. She recoiled from his touch. 'We can't just abandon her.'

'I'm sorry, Ruth, Vicky's gone. There's nothing we can do.'

Vicky found herself in an unexpected patch of inner-city woodland. An obviously well-maintained place pre-apocalypse, it was wild and overgrown now, but she was still able to make out defined walking paths. The bulk of the deceased population remained distracted by the activity at the docks, and apart from the occasional cadaver she found trapped in the undergrowth or snagged on jagged branches, she was largely alone. She kept moving, knowing the absolute worst possible thing she could do was stop.

Her knowledge of this part of London was sparse, but she knew the twists and turns of the Thames were such that if she kept heading north, she had a chance, albeit slight, of reaching the river ahead of the clipper. If it worked, she'd try and attract the attention of the others from the shore.

She recognised this place. Stave Hill, it was called. She'd seen it on TV once: a man-made mound with a viewing point on top. It was directly ahead of her now, and she raced towards it, figuring that, though it would eat up a few precious minutes, it should also give her an indication of whether she could beat the boat or not. She ran around its circular perimeter until she reached a steep, straight set of steps, then dragged herself to the summit, clinging onto the handrail and pulling herself along with effort.

The view from the top was stunning, but useless.

She knew where the Thames was; what was left of Canary Wharf was visible on the other bank, but the trees and buildings between Stave Hill and the river prevented her from seeing the water at all. In the deceptive stillness she could hear the clipper on the move, beginning its return trip. She followed the sound as it swirled around her, over to the east at first, then beginning to move north. The engine noise increased her feelings of desperation. She accepted the logic of them leaving without her, but the realisation that she was completely alone on the south bank now was like a punch to the gut.

She was exhausted. Struggling to keep going. Pain washed over her in waves. She tried to run, but no longer had the legs. She knew it wouldn't make any difference now. The view from the top of the hill had given her an improved sense of perspective. Even if she'd been able to sprint north with Olympic speed, clearly, by the time she reached the river, the boat would be long gone.

25

They were refusing to play ball. Marianne and the others had shut themselves away downstairs in the hotel meeting room. It meant no access to food or other supplies in the short term, but they figured that was a small price to pay to stay alive. A furious Piotr had sent Stan over to try and talk some sense into the group, but negotiations had gone as badly as expected. Stan was an inherently selfish and inflexible old git who couldn't understand why none of them were prepared to go out and clear the streets again, even though he'd barely left his plush apartment in the last few weeks, other than at mealtimes.

'Be reasonable,' he said. 'We've all got to play our part.'

'And what exactly is your part, Stan?' David asked. Marianne had coaxed him down from his room, but his mood was not improved. 'See, I'm at a loss there. In all the time I've known you, I haven't seen you lift a bloody finger. I can't see the point of you being here at all. And, for the record, I am very reasonable, I just don't have a death wish.'

'I play my part, you know. I help in other ways. I'm an advisor. I've got a lot of useful experience. And let's be honest, I'm too old for fighting.'

'Too old or too scared?'

'If you're just going to throw silly insults around, I'll leave.'

'I wish you would.'

'Look, all Piotr's trying to do is keep us all safe.'

'Really? I'm starting to think he's trying to keep himself safe by using us as human shields. It's alright for you and Damien and everyone else over there in your fancy apartments, but we're right on top of the area where most of the problems are happening. When things go tits up, we won't stand a chance.'

'Then *help*, for goodness's sake. One more push and the whole of the area behind the hotel will be secure.'

'Christ, you're even talking like him now. What Piotr's planning isn't helping. He's only making things worse.'

'Well, I disagree,' Stan said, shaking his head.

'Well, I don't care,' David told him. 'I've been out there, mate, and I'm not going out again. What's it going to take before you wise up? There are no half measures with Piotr. Time and time again I've watched his plans turn to chaos.'

'And what would you do different? How else do you expect to get out of this stinking hotel without getting rid of all those horrible things outside?'

'I'd rather stink of sewerage and be safe, if that's what you're asking. Look, Stan, it really doesn't matter, because Piotr will do whatever he wants. He wants to take back the whole of London when we only need a few streets. Until there's a change of tactics, I've made a conscious decision not to get involved. Same as you have, actually.'

Stan was about to say something but was interrupted when Sanjay burst into the room.

'Any sign?' Marianne asked.

He shook his head. 'Nothing.'

'What's wrong?' asked Stan.

'Omar's missing.'

'That little bugger could be anywhere,' Stan said, unhelpfully. 'He's a little sod, that one. He's probably pinched a load of food and shut himself away somewhere. I wouldn't trust him as far I can spit.'

'He speaks just as highly of you.'

Stan shook his head. 'I'm getting nowhere here. There's no point wasting my breath.'

'At least that's one thing we agree on,' Marianne said. 'Just leave us alone, Stan. We'll keep ourselves to ourselves. We don't want any trouble.'

'And neither does Piotr. Look, I've tried to keep this friendly and positive, but the reality is we've got our backs against the wall. I asked him to let me come and talk to you because I thought you might listen to reason. Thing is, he's going out there to clear more of the streets behind this place, and you're going to have to help whether you like it or not. Harjinder said he'll come and drag you out there himself if he has to.'

Stan's last comment made David bristle. 'Fucker can try.'

Marianne was losing her patience. 'For goodness's sake, what's happening to us? The enemy is those foul things out there, not each other. We need to cooperate, and we *all* need to take other people's views into consideration. If Piotr thinks he can send his bullyboys in here to start throwing their weight around, then he can—'

She stopped talking when Selena appeared, breathless. 'There's a boat coming,' she gasped.

The mood changed immediately; arguments put on pause. People poured out of the hotel and joined many others already on their way down to the pier. 'Are we sure it's them?' Stan asked, watching the Thames Clipper approach. His question was redundant, because there was no mistaking Dominic Grove hanging over the safety rails near the bow of the vessel, waving like some highfalutin dignitary.

'Who the hell does he think he is?' Lynette said to no one in particular.

Allison sailed past then turned the boat around in a gentle arc, nudging the bow through floating corpses and other flotsam and jetsam. She moored at the Tower Pier, facing downriver. Marianne assumed it was to make unloading easier because of the proximity of Tower Place, but the cynic in her couldn't help wondering if Dominic had asked Allison to take him on a victory lap before heading into port.

Piotr was at the front of the queue, inevitably, ordering someone to tie up the boat and telling someone else to stop too many folks crowding onto the pier. With Chapman's help, Dominic lowered the steps and was the first to disembark, looking like a long-lost explorer, returning home after years away at sea.

'He's every inch the politician he claims not to be,' Marianne said to David, and he agreed. When Dominic spoke, his words sounded disingenuous and over-rehearsed.

'Thanks to Marianne and Lynette for suggesting Surrey Quays, and everyone who went over there with me and risked so much over the last couple of days.'

'Well?' Marianne asked, impatient. She could see the cabin of the boat was piled high with boxes and trays, though, from here, she couldn't make out any useful detail.

'We did it.' Cue much cheering and congratulations on the pier. Dominic gestured for people to quieten down. 'I'd be lying if I said it had been an unqualified success, because we haven't all made it back. I'm sorry to say, Vicky's not with us. We think she's fine, but she got cut off from the rest of us and couldn't get back to the boat.'

David pushed his way through to the front. Dominic kept talking, anticipating his questions.

'I'm sorry, David, I really am. We think she's probably okay. Like I said, she got split up from the rest of us and couldn't make it back. We kept the dead at bay for as long as we could, but they broke free as we were loading up to come home. We had no option but to leave. She knew the risks. We all did.'

'And that's it? You just abandoned her?'

'There's every possibility we'll be going back.'

'When?'

'I can't answer that, it's for the council to decide. I'll explain more later. There's a lot to unpack, figuratively and literally, but right now we need to get Mihai down here to start getting everything into storage. We've brought back a boat full of food, and our short-term future is now so much more secure. If we're sensible, there should be enough to keep us going through most of the winter, if not right through to next spring.'

'This is bullshit,' David said. 'They'd have gone back if it was you that got left behind.'

Ruth got off the clipper. Sensing trouble, she ushered David away. 'Come on, mate. I'll tell you what happened, and you can explain to me why you look like you've been mugged.'

26

Vicky was struggling to keep moving; wasn't even sure if it was worth the effort. It felt like the harder she tried these days, the less she achieved. Tempting as it was to stop, though, rolling over and giving up just wasn't in her nature. If that had been an option, she'd had done it already.

The area through which she was walking now was eerily quiet. She went unnoticed; a speck of dust being blown across a landfill site. She looked up at the houses she passed – decent, desirable places once – and wondered if she could find one that was in good enough nick that she could hole-up inside with enough supplies and books to see out her time. One last push and a final risky trip to the supermarket and she would be sorted. No more fighting. An end to the constant effort it took just to stay alive in this hellish place. And then, as always happened when her mind started wandering like this, she heard Kath's voice in the back of her head, berating her. She could hear her nagging, going on about getting Selena to bloody Ledsey Cross, despite the fact they'd known from the start that getting out of London was going to be all but impossible, never mind anywhere else.

Now that the clipper had gone and there was no longer any point heading for the river, she turned back towards Surrey Quays. She was going to spend tonight in the supermarket, if it was safe. They'd left behind shelves full of treats and luxuries to focus on necessities. Chocolate and booze, that was what she fancied most of all. More cigarettes. And crisps, too. She hoped she'd find a few packets that were still in date, or close, anyway. Tubes of foil-packed, preservative-heavy Pringles would be okay, wouldn't they? It was sad to think there'd be a day in the not-too-distant future when all the comfort food she craved would no longer exist.

Almost all of the dead were looking the other way, still fascinated by the aftereffects of what had happened at the pier and around the dock. Dumb fuckers. The excitement was all over now, had been for an hour or more, and yet they continued to congregate there *en masse*. Vicky walked in a wide loop along maze-like streets to avoid the bulk of them, only cutting back south when she thought she was level with the shopping centre again. This part of London was in stark contrast to the places she'd known on the other side of the river. Over there, new buildings were crammed into the gaps between old ones, roads twisted around relics. To the north, London often felt haphazard, barely planned at all. Here, though, vast areas had been redeveloped with a structure and order that was absent elsewhere. She was walking along a canal which ran between tall, uniform-looking apartment blocks on either side, functional, consistent, and visually appealing. This was what she'd been led to believe Wapping would be like. It made her wonder why they were risking so much to seize the streets on the north bank, when this side of the river could have been theirs for the taking.

Vicky was starting to enjoy the space around her. It made her feel even more antisocial than usual, and she liked it. When this place had been constructed, the population of the city had no doubt warranted huge housing stocks. These days, the remaining population of London could likely fit into just one of these buildings, though if everyone she'd left on the north bank had been living in the block up ahead of her now, she'd still have wanted to find herself another building elsewhere. She was so done with people.

The towpath ran under a road. When Vicky saw that there were hardly any corpses on the road above, she decided to risk going up to get a better view and properly orientate herself. She climbed a set of steps onto a completely empty street. The desolation didn't feel right. There should have been more bodies than this... had she become disorientated and ended up miles from where she'd expected to be? Surely the distraction at the docks couldn't still be drawing the dead away from everywhere else, could it?

Hang on.

These roads had been blocked.

There was no question. This had to be something to do with the people who'd tried (unsuccessfully) to prevent them getting into the supermarket, and who'd coordinated the subsequent flood of death that had resulted in her being stranded here. It made her feel uneasy. Prone. Were they watching her now? Had they been watching all along? There was no reason to think that would be the case; they were most likely unaware she'd been left behind. Strange as it was, she didn't hold any grudge. If anything, she admired the circumspect approach of these people. It was a welcome contrast with the bombast of Piotr and Dominic's would-be war machine over on the north bank. Whoever was responsible for defending this area had developed a plan that was startling in its simplicity. Rather than being held back, the dead here were being guided along certain streets, kept constantly moving. They'd been allowed to circulate around the vicinity along specific veins and arteries like blood in a body, lines of vehicles placed across certain junctions to prevent them from straying. She smiled at the irony of her metaphor, death mimicking life, but it was true. The dead formed the active population of London now.

Vicky came across a large, fenced-off construction site. There were two sets of gates, one on either side of the vast, open area, both left propped open. More vehicles had been used to corral corpses in and out. The site appeared to have been used as a holding pen of sorts, a relatively clear space which had filled with corpses then gradually emptied, regulating their flow. She was sure that was what had happened because the ground inside the fenced-off area was awash with stale blood. There were some stragglers here too, partial bodies that hadn't had the strength (or enough limbs) to keep moving and follow the rest of the crowd. If she'd had the time and inclination, Vicky expected she'd find other, similar holding pens nearby. The extent to which the putrefying population had been shepherded around the local area was only beginning to become apparent. It was genius, really. The survivors here had avoided becoming the focus of undead attention by keeping the corpses focused on themselves. In the absence of distractions, they just kept walking round and around... it explained why their activity at the dock had generated such a devastating reaction.

She'd allowed herself to lose focus, and that was never a good idea these days. She looked around and saw a sports clothing store across the street. It made sense to stop there and shelter for a while, to take stock and carefully plan her next move. Given what she was seeing here, was heading back towards the shopping centre alone a smart idea?

She entered the building through an underground carpark, an unusual luxury in this part of the city. It was dark and cold down there, but the anonymity the low light provided was welcome. She walked past the windows of the tiny security office and peered inside. The husk-like remains of a uniformed guard sat slumped in a chair; he clearly hadn't moved since the day he'd died. It didn't look a particularly comfortable spot, but she thought it might make a decent subterranean bolthole for tonight.

Vicky went up onto the shop floor. It was reassuringly dusty and untouched, and she became distracted walking around the displays. Funny how sports stores had never been particularly high on their list of useful places to loot, because there was so much here worth taking. She found herself a complete change of practical, comfortable clothing and a pair of sturdy walking boots to replace the blood-soaked trainers she'd been kicking around in for weeks. Fresh clothes that fitted her scrawny frame, clean socks... oh, the luxury! She peeled off the filthy leggings she'd been wearing for longer than she could remember and threw them in a bin. If only she could have had a shower... she thought as she put on a support bra and several thermal underlayers. She found a decent rucksack that she filled with spare kit, then put on a climbing harness from which she hung her crowbar.

The pièce de résistance came when she discovered a couple of untouched, cobweb covered vending machines tucked away in a corner by the checkouts. She crowbarred them open and helped herself to energy drinks and chocolate. Sure, it wasn't quite the height of indulgence she'd pictured in the supermarket, but for now it was good enough.

She grabbed an all-season sleeping bag and a rolled-up ground mat, then she looked around for a brighter alternative to the underground security office she'd been considering. She desperately needed to rest.

When she turned around, there was someone standing right behind her, just inches away.

'You got everything you need?' he asked.

27

The man was French-Canadian, and Vicky had known from the moment he'd opened his mouth that he didn't pose a threat. His name was Eric Layette. He was shabbily dressed (wasn't everyone?) and behind the shaggy hair and even shaggier beard, she estimated he was probably in his mid-forties. He talked incessantly when it was safe to do so, and kept his mouth shut the rest of the time. 'We had a few looters come here before you,' he explained. 'Mostly ones or twos at a time. You're the most organised.'

'Sorry for taking your stuff,' Vicky said. 'We didn't realise anyone had staked a claim to it.'

'What, even after we put a new padlock on the door to replace the one you broke?' He shrugged. 'Doesn't matter. We like to stay quiet and stay local. Keep ourselves to ourselves. Don't want any trouble.'

'You don't sound very local.'

'What, the accent?' He smiled. 'I'm from Terrebonne, Canada. Came to England with some friends to see a band, and now I'm stuck here. Trip of a lifetime, believe it or not. Didn't realise it was going to last a lifetime, though.'

Vicky shook her head and smiled. Eric was instantly disarming, very matter of fact. She got the impression he was just telling her like it was, no need to impress or exaggerate, and his modesty was refreshing.

'So, I get stuck thousands of miles from home, but it's not all bad news. I've lost a hundred pounds, I think.' He lifted his baggy T-shirt to reveal an equally baggy belly. 'Look at me, I'm ripped!' he laughed, though he instinctively kept the volume down to a whisper.

'Where are we going?'

'To the others.'

'How many?'

'Just six. Seven now, with you. Works better with just a few, I think. Started off with just me and Brian and Doreen. Brian's a smart guy. He was a teacher. Old, though, but not as old as Doreen. I like Doreen; she's lived around here forever. The others found us like you did.'

'You found me, actually.'

'It wasn't difficult.'

The streets they'd been walking along remained almost completely silent. Barely any bodies at all. Clouds of smoke still drifted across from the Canary Wharf fires. Sometimes it was dense enough to make Vicky's eyes water.

'It's so quiet here,' she said.

'It's quiet everywhere.'

'You know what I mean.'

'You're talking about the dead folk? For a long time, they were easy to deal with. Did you find that too? We just pushed them around and blocked a few roads, so they kept going in circles. We made sure we could get to the shops and back.'

'Until you set them on us today.'

'Down by the dock? No, we didn't set nothing on nobody. We fixed things so they wouldn't bother us. It was you that drew them that way with all your noise. Sorry if they caused you trouble, but it wasn't our doing. Like I said, they heard you. You were being pretty loud, all things considered.'

Vicky decided to reserve judgement. Eric's accent and the words he used made everything sound innocent, comfortingly pre-apocalyptic. It was a stark contrast with the aggressive talk she was used to on the other side of the Thames. He seemed worried that he'd upset her and did what he could to prolong the conversation.

'You have a lot of people where you're from?' he asked.

'Hundreds.'

'Hundreds! No shit! Jeez, I would not like that. All that noise... I bet you see a lot of trouble.'

'Tell me about it.'

'It's much better this way. Just a few of us, and a heck of a lot of space.'

'I'm starting to think you might be right.'

'Are you going to try and get back?'

'I... well, I'm not sure yet.'

'Are your people far?'

'By the Tower of London.'

'Wow, that's such a cool place. I was supposed to visit there, but the world went crazy. A day or two later and I might have been over there with you, maybe. The other side of the river, though, that's a long way these days. Almost Terrebonne distance.'

'Not quite, but I know what you mean.'

Eric stopped and gestured towards a line of cars parked nose-to-tail along a stretch of pavement. 'Home sweet home,' he said.

It took Vicky a few seconds to work out what she was looking at. What had initially appeared to be a typical street scene was, on closer inspection, much more. The vehicles had been left parked in such a way that they were all touching, preventing undead access to a large, open, concrete and grass-filled space just beyond. At the centre of it all, yet another tower block. It looked old – sixties or seventies, she thought – different from the patch of the more recently constructed places she'd just walked past in the surrounding area.

Eric double-checked, making sure no one was watching, then he opened one of the cars, slid across the back seat to the other side, and let himself out. Vicky followed, closing the door onto the street behind her.

It might not have looked much aesthetically, but Vicky immediately realised the value of the drab-looking, grey brick building they were walking towards. It was in an oasis of space, protected by the rows of vehicles across the front, and by other, fortress-like apartment blocks on the remaining sides. The approach roads had also been blocked, as she'd seen elsewhere in the neighbourhood. With quick and relatively corpse-free access to a huge store of supplies just a short distance away, this place looked ideal for a small group of people. In fact, it looked like somewhere people could set up permanently. She didn't admit as much, but she was jealous as hell. It was an urban paradise in comparison to the shithole she'd left behind on the other side of the river. She was already making plans to find a way of bringing Selena, Ruth, and a select few others over here, rather than working out how she was going to get back.

'This is John Kennedy House,' Eric announced. 'Named after the president.'

'You don't say.'

They accessed the building through a rear entrance, not the obvious main doors, which had been blocked. Inside, the place was gloomy, though not as dark as Vicky expected. They climbed the stairs and she saw that the doors to many of the flats on the lower levels had been left wedged open, letting maximum light spill into the communal spaces.

'We're up top,' Eric explained. 'We have our own places, but we spend a lot of time together too.' Vicky noticed that he was already wheezing with the effort of the climb. Perversely, she even took that as a good sign. She'd been living on the edge since the beginning of September, potential threats lurking around every corner. Judging by the apparent exertion, she suspected that Eric and his friends, after their initial burst of energy to secure this place and block the nearby roads to keep the corpses flowing, had done very little. Again, she was jealous. She shook her head. Imagine being able to sit back, gorging on pilfered food, watching the rest of the world decay. It occurred to Vicky that by taking a completely opposite approach, these people appeared to have succeeded where the Monument group had failed. Start small, build slow, stay safe. She thought Dominic and Piotr could learn a lot from these folks.

After a midway break for Eric to catch his breath, they reached the landing on the top floor. 'Here we go,' he said. Vicky hesitated slightly, not least because it was darker up here, the doors to all the individual flats left shut. Again, she thought it through, and it made sense. The people up here would want privacy.

Suddenly she became mistrusting, though she hated herself for it. It was better to stay cautious; this place was too good to be true, wasn't it? These days things only ever went wrong, never right, and she braced herself for the inevitable denouement. Maybe Eric was crazy – he was certainly the happiest person she'd met on this side of the apocalypse – and those other people he'd talked about were, in fact, dead. She pictured him ushering her into the lounge of one of these flats, introducing her to writhing corpses strapped to chairs dotted around the room, his so-called friends. Or maybe there wasn't anyone else here at all, his companions existing only in his head. Or, and now this seemed most likely, this was a honeypot trap and there was a whole load of fuckers about to beat her and kill her and maybe even eat her the moment she crossed over the threshold. Although the close proximity of a fully stocked supermarket seemed to cast doubt on that theory, she tightened her hand on her crowbar, just in case.

Against the odds, Vicky was completely wrong on every score.

'Excuse me, everybody,' Eric announced as they entered the flat. 'House meeting, please. We have a visitor.'

There was an old guy sitting in an armchair facing the window. He jumped up as soon as he heard Eric's voice. He was reasonably smartly dressed, with a shock of white hair. Vicky noticed he was clean shaven. Very few men had the time, resources, or inclination these days, so much so that she'd started to think shaving was in danger of becoming a lost art. 'Nice to meet you,' he said, enthusiastically holding out his hand. 'I'm Brian.'

A young girl entered the room from the kitchen. She was carrying a can of drink and a bowl of snacks. 'Hiya. I'm Joanne.'

'Vicky,' she said, punch-drunk.

'You want something to eat?'

'Later, thanks.'

'You sure? Shanice is in the kitchen. She'll fix you something.'

'I'm good, thanks.'

On hearing her name, Shanice popped her head around the door. 'Sorry, I had my headphones in,' she explained. 'I'm Shanice.'

'Hi.'

She came around the corner then and hugged Vicky. Vicky remained starchy-still, wanting so much to relax, but unable to quite let go. Shanice seemed to understand and went about her business.

'Where are the other two?' Eric asked.

'In their flats,' Brian replied. 'I think Doreen's asleep. She usually is.'

'I'll go and tell them.'

'Probably best to leave her to rest,' Brian started to say, but Eric had already gone. 'Bit of a force of nature is our Eric. Lovely lad. He means well.'

'Well, I'm very grateful he found me.'

'We saw all the commotion earlier. You're alright, I take it?'

'I'm fine.'

'What about your friends? I assume you weren't alone?'

'They've gone. We came by river.'

He nodded thoughtfully. 'Sensible. Probably the safest way to get about right now. That's if you feel you need to travel, of course.'

'And you don't?'

'We've got everything we need here,' Joanne said, and she plonked herself down on a sofa and picked up a book.

Vicky was on the verge of launching into a tirade about how there were other people out there suffering, and how selfish it was of them to sit here in relative comfort when there was so much pain and devastation elsewhere... but she didn't. She stopped herself and sank into a gloriously comfortable chair and just looked around the room. It was like she'd travelled back in time, as if nothing had ever happened.

'Are you okay?' Shanice asked, concerned.

Vicky nodded. 'Think so. Bit overwhelmed.'

'I'll get you a coffee,' she said, and she went back into the kitchen.

Vicky found herself thinking about her dear, departed friend, Kath. If they'd found a place like this at the beginning, they could have stayed there with Selena. Maybe Kath would still be alive. It was a dark train of thought to follow, but she couldn't help it. She felt wracked with sudden guilt; the three of them had decided collectively to stay together, to keep moving and try to get out of London, to make the trip north to Ledsey Cross. They'd planned to travel hundred miles together; now one was dead and the other barely speaking to her.

Eric was so loud coming back into the flat that she wondered how he'd managed to survive so long. She got to her feet to greet whoever it was he'd got with him.

'Fuck,' she said.

'Fuck,' he said, grinning at her.

'I thought you were dead.'

'Sorry to disappoint.'

Sam Miller reached out for Vicky and held her tight. And despite the friction that had previously been so evident between them, despite the fact she'd thought he was an opinionated gobshite, and that he'd thought she was a miserable, defeatist bitch, they melted into each other's arms.

28

Across the water, food had temporarily calmed tempers and repaired frayed nerves. Love him or loathe him, there was no denying the fact that Dominic Grove had a public presence like literally no one else left alive. With a liberal application of bullshit and positive vibes, he'd managed to placate just about everyone. His tone and manner encouraged positivity from the masses, and his playing to the crowd meant that heavy conversations could be avoided, difficult decisions temporarily deferred. He made sure everyone heard what had happened over on the south bank, then picked up his food and took it elsewhere to eat.

He left behind a mess hall filled with noise and excitement. For a short time, rich and delicious smells masked the foetid stink of dead London. Phillipa had spent hours coordinating her team, cooking vats of rice and pasta over large wood fires, adding all manner of sauces that had been brought from the supermarket on the south bank. And the best part of it was, they'd barely even made a dent in their newly bolstered stocks. They had enough food for everyone to be able to eat like this for weeks, maybe longer.

Funny how food changed everything.

People who'd kept themselves shut away had emerged from their private spaces and were chatting away to other folks for the first time in ages. It felt good. It felt right. It felt long overdue.

But the celebrations were tempered by loss. Audrey Adebayo had said a few well-intentioned words of tribute for Vicky before the food had been served, talking about her as if she was gone forever. She spoke about Holly too, though few people had known who she was talking about, and fewer still had noticed she wasn't there.

Piotr and around twenty others ate in the White Tower, the keep at the centre of the grounds of the Tower of London. It was the oldest, safest part of the castle. Piotr had become something of a history buff since they'd ended up there. Some of the walls of the White Tower, he'd learnt, were several metres thick. Most of the people who'd spent time there with him were less concerned with the fortifications and more interested in the displays of ancient armour and weaponry, most of which had already been pilfered and used in their battles to take back Wapping. Tonight, though, Chapman was the centre of attention, Piotr insisting on him giving them a blow-by-blow, spin and bullshit free account of what had happened at Surrey Quays.

Once she was sure Chapman was in full flow and everyone else was busy, Orla fetched Marianne from the hotel. The two of them met Lynette in the atrium of Tower Place as agreed. 'He here?' Orla asked.

'He's always here,' Lynette replied, and they went up to the boardroom. When the door opened, Dominic looked up, concerned.

'What's this? Looks like a deputation.'

Marianne sat down next to him. 'Nothing to be worried about, Dom. We just want to know what you saw out there. We wanted to know what you're thinking.'

'Did you not hear me at dinner? I already told everyone.'

'We saw the public performance, yes, but we've also spoken at length to Gary and Ruth, so we know things aren't as rosy as you'd have us believe. We need to know if there's any substance to what you were saying or—'

'Or if it was just your usual crap,' Lynette interrupted. 'Let's not beat around the bush. Were you just telling people what they wanted to hear?'

'I wouldn't do that,' he protested, shocked at Lynette's brusqueness. 'Is something wrong, Lyn? This isn't like you.'

'Nothing's wrong. I've had enough lies, that's all.'

'I don't lie. You should know me better than that.'

'Okay then, I've had enough deception, enough misdirection, and certainly enough bullshit. I know how you operate, Dominic.'

'I've got nothing to gain from deceiving anyone. No, maybe that's not right. Let me put it another way. We've all got as much to lose if we're not honest with each other.'

'So cut the crap, dial down the rhetoric, and just tell us,' Orla said.

Dominic pushed away his plate, got up, and walked to the window. It was dark outside. The light from the lamps on the boardroom table meant that all he could see was his own face reflected, standing before the faces of the others waiting for him to speak. 'Very well. As you have guessed, things didn't go as well as we'd hoped. I'm devastated Vicky didn't come home with us, and that we couldn't finish the job. That aside, the positives are huge. We have Allison and the boat now, for starters. That's opened up so many options.'

'There you go again, Dominic,' Lynette said. 'Calm down. Stop talking to us like you're delivering a speech at the party conference. Just give us the facts. We want to know what happened, not what you hope is going to happen next.'

He turned back to face them again. 'Truth is, ever since you two mentioned it, I'd been pinning my hopes on Surrey Quays providing for us for a decent length of time. That still might prove to be the case, but it's not going to be as easy as I'd hoped. Getting the food was relatively straightforward, getting it back to the boat was where we hit problems. That was where we tripped up – or where we were tripped up, I'm still not sure which.'

'Ruth told us you left the dock in quite a state,' Marianne said. 'Will we even be able to go back?'

'Hard to say. But, truthfully, even if we have to start looking elsewhere, we've the ways and means now of going further afield without taking such a risk. The dead on the other side of the river, they were different... far fewer in number, more spread out. I know they got the better of us in the end, but even so there was

166

'nothing like the crowds we're used to.'

'She said something about another group?'

'Yes, and I need to talk to the council about that. There are people over there; we didn't get the impression there were many of them, and, apparently, they're not confrontational. They did just enough to let us know they were there, but they kept out of our way. Ultimately, we outstayed our welcome and they'd obviously had enough, so they released a flood of corpses down towards the river to shoo us away. Part of me thinks we can still build bridges — if we can get them to talk to us. Once they see what we've got over here they'll—'

'They'll run a bloody mile if they've got any sense at all,' Marianne interrupted. 'See, this is what I'm worried about. You're in danger of losing focus here, Dom, we all are. I'm struggling to see that we've got anything left here worth fighting for. We've got numbers, yes, but it sounds like the people on the other side of the river are doing much better with fewer of them.'

Dominic shook his head. 'And you think I'm the one who's losing focus? Just listen to yourself. There's safety in numbers. The fact there are so many of us here makes us so much stronger. Say there's only a handful of people on the south bank... what happens when one or two of them fall ill or get injured? And when the dead are gone and they're left to fend for themselves, how will they cope when they hit a bump in the road?'

'You mean when three hundred of us knock on their door again, demanding food?'

'That's not going to be an issue. Did you not see how much we brought back with us?'

'I saw,' Lynette said. 'I also spoke to Mihai. He doesn't think it'll be enough.'

'Mihai is very "glass half-empty". And that's not a bad thing. We need a quartermaster who's realistic.'

'You weren't so happy about him being realistic the other day. You came down on him when he told you he didn't think we'd be able to find enough food over here.'

Dominic was dismissive. 'Lots of things get said in the heat of the moment. The fact is, we now know where to find more food. Like I said, it might not be easy, but we can go back for more if we need to. If it's not Surrey Quays, we'll get in the boat and go somewhere else. Honestly, people, the world is starting to open up for us again.'

'Jesus Christ, now I know for sure that you're still a politician,' Marianne said. 'And I hate to piss on your parade, but that boat won't hold all of us. Right now, I'm seriously considering finding myself a little tug and sailing off into the sunset.'

'Now that's just stupid.'

'You really think? We've heard plenty about what you got up to while you were away, but has anyone told you what's been happening here?'

'Yes, Piotr brought me up to speed. He told me about the problems we've had with the dead around the docks. And before you start, yes, he also told me that things hadn't gone as well as he'd hoped.'

'Did he explain why? Did he tell you that he attacked David this morning?'

'He attacked David?'

'Yes, because he dared to have an alternative opinion to his and spoke his mind. The poor bloke is distraught. He's spent most of the day shut away in his room since it happened.'

'I know Piotr can be very direct, but—'

'Being direct isn't the problem,' Orla interrupted, 'the fact he's not listening is the issue. He needs to be brought under control. He seems to think he has a free rein here.'

'I'm not as naïve as you think I am. I know Piotr can be abrasive.'

'Oh, I've never had you down as being naïve.'

'What then?'

'She's saying she doesn't trust you, Dom,' Lynette said. 'And to be honest, right now I don't think I do either.'

He shook his head. 'I don't know where all this negativity is coming from. It's misplaced, it really is, tonight of all nights. Now that we've got a decent store of food, we're in a far, far better position.'

'Some of us, maybe. Did you hear about Holly?' Marianne asked.

He shook his head. 'Is she that young girl? Tall and willowy? Slight accent? What about her?'

'She killed herself, Dominic. Slit her wrists. But that's clearly nowhere near as important as anything the mighty Piotr's been up to, eh?'

Dominic shook his head and looked down. For a moment he seemed genuinely distressed. 'I'm sorry. I didn't realise.'

'And Omar,' Lynette said. 'He's missing.'

'I did hear about that. He's probably just hiding somewhere, little bugger.' Dominic paused to collect his thoughts, then spoke again. 'It's tragic, Vicky and Holly especially... but I don't know what you expect me to say? We've lost a lot of people over the months. Far too many.'

Marianne shook her head. 'We don't necessarily want you to say anything. You usually say too much. What we want is for you to consider other people's points of view, and not just agree with everything Piotr says. He doesn't think things through properly, and he doesn't respect the council. Liz challenged him, but his attitude was that, because you weren't here, he was in charge. It can't be like that.'

'I know what you're saying, but—'

'Everything Piotr's doing is driving the dead wild,' Lynette said, 'and he doesn't seem to care. Honestly, I think it fuels him. If he goes off half-cocked he could put all of us in real danger, and as you say, we've lost too many people already.'

'It's worse than that,' Orla said. 'Piotr's getting cocky, and so are his cheerleaders. The more arrogant they get out there, the bigger the risk of them fucking up. They're not just playing with their lives, they're putting all of us in danger too.'

'I understand that.'

'Do you?'

For once, Dominic didn't respond immediately. The hesitation was uncharacteristic. It made Orla uneasy. He cleared his throat. 'Fact of the matter is, I'm one hundred per cent behind Piotr's actions. He's doing the right thing, for the right reason, and he's doing it with my blessing. I've seen what the rest of the world looks like today, and it's made me feel more hopeful for our future than at any time since this all began back in September. Our plan has always been to get through the winter first and foremost, then strike out. I know I've been guilty of letting my imagination run wild and trying to build some brave new utopian world for us here, and I know now that's not going to happen. More to the point, it doesn't need to. For now, I've asked Piotr to continue the planning work and make sure the area around St Katharine's Dock is secure, because that's all we'll need. We'll get everyone into better accommodations, then sit tight until all of this is over. One more push is all it's going to take.'

29

Wrapped up tight against the cold with a facemask on to keep out the smoke and ash, Vicky sat on the balcony of the flat Sam had claimed for himself on the floor below the others. The apartment itself was underwhelming – small, one bedroom, a little damp – but the view east was spectacular, despite the fading light. One of the Canary Wharf towers had collapsed in the last couple of hours, and now the flames were ripping through its nearest neighbours.

'Here you go,' Sam said, handing her a mug of coffee. He took a selection of chocolate bars from his jacket pockets and dumped them on a small table between the two seats, then sat down. 'So, where do we start? It's only been about a month, but it feels like forever since I last saw you.'

Vicky pulled her mask down so she could talk. She started coughing and swigged her Benylin before touching her drink. 'Start with you. How did you end up here?'

'Truth be told, I never much fancied the idea of locking myself up with all those other people at the Monument, and when those explosions went off... I guess it was just a spur of the moment decision. I still thought it was probably the right thing for everyone else, just not for me.'

'So, there's me thinking you were being all heroic trying to block the bridge, but the reality was you were just looking for a get out?'

'That's a bit harsh,' he said, stung. 'But you're not a million miles from the truth. The bridge clearly needed blocking, I could see that, and the only thing I had to hand was a bloody big London bus. It seemed like a logical solution, and it gave me an excuse not to shut myself away. To be honest, I didn't think it through any further than that. I improvised the rest.'

'You don't say.'

'Those things out there that day, they were ferocious, you know.'

'Believe me, I know.'

'They still getting worse?'

'Hard to say... around the base a lot of them have been worn down to mush, but when others, the ones that have been more sheltered, get through they're...'

He didn't like that she hesitated. 'They're what?'

'It's hard to explain. More controlled.'

'Don't like the sound of that.'

'I know they're all going to rot away to nothing eventually, but I worry how dangerous they'll get before they stop being a threat.'

'Jesus,' Sam said.

'So, carry on; what happened?'

'I lost control of the bus and it ended up on its side. I hit my head and injured my leg, and I couldn't immediately see any way of getting out. So, I thought, fuck it, and I stayed where I was. They were mostly *around* the bus, hardly any of them on top of it, so I took my time and made myself a cosy little nest so I could sit things out. I hadn't intended stealing half your supplies, but I ended up with a heck of a lot of stuff onboard, so I wasn't going to go without. I had just about enough to eat and drink, enough clothing and bedding to keep myself warm... I managed to patch myself up, so I thought I'd see how things went, then try and get out.'

'And how did things go?'

'It was crazy, you know. I left it for as long as I could; managed to sit tight for almost a week before I cracked.' He paused, then asked, 'Did you know glass is a liquid? Kind of, anyway.'

'I didn't. What's that got to do with anything?'

'You talking about the dead having been compacted just reminded me. Glass is actually an amorphous solid. It flows very,

very slowly, like the dead do when they're stuck somewhere in large numbers. I couldn't get that word out of my head all the time I was trapped on the bus. It was the way they were slowly spreading all around it... they didn't seem to be moving at all, but when the sun came up every morning, they'd have all slightly shifted a little further along. Frigging terrifying, it was. Eventually I couldn't stand it any longer. I broke a window and climbed out onto the top of the bus – the side of it, really – and all I could see was more of them in both directions along the bridge. Lucky for me, there's anti-terrorist barriers on the pavements up there, so there was a little free space. I managed to jump across, knackering my leg again in the process. Dropping in on you lot seemed way too dicey, so I went south. I had to balance on the railings at some points, like a bleeding tightrope walker I was. I thought someone might have seen me. Bit of a mad limp across the bridge, then I took my time. I went building by building as far as I could.'

'And you ended up here.'

'Eventually. I found the shops on a map and thought it would be a good place to head for. I was trying to find a way of getting inside when young Eric spotted me hobbling down the road.'

'Yeah, he spotted me, too. It all feels a bit contrived, don't you think? A little too convenient?'

'It's perfectly logical, if you think about it. I'm surprised more people haven't found their way here. I wish we'd known about it sooner. River access, loads of food... this place should be a magnet for survivors.'

'Says something that no one's come.'

'Yeah, it says: depressing. So, tell me, how are things over the water? Everyone safe?'

'No one's safe these days, Sam.'

'I figured that much. Did it turn out to be the promised land you were holding out for?'

'Don't take the piss. I never said that. I just thought we'd stand a better chance if we were all together. Turns out the opposite's true.'

'The place is still standing, though?'

'More or less.'

'And all those explosions?'

'You know yourself, there are some big characters calling the shots over there. They managed to piss off some lone wolf vigilante just before we arrived, and he got his own back. We're told they killed him.'

'You don't sound convinced.'

'I don't believe anything I'm told these days, especially when there's an ex-politician involved.'

'And is everyone alright? Christ, I should have asked sooner. David, Marianne, Sanjay... they all okay? And what about that little shit Omar? Selena?'

'They're all as well as can be expected.'

'That doesn't mean anything.'

'So what do you want me to say? Want me to tell you they're having a grand old time, really living it up?'

'Things that bad, eh?'

'It's getting that way. Lots of testosterone-fuelled posturing going on.'

'Pathetic. Nothing ever changes.'

'My sentiments exactly.'

'So, how come you're here?'

'They had a decent stock of food, but then our lot turned up and inflated the numbers. The plan was to start reclaiming sections of land then strip them of anything of value. Sit tight through the winter, strike out in spring.'

'Sounds sensible.'

'It would have been a good plan if there weren't so many mouths to feed. With hindsight, we were never going to be able to gather enough to feed three hundred-plus people for several months. We only started about a week ago, but it didn't take long to see it wasn't going to work out.'

'Hence the away day over here.'

'Exactly. And, of course, the dead reacted in the same way they always do. The more active we've been, the worse they've got. They're the one constant in all of this, but the goons calling the shots don't seem to understand. That might change now, though.'

'How so?'

'Dominic Grove was over here with us. I think it opened his eyes to how shitty things are getting back there. We've lost quite a few folk in the fighting, and we've all been working our butts off for relatively little gain. Loads of territory taken back, but it's food that people need, not space. Marianne and Lynette suggested coming over here. Typically, though, we overstretched ourselves. We should have taken half as much. We'd have caused far less of a distraction, and we'd have been able to come back for more later.'

'And that's how you ended up stranded?'

'Yep. Got myself cut off from the others. Could have been worse, though. I thought I was screwed when they first left me here.'

'Thank goodness for Eric, eh?' Sam leant a little closer and whispered to Vicky, though there was no need. 'This lot here, you know, they're awful polite. There was a lot of talk about confronting the looters, but in the end, they just went all passive-aggressive and locked the supermarket doors once you'd disappeared.'

'It didn't work.'

'Clearly not. And now you've given the dead the run of the docks, as I understand.'

'Not me personally, but yes.'

'And what about you personally?'

'What about me?'

'What are you planning to do? Going to stay here or try and get back?'

'Don't know. Haven't had chance to think about it yet. I can't see an easy way back, to be honest.'

'What do you want to do?'

'Don't know,' she said again.

Sam nodded and passed her a bar of chocolate. 'Here, have this. Make the most of the break.'

It hardly felt like a break, but she knew what he meant. It was important to take advantage of this unexpected opportunity to rest and take stock.

Midway through demolishing a Twix, Sam pointed towards the belching clouds of smoke on the other side of the river. 'Seen that?'

'It's pretty hard to miss, Sam.'

'Scary, don't you think?'

'It's just a fire.'

'Yeah, but there's no such thing as just a fire anymore, is there? There's no fire service to sort it out. The city is pretty much an endless source of fuel. There's nothing to stop the flames but the rain, and we've had hardly any of that since the second of November.'

'Sounds like you've been keeping records.'

'I have, as it happens. There's not been a lot else to do around here. I was laid up a while with my leg, you see.'

'Better now?'

'Getting there. I was thinking about going out for a run later.'

'Seriously?' she asked in disbelief.

'No,' he replied, laughing. 'What do you bloody think?!'

Vicky helped herself to more food and sank back into her chair. The moment felt bizarrely normal, and yet it was anything but, because everything that had been trivial and mundane in the past was now the exception rather than the norm. The familiar had become unfamiliar. Vicky felt herself beginning to relax, but the space allowed her too much time to think, and her mood became fragile. The guilt took hold, then frustration, then resentment, and then anger. Sam watched her face, studying her changing expression.

'It's okay. You are allowed to let go, you know.'

'What's that supposed to mean?'

'Stop holding it all in. While you're up here you can forget all your troubles, even if it's only temporary.'

'I can't. I feel like I'm abandoning the others, like I'm turning my back on them all.'

'No one's thinking that but you. I'm not saying you won't be missed, but they're not all going to be crying into their dinner tonight. We're all expendable these days. I don't reckon they'll be planning a rescue mission anytime soon, either.'

'I'd forgotten how much of an asshole you can be.'

'I know exactly how annoying I am. Harsh as it might sound, I'm just being realistic.'

'I know that, but you're not helping.'

'People don't matter to people anymore, not like we used to. None of us do. I can't imagine too many tears were spilled when I did what I did. I reckon you were probably cheering.'

'I wouldn't go that far. To be honest, back then we were all just relieved to still be alive. No one had time to think about the ones who didn't make it.'

'My point exactly. And that's how it should be.'

Vicky looked angry. She chewed her lip to stop herself saying something she might regret, then said it anyway. 'The thing I hate most about you, you annoying bastard, is that a lot of the time you're right. It's really frigging annoying.'

'Sorry,' Sam said. 'I think.'

Suddenly, she was crying. That shocked him. All he'd ever had from her was aggression, opposition, attitude. He hadn't expected to find any cracks in her ice-maiden façade.

'I just keep thinking about Selena. I promised Kath I'd look out for her.'

'And you will. In a weird way, this *is* you looking after her.'

'How do you work that out?'

'You're recharging. And when you're ready, you can go back. If you want to, that is.'

'I don't know what I want. Right now, what I'm feeling most of all is sorry for the rest of them stuck over there. I can only see things going one way.'

'Look, I'm sure we can convince Brian and the others to come to some agreement so we can share what we've got here. There's too much for just a handful of folks, and it's like we've been saying all along, just get through this winter and things will be different. Fact of the matter is, once the corpses are gone, they're gone. All we need to do is stay alive until they're no longer the threat they are now, then things will get easier. Let's be honest, they're only a problem right now because there are so bloody many of them.'

'True, but...'

'Alternatively, we could sneak a few people out and get them settled over here with us. The people you give a shit about.'

'I know, Sam, I know. All that sounds perfectly sensible and reasonable, but you're forgetting that we're not dealing with sensible and reasonable people. We're dealing with Piotr and Dominic Grove, mouthy bastards who both think that their way is the only way. If they get a sniff of what you've got going on over here, they'll be plotting a full-scale invasion.'

'And on current form, they'll fuck it up. Anyway, do you not think they'll take one look at the docks and turn back? It's going to take an age for all those bodies to calm themselves down again. Like I said, we just need to get through the winter. Give it six months and—'

'But what if we don't have six months?' she said, cutting across him. The strength of her reaction caught him completely off-guard. Tears were flooding down her face.

'Six months isn't long. It's already been almost three months since it happened and...'

She was shaking her head.

'It's different for me.'

'I don't understand... different how?'

'I've got cancer.'

'Fuck.' Sam looked like he'd been hit by a train. 'I'm sorry, Vic... I didn't know.'

'Nobody knows. You're the first person I've told.'

'When did you find out?'

She shrugged, appearing remarkably nonchalant, given that she was talking about something indisputably huge. 'It was a couple of weeks before everyone died. Remember I told you I was in a hotel the night before it happened?'

'Yeah, I remember you saying.'

'I'd had a hospital appointment first thing. I'd already been given the bad news, but they'd called me back, so I knew it could only be *really* bad news. I knew I was going in for the "How long have I got?" conversation.'

He tried to ask her for more detail but struggled to find the right question. 'What kind of cancer... I mean, do you know how... advanced it is?'

'Lung cancer. Very shitty. The odds weren't good even with treatment. I'll be lucky to be here for much of next year.'

'Shit, Vicky, I don't know what to say.'

'You don't have to say anything. I guess I just wanted you to understand. Things are different for me now.'

'Explains why you're so fucking angsty all the time,' he said, and she laughed, then cried again. 'Why'd you keep it so quiet? That's a hell of a thing you've been carrying.'

'Turn that on its head, Sam, why bother talking about it? What difference is it going to make? We're all at risk of dying every day. I nearly copped it today. The sad reality is, I know I might not have six months left, but there are plenty of relatively healthy people I'll more than likely outlive. People who should have had their whole lives ahead of them. It's all so fucking unfair.'

'You're not wrong there.'

She lit a cigarette and waved it at him. 'This is the one positive. Nothing to worry about anymore.'

'Except where you're going to get your next pack.'

'Fair point.'

'I'm surprised, Vic.'

'That I've got cancer? I wasn't.'

'No, that you told me.'

'I didn't mean to, to be honest. It just came out. It's different over here, I guess. It feels like there's less at stake.'

'Fewer dead bodies?'

She shrugged. 'Fewer people. I don't want to spend the rest of my days with people treating me differently just because I'm sick. I can't stand the thought of being side-lined, watching everyone else doing all the work. I need to keep myself busy for as long as I can; I'll go crazy if I have too much time to think about what's coming.'

30

Gary limped up the hotel staircase to David's room, Marianne close behind. It was almost pitch black inside the building, a little light seeping in from flickering bonfires outside. Muted celebrations continued elsewhere in the compound – full bellies having restored a little optimism – but this foul-smelling ruin of a building was largely a positivity-free zone.

David took an age to come to the door. Even then he didn't open it fully. 'What do you want?'

'To talk to you,' Marianne said.

Still nothing.

'I've brought you some food,' she said after a few seconds had passed. He let them in.

'I'm really not in the mood,' David said.

'None of us are, but we need to talk.'

Resigned, he gestured for them to sit down.

'We spoke to Dominic,' Marianne explained.

'And?'

'And he's backing Piotr one hundred per cent.'

David picked at the food they'd given him. 'Dominic Grove is a fucking moron,' he said.

'He only sees what he wants to see,' Gary said. 'I mean, I know it's important to try and stay positive, but he's borderline delusional at times.'

'I don't think he's delusional. I think he knows exactly what he's doing,' Marianne said.

'So, did you disturb me just to tell me things I already know, or is there a point to this visit?'

Gary ignored his cynicism; it was entirely justified in the circumstances. 'We think we need to talk through our options.'

'Do we even have any?'

'Three, as far as I can see,' Marianne said. 'We can either play ball and see what happens, refuse to play ball and risk the consequences, or we try and get out of here altogether.'

'Is that a realistic possibility?'

'We left Surrey Quays before things got too dangerous,' Gary explained. 'The docks were swarming, but that was down to us shifting stuff from the shopping centre to the boat. I've been thinking... we don't need to use the same pier, do we? We could go further along the river and find somewhere else to moor up. There will be plenty of bodies wherever we go, but from what I've seen it's nothing compared to what we're dealing with here.'

'Would Allison go back?'

'I don't know. I do know she showed Chapman the ropes, so he might if she won't.'

'I don't trust him,' Marianne said. 'He's too close to Piotr.'

'Well, he might be our only option if Allison can't or won't do it. I really feel for her. She did a great job, don't get me wrong, but I think she'll find it harder when she has to go out there again. She'll know what to expect next time, and that'll ramp up her trepidation and nerves.'

'You said you'd go further down the river. What about Vicky?' David asked.

Gary shook his head. 'Hate to say it, but I think she's a lost cause. I don't see how we can risk trying to help her. If it makes you feel any better, and I know it probably won't, she won't be expecting any rescue missions or anything dumb like that. She's smart. I think she'll hole-up at Surrey Quays and wait. There's more chance of her finding us than us finding her.'

Marianne was exhausted. She sighed and rubbed her eyes. 'Okay, so do we stay here as we are and let Piotr keep calling the shots, do we try and strike out on our own, or...'

It was as if she'd lost confidence in her own voice.

'Go on, say it,' Gary urged. 'Tell us what you're thinking.'

'Or do we to try and build up some support then get rid of Piotr and Dominic.'

'Bloody hell, it's all starting to feel a bit mercenary, don't you think,' David grumbled.

'I'm not saying we should, I'm just putting it out there as an option. I don't know what to say for the best. We have the council, but it's clear that Piotr and Dominic will do whatever the hell they want, with or without approval.'

'The idea of getting rid of the top dogs definitely appeals,' Gary said, 'but it wouldn't be easy. They've got a core of lackeys we'd need to get rid of too, and they're always up for a fight. Even if we had a couple hundred people behind us, I still wouldn't fancy our chances.'

'I think you're right,' she agreed. 'I'm sure we'd have enough support in theory, but Piotr has all the muscle. The number of the people who'd be cheering us on would be doing it from the safety of their rooms. And I should know because I'm one of them. The thought of getting involved in any kind of physical confrontation terrifies the crap out of me. I'll be completely honest with you both, I really don't think I could do it.'

'You would if you had to,' David said.

'I'm not so sure. Christ, it's a nightmare situation we've got ourselves backed into here.'

Gary agreed. 'I think we need to give it a little longer, see if it anything changes now that we've got food in the stores. Whatever we decide to do in the end, we're only going to have one shot at it. We need to make sure we've got all our bases covered.'

The morning came too soon, many people having hardly slept. Yesterday had been a maniacal day of contrasts: elation at finally being able to eat properly, tempered by the loss of Vicky and the fact that Omar hadn't yet returned. Although very little alcohol had been recovered in the haul taken from the south bank, there'd been a decent amount held in reserve and, until yesterday, no reason for celebration. Dominic had given agreement for the booze to flow freely last night, and plenty of people were worse for wear as a result. They didn't get to drink that often these days; they'd all become lightweights.

The noise had kept Selena awake for hours. She got up and walked the short distance to Tower Bridge, heading for the lookout point Lynette had shown her. She was surprised to find Lynette already up there, and she might have tried to slip away again unnoticed had Lynette not heard her approach. Selena thought she looked terrible, like she'd been out here all night. Lynette reached out and hugged her.

'Sorry about Vicky, love.'

Selena disengaged herself from the embrace, uncomfortable. 'Doesn't bother me. It's not like she's my mum or anything.'

'I know that, but I know how close you were.'

'I think she was closer than I was.'

Lynette turned back to look out over the river.

'I know you better than you think I do, Selena. Vicky meant more to you than you're letting on. I know how much you've been clinging on to the hope of getting out of London and going to that place you're always talking about. What was it called again?'

'Ledsey Cross.'

'That's right.'

'I'm still going. Kath's friend Annalise is waiting for us.'

Lynette shook her head. 'I'm not so sure there's anyone else left alive out there and it'll be a lot harder without Vicky to help you. She was the one who was really pushing to go.'

'Don't care. I promised Kath. I'll find another way. I'll find other people to go with.'

'Be careful, though, love. I wouldn't want you doing anything that'll get you into trouble with Dominic and Piotr, you know what they're like.'

'Look, those pigs are not the boss of me and I'm not bothered about them. I can't just keep my mouth shut and put up with it. I'm not like you, Lynette, no offence.'

'None taken. When you get to my age and you've put up with as much shit as I have over the years, you start to realise that keeping your mouth shut is the only option sometimes.'

'That's not what Kath used to say. She said the opposite. She said that not speaking out was what took all the effort and caused all the hurt. Think that's why I've got so gobby. Vicky's the same. Vicky *was* the same. If we just put up with other people's shit, then that makes us just the same as them. Practically makes us as bad as the dead.' She waited for Lynette to react, but she didn't. 'So, like I said, I'm still going to Ledsey Cross. Don't know how, don't know when, but I'm going to go. Come with me if you want.'

Lynette's expression finally changed. She broke into a smile. 'Yes, love, of course. Put me down for a place. I'd love to go.'

32

Yesterday's planned offensive had been called off at the last minute when the group returned from Surrey Quays, Dominic and Piotr both agreeing that it made sense to allow people to rest and refuel. Now, with their stomachs filled and the promise of more food to come, there was no shortage of volunteers to take on the dead again today.

Dominic called an impromptu council session to discuss today's initiative. The hastily convened meeting took place not in the boardroom for once, but on the roof of 1, St Katharine's Way, a long strip of a building at right angles to the hotel. From up here, they had a clear view out over the docks, right across the next area Dominic planned to seize back from the undead. As he called the meeting to order he seemed a little subdued, embarrassed, even.

'Listen, everyone, before we start, I spoke to a few of you last night, and I wanted to apologise. What you said caught me off-guard. I got so wrapped up in the excitement of the day and, with hindsight, I think I probably came across as being a little, how can I put this... a little dictatorial, I suppose?'

'That about nails it,' Marianne agreed.

'So, I wanted to bring you up here to better explain what I think we should do now, and to ask for the council's agreement. Piotr, talk everyone through the plan please.'

Piotr pointed out the clear space along East Smithfield to the north, and the area south of the docks that had been more recently reclaimed. 'Thomas More Street connects the spaces we've already taken, and it's where we had the breach the other night. We clear out the bodies there, then we go one more street further east to Vaughan Way and do the same again. Then we stop.'

'What's so special about Vaughan Way?' Liz asked.

Dominic explained, 'Between that and Thomas More Street are those office blocks you can see.'

'All I see everywhere here is office blocks,' she grumbled. 'This city is nothing but bloody office blocks and high-rises. Surely you don't think we need more buildings? Haven't you repossessed enough real estate yet?'

'The point of seizing those particular buildings is precisely that we *don't* need them. They mark where our eastern boundary is going to be. Easy to defend, and hard for anything to get past. Effectively, those buildings are going to be our city wall.'

'Today, we go back out to Thomas More Street and secure our position,' Piotr continued. 'From there, we move across into Vaughan Way which we clear all the way south down to the river. Then we clear the area Dominic just showed you.'

'And after that?' Marianne pressed.

Piotr shrugged his shoulders. 'After that, nothing. Job done.'

Dominic turned to face the rest of them. 'The dynamic has completely shifted now that we know we can keep everyone fed. I'm not saying we've got enough food, but the difference now is we know we can get in the boat and get more when we need it. So, this could be our final push. Taking that plot of land will give us all the space and security we need. One more focused burst of effort, then we're home and dry. Once we've secured this space, we can properly start rebuilding, making life more comfortable for our people, particularly for you poor buggers stuck in the hotel. I'm under no illusions; it's going to be another few tough days, a few *really* tough days, but once we're done, we'll effectively go into hibernation. We'll be able to take stock and build up our strength because Christ alone knows, we're going to need it next year.'

33

Early afternoon. Marianne was back in her hotel room, nerves clanging. She hated it when the others went out to fight. She had a bottle of drink on the bedside table left over from last night, and much as she wanted to take a nerve-calming swig or two, she resisted the temptation. She needed to keep a clear head. With David down the hall holed up in self-imposed solitary confinement in his room, Gary injured, and Vicky lost, she was feeling the pressure more than ever. It was beginning to feel like it was all on her now. It wasn't, she knew, but that was how it felt.

She wished she was more physically able. It was horrible watching the others going off to fight and having to stay behind. Not that she'd have been any use out there. She could talk rings around the lot of them but, physically, her best days were far behind her. Sanjay, Ruth, and numerous others had dutifully headed back out to the frontline. Though taking part in today's offensive had, on the face of it, appeared entirely voluntary, the consequences of constantly being seen bench-warming were becoming increasingly clear.

From her window at the far end of the hotel, Marianne watched them marching out along St Katharine's Way. She could see Sanjay hanging back near the rear of the group. *If I'm feeling nervous,* she thought, *how must he be feeling?*

And then she froze.

Someone was knocking at her hotel room door.

She didn't want to see or talk to anyone. Could she pretend she wasn't here? She tiptoed across the room and peered through the peephole. There was a diminutive and instantly recognisable figure standing outside, looking up and down the corridor anxiously.

Jesus Christ. Omar.

Marianne opened the door and the kid rushed in. 'Where the hell have you been?' she shouted, sounding angrier than she'd intended. Despite the fact he was covered in all kinds of glistening muck, she grabbed hold of him and wrapped her arms around him. Omar typically recoiled from any physical attention, but not today. For a while he was the one who wouldn't let go. Marianne sat him down on the end of her bed, the size of the king-sized mattress emphasising the boy's smallness. She passed him a bottle of water which he quickly drained between breathless sobs.

'You look terrible, Omar. What happened?'

'Frigging Piotr.'

'What about him?'

'Shithead threw me over the wall. We was up on the train tracks and he hung me by my neck and tossed me over.'

'*He did what?!* My god, Omar! What were you doing up there?'

'Having a go at him after what he did to Dave.'

'You little idiot,' Marianne said, seething.

'What are you so mad about? Dickhead Piotr's the one what tried to kill me.'

'I'm sorry, love. But that man is insane. What did you think you were doing approaching him like that?'

'I was trying to stop him being such an asshole.'

The kid's energy was returning almost as Marianne watched.

'He is an asshole,' she agreed, 'but being an asshole is irrelevant when you're as vicious and nasty as Piotr. Now you say he *threw you over?*'

'Yep. I'd have hit the road if it hadn't been for all the bodies.'

Marianne screwed up her face. 'I know this building stinks, Omar, but you smell even worse. You could do with a dunk, get yourself cleaned up.' She stopped, the surprise of his sudden return finally beginning to fade, allowing her to think straight. 'Wait, how did you get back?'

Omar wasn't listening; too busy talking.

'None of you even bothered looking for me.'

'It was a while before we'd realised you'd gone. You're always disappearing into some hidey hole or other.'

He carried on, still not listening. 'I got into a building, and I climbed up so you could see me. I was banging on the windows, trying to get you lot to hear me, but you never did.'

'You still haven't answered my question. How exactly did you get back inside?'

'It ain't as bad as you think out there. Them things are falling apart, and they're all packed in tight up close to the walls. I was crawling all round their legs, and they didn't even know I was there.'

'But how did you get back over?'

'There's this pub-restaurant-thing, goes right under the train tracks, one side to the other. There was this beer garden he showed me on the other side what's been blocked off. It's got a wall around it and the dead can't get in. It's been there all along, right under that thick fucker Piotr's nose and he never even noticed. That's how we did it.'

'Wait, how *we* did it? Who helped you? Who brought you back, Omar?'

'I didn't know who he was at first, but I weren't that bothered coz I was just happy someone finally come. He said he saw me up at the window. I was banging and banging for hours and you lot never even frigging looked up or—'

Marianne cut across him. 'Omar, who brought you back?'

'Taylor.'

'What?'

'He's alright, once you get talking to him. He told me loads of stuff. He knows everything what's going on here. Piotr keeps telling people he's dead, but he ain't. It was him what blew up the wall of the train station so yous lot could get in, remember? I said to him he's the kind of bloke we need on our side, but he said he don't take sides. He says he tries to keep out of it. He says that was all he was ever tryin' to do.'

'What did he look like?'

'Keeps hisself all covered up. I never really seen his face.'

'And you're sure it was him?'

'Dunno. Suppose.'

'You think he'd talk to us?'

Omar began nodding furiously. 'Yeah... that's what he wants. He says there's stuff we need to know. He says to meet him down at The Highway an' he'll talk. He's there now, waiting. He says you or Dave would be best. Where is Dave? Is he out there fighting?'

'He's in his room. Wait, how does Taylor know his name?'

'He knows all our names. I told you, he knows everything what's going on here. Honest, he come into the building to get me and he's like, "Alright, Omar? How's it going?"'

'I'm amazed no one's seen him breaking in if he's here that often.'

Omar was shaking his head. 'You don't get it, do you? It ain't like that. He don't use the pub to get in, that's how he gets *out*. He's in here with us. He says he's walking round with us all the time. He's like some kind of superhero out there, but in here he don't wear a mask. He says he walks around here like bleeding Bruce Wayne or Peter Parker.'

'Clever bastard,' Marianne said, appreciating the analogy. 'Think you could identify him?'

'Don't know. Maybe when he talks. Got an oldish voice, you know what I mean? Weird accent.'

'He's smart, I'll give him that much. He could be anybody. Nobody.'

'Exactly. He says it's all about blending in, not standing out. He kept saying that.'

'What else did he tell you?'

'He said to tell you trouble's coming. That's what he needs to talk about. He says if Piotr keeps pushing the dead away like he's planning, they're gonna push back.'

34

Piotr split his troops three-quarters, one-quarter. The smaller group was dispatched along The Highway to guard the blockade at the north end of Thomas More Street and deal with any stragglers that managed to get through. They anticipated a relatively easy ride, because the dead could be reassuringly predictable at times. When the larger group launched their main offensive to the south, the whole damn lot of them would be clamouring to get closer to the chaos. Dumb fuckers would be fighting with each other to be next to be cut down, sliced up, and chucked on the fire.

The larger group of fighters marched out along St Katharine's Way towards the junction with Thomas More Street and Stockholm Way to the south. It was there that temporary barriers had been installed after the most recent skirmishes, and it was from there that the drive to clear the remaining three hundred metres of flesh and bone would begin. Piotr didn't think it was going to take long. It was worth putting in these few hours of effort today so that they could focus on Vaughan Way tomorrow.

They were running short of vehicles that still worked. The otherwise useless wrecks of old knackers had been used to block the road here. A confusion of two, broken down family saloon cars and a mini-SUV prevented the dead from getting past, though they tried incessantly to break free. The walls, fences, and railings that lined the sides of Thomas More Street had channelled the flow of flesh to this specific point. Decayed arms constantly stretched through the narrowest gaps between the vehicles, grabbing at the air as if each of the corpses was saying *pick me, pick me, pick me...* desperate for attention.

The advancing crowd of fighters parted when they heard the

laboured groan of the trusted backhoe loader approaching. One end of a chain was attached to the loader, the other coupled to one of the blocking vehicles. Kevin reversed back, dragging the carcass of an ancient grey Audi out of the way and opening the floodgates.

'Move up,' Chapman bellowed over the engine roar, but his orders were superfluous as the army of fighters had already obliged. As crowds of corpses slid, slipped, and slithered towards them, folks who had been re-energised by a decent meal and the unexpected optimism of the last twenty-four hours, raced into battle and began to batter the dead with glee, appearing to genuinely relish the one-sided conflict. No one dared say it out loud, but they could feel it in the air today: the tide was turning.

Fighting hadn't come naturally to most of these people. Hardly any of them, truth be told. In the months since the world they'd known had crumbled, though, necessity had forced perspectives and attitudes to change. Now they fought because they had to, knowing it was down to them and them alone to keep themselves safe. The collapse of society had stripped away every safeguard, all other protective layers, and had crushed any illusion that others had their backs. Out here today they knew they were the last line of defence. In the days since the offensive against the dead had begun, these folks had become confident and assured while the inexorable decline of their enemy had continued. Not only had the warriors become stronger and more capable, but their enemies were less human-looking than ever, one less hurdle for the killers to overcome. The dead were no less aggressive, but they were becoming physically weaker by the day.

There was a woman fighting alongside Richard, armed with a scythe. Where she'd found a scythe in the middle of London was a mystery, but right now that didn't matter. It was adept, perfectly suited for its current use. There was little doubt that the impulses and triggers that kept the creatures moving still had to follow established routes from the sense receptors to the brain then around the body, so she hacked at the neck of each corpse, the vicious curved blade inflicting maximum damage with minimal effort. Total decapitation, though satisfying, wasn't necessary; all she had to do was slice deep enough to sever the nerves connecting body and brain. There was a slick beauty in the way she cut them down, as if she was harvesting the last of a spoiled crop.

Richard, though equally efficient, demonstrated no such finesse. His weapon of choice today was a lump hammer. Though blunt and heavy, he persevered because it was damned effective. A single good crack to the skull was typically all that was required. Brute force shattered fragile bone like eggshell. His targets were closely packed, his next victim always in easy reach. It was as if they were lining up to be put out of their misery.

Sanjay hadn't caught the infectious optimism and renewed drive some of the other fighters demonstrated, but he knew this had to be done. Unlike their other recent land-grabs, this time it felt like they had a finite number of corpses to deal with, and each one they re-killed put a little extra safe space between the living and the dead. He hadn't wanted any part of the fighting today, but even he had to admit it was satisfying to see so many of the vile aberrations lying in pieces around him.

And then, an unexpected break.

It seemed impossible to believe that positive things could still happen after they'd had their backs against the wall for so long, and the fact they hadn't noticed this place before made it harder to accept such a sudden change in fortune, but there it was: an overlooked gem buried deep within the grime-covered wasteland. Maybe they'd missed it because the neon signs were no longer lit? Maybe it was because they'd been focused on so much else, up to their necks in gore, that they just hadn't been looking? Maybe it was because all the obvious pedestrian approaches had been blocked by sheer chance, abandoned vehicles and other obstructions funnelling the dead away? Whatever the reason, all that mattered was that they'd found it now: a perfectly preserved supermarket. Though nowhere near the size of the Tesco superstore over on Surrey Quays, this branch of Waitrose felt like an oasis.

They'd been scrapping around the back of the building for almost the whole time they'd been clearing St Katharine's Way and hadn't even known it was there. It butted up against the rear of the apartments that lined one side of Stockholm Way, forming the bottommost tip of the area Piotr had his sights set on reclaiming. Chapman ordered the group pushing north to hold the line, then sent word to Piotr and Dominic.

Mark Desai sprinted through St Katharine's Dock at breakneck speed to speak to the chiefs. Dominic, Piotr, and Mihai were in the boardroom. As soon as he heard the news, Dominic decided there was no point calling the council together; this wasn't the time for endless, wearisome, looping conversations; this was a decision he needed to make fast.

Mark stood at the window and looked out over the heart of the compound. It felt so calm here this afternoon, almost peaceful. It was a million miles removed from the bloody chaos he'd just left on the frontline. He swigged a bottle of water while he waited for them to decide on their approach, enjoying his moment. Every second he spent in here was one not spent out there, among the dead.

Piotr called him over too soon.

'Go back and tell Chapman to forget about clearing the road for now. Hold the line and focus on the supermarket. Take every scrap.'

35

David skulked along Cable Street, north of East Smithfield and The Highway. It had taken all of Marianne's powers of persuasion to get him to leave his room, and even now he was in half a mind whether to keep going or turn around and go back to the hotel. Was it merely curiosity, or was it some bizarre masochistic desire to keep hearing bad news that was keeping him moving forward tonight? Had Omar really been saved by Taylor, or was it just some smartass fucking with them? Finding reliable, verifiable answers to anything was all but impossible these days.

The sun was starting to set. After almost losing his life when he'd been caught in the breach at the end of Thomas More Street around this time of day, he didn't want to be out here long. He was looking anxiously around every corner for advancing bodies, double-checking every shadow, always anticipating an attack.

'Taylor says he'll be waiting up near McDonalds opposite Cannon Street Road,' Omar had told Marianne, and those instructions had given David a small crumb of comfort. As far as he was aware, the kid hadn't known any of the details of the trouble they'd had there when they'd cleared The Highway. But that pathetically small reassurance disappeared fast and was replaced with even more unease. Had Taylor been there that day? And since when had relying on anything Omar said been a good idea?

He followed the train track along the border until he reached the junction with Ensign Street, far enough east to have bypassed the activity around Thomas More Street. As he walked south towards The Highway, it struck him just how everyone had bought into Dominic's bullshit without question. On the politician's advice, they'd willingly confined themselves to a grubby patch of land around the Tower of London, from Tower Place across to St Katharine's Docks. Had it really been necessary to be so restrictive? The road he was walking along now had decent-looking flats on one side, and a primary school on the other. Why had they spent days and weeks struggling in the hotel, uncomfortable and unhygienic, when there had been better places out here that they could have moved into instead? Sure, there was an argument for keeping maximum distance from the dead, but considering they'd been swarming all around the back of the hotel even then—

'David?'

The whispered voice came from nowhere, startling him. David looked around but couldn't see anyone, couldn't even tell which direction it had come from.

'Hello?'

Taylor – the person who claimed to be Taylor, anyway – stepped out of the shadows. He'd been waiting behind an open school gate. In the low light, David couldn't make out much detail. He presumed that was intentional.

'Thanks for coming. This way.'

'Wait, do you seriously expect me to accept you're Taylor and just follow you like this? You could be taking me anywhere.'

'It's up to you, pal,' Taylor said, walking away.

Did he resist? Refuse? Attempt to stamp some authority on the situation? There didn't seem to be any point objecting. What else could David do but comply?

He followed the man down towards The Highway, studying him, looking for clues. Taylor was shorter than he'd expected (why he'd assumed any of Taylor's physical traits was beyond him), and the few words he'd said had been spoken with a trace of a Liverpudlian accent. David had hoped there'd be something more distinctive about him – a limp, a stutter... anything – but there was nothing. He was just like the rest of them, just another survivor. Except a little smarter than most, perhaps, and more dangerous, too.

The familiarity of this section of The Highway increased David's unease. He remembered when he'd last been here, fighting alongside poor Holly and Marie and the others. He felt no safer this evening, just a different kind of fear.

They walked back in the direction of the base but stopped just before they reached a boxed junction. The road to the south had been blocked on the first morning of the fighting, and people had been out here strengthening the barriers in the days since. This, David realised, was the other end of Vaughan Way, the outermost edge of the territory Piotr was dead set on reclaiming tomorrow. There was a hoarding outside a ubiquitous-looking block. 'Look at this,' Taylor said, and he read from the sign. 'Discover city living in one of the capital's most exciting new neighbourhoods... what do you reckon?'

'I've had enough of city living,' David said, and he thought he detected a laugh, but it was hidden behind Taylor's face mask. He tapped on the nearest window, and David saw that the ground floor of the building was busy with corpses. 'I'm not going in there,' he said quickly.

'Neither am I,' Taylor agreed. 'That would be monumentally stupid. We're going upstairs.'

There was a row of trees in front of the building. Taylor climbed the second one along and, perched between two branches, stretched across, then climbed through an open first-floor window. He made it look easy. David followed, struggling to get over.

Taylor was waiting for him just inside. 'We can talk properly now,' he said, though he still didn't remove his mask. 'I'm Tony.'

'Good to meet you at last,' David said.

Taylor's face remained hidden; the tone of his muffled voice frustratingly hard to read. 'If there's one thing you know about me, it's that I try not to mix. I wouldn't be doing this if I didn't have to.'

'I assumed as much. So why me? Why not go straight to the big boys?'

'Because you'll listen, they'll just react. Anyway, Dom and Piotr can't talk to me without looking stupid. They've been telling people for weeks that I'm dead. Imagine how pissed off they'd be if they knew we were having this conversation.'

'And how do I know you really are Taylor?'

'You don't. There's always the possibility that I'm just some chancer trying it on.'

'True. I'm taking you on trust, so give me something.'

'Like what?'

'Reassure me you're on the level. Tell me why you blew the barricades around here and put everybody at risk? Did you know we were on our way here when you did it?'

'No, I didn't. And I'm genuinely sorry about that. I know now that I made things much, much harder for you as a result, and that was never my intention. But you're right, I guess, an explanation would be in order.'

'Revenge. That's the rumour I heard.'

'Yes, that's what I've heard, but it's not true. When this all started, I built myself a shelter up near Spitalfields. I took in a girl who was badly injured and had lost her way. She was lame, and she'd gone a little bit crazy, and with the best will in the world, I was never going to be able to nurse her back to health. Poor kid was a danger to herself, and I didn't think she had long left, so I kept her isolated, kept her supplied with food and water, tried to make her as safe and comfortable as I could. It was about then that our friends Piotr and Dominic started causing me problems.

'I worked out early on that the best way of staying alive was to stay on my own, but I kept getting dragged into their dramas. They sent a kid up here on a bike to draw the dead away, and she got herself into trouble on the defences I'd put up around the building to protect Helen. When the girl died, I made a mistake. I should have just left her, but I was sure they'd come mooching around, so I tried to warn them off. I took the body back to them and left a message telling them to stay away. You'd have thought they might listen, but not Piotr. Oh no, that frigging Neanderthal couldn't lose face. He ended up sending more people up here and things sort of spiralled out of control. Helen panicked and started throwing petrol bombs, I ended up getting a bit trigger happy and—'

Taylor stopped.

'What's wrong?' David asked.

'Am I talking too much? It does me good to explain. It's been a weight on my mind. I chewed young Omar's ear off earlier.'

'It's fine. I still want to know why you thought it was a good idea to blow the place up.'

'It *was* a good idea,' Taylor insisted. 'In the circumstances, anyway. Like I said, I made a mistake. I realised two shots too late that a shooting match with Piotr was only ever going to end one way. He's like a dog with a bone, never knows when to stop. I also saw the danger of him trying to manhandle hundreds of thousands of corpses. He didn't fully understand what he was doing, still doesn't get it, actually. I had to accept that the safest option for everyone – me included – was to fully lockdown somewhere and wait for the dead to neutralise themselves. And then those bloody idiots started trying to spread their wings again. They killed Helen, and I tried to warn them to stop... but by then it was too late. I put holes in their outer barriers, because I thought that getting the dead up close again would keep the group locked down by the Tower, and that had to be safer for everyone.'

'So, you're telling me you blew the barriers and the bridge up to clip Piotr's wings, and you thought locking yourself away with all of us was your safest option too?'

'That's about it. And I'm sorry for the shitty timing, by the way. I truly didn't mean for you all to get caught in the crossfire.'

David didn't know what to think. 'I have to admit, this wasn't the conversation I expected to have today. They all reckoned you were a vigilante, killing for sport.'

'Sorry to disappoint.'

'All we've ever heard was stories about snipers and grenades...

you definitely don't match the public image they've built up for you.'

'I know. I've heard it all too, remember. It's been hard keeping a straight face at times. I worked in demolition, and shooting used to be a hobby of mine, that's all. It's funny how people still like putting two and two together, coming up with completely the wrong answer and defending it with all they've got.'

David checked himself. He'd become distracted. He was on his own with a man of increasingly dubious character, on the first floor of a building he knew nothing about, on the very edge of dead territory. 'Remind me what I'm doing here again?'

'Of course. Yes. Sorry. Follow me.'

Taylor led David deeper into the building. It was a nondescript, open plan office, everything covered with a snow-like layer of dust. Nothing had been disturbed, but David noticed many sets of identical footprints. Taylor had clearly been here on several occasions before today.

They were on the other side of the building now. The sun was sinking across the Thames, filling the office space with a final few minutes of bright orange daylight. Taylor positioned himself between David and the windows, the shadows obscuring his face. 'I need you to talk to Piotr and Dominic, and I need you to make them understand. For obvious reasons I can't do it, and from what I've seen, I think you're one of the few people they might actually listen to.'

'I think you might be disappointed there...'

'Well, whatever. You've got more chance than I have. Fact is, they need to know about this.'

'About what, exactly?'

Taylor stood to one side to let David get closer to the window. He looked down and felt his legs weaken. He'd seen vast crowds of corpses before, huge numbers of them at a time, but never anything like this. The size of the crowd below was impossible to quantify. They were everywhere down there, tripping along every road and alleyway, spilling into every empty space... Christ, there were even some up on the roofs of buildings (*how the hell did they get there?*), and others traipsing over parks, wasteland, construction sites... they were everywhere.

But it wasn't so much the number that terrified David, it was the intent. Whenever he'd seen large crowds before, there'd always been pockets of distraction and hesitation, where something unseen had captured the attention of anything from a handful to a few thousand corpses. Here, though, it seemed that every single one of the damn things was unquestionably moving west towards the Tower of London. Taylor took David up another few floors. The higher in the building they climbed, the more of the dead were revealed. The enormous gathering outside was without a visible end. Shadowy movement was visible for as far as he could see into the distance.

David was struggling to find words to express the enormity of what he was seeing. 'Fuck me,' was all he could manage.

'Yeah, that was pretty much my initial reaction,' Taylor said. 'Trouble is, David, no matter how bad you think things are out there, in reality, they're infinitely worse.'

He still couldn't avert his eyes, couldn't bring himself to look away. 'How so?'

'It's a question of geography and physics, you see. The dead can't go any further south because of the river, and because East Smithfield and The Highway have been cleared and blocked now, they can't go any further north, either. So, what's happened is this huge, massive number of them have been forced into a relatively narrow slice of London. At the same time, because of the trouble he's been having around the docks, Piotr's focus has been on a relatively small area. So that slice of London I was talking about has effectively been tapered to a point, and that's increased the pressure even more.'

It made sense when Taylor explained it. Jesus, looking down, David could see it for himself.

'It gets worse,' Taylor said.

'Go on.'

'Aside from the obvious problems you'd expect when you're trying to fit a couple million bodies into a space that'd struggle to hold a fraction of that, I'm also worried about the noise. Listen.'

He slid a window open. Even from this distance and this height, the frantic activity along Thomas More Street was clearly audible.

'My thinking,' Taylor continued, 'is, that noise can likely be heard for quite a distance.'

'Jesus Christ.'

'I know. Sobering when you see the scale of it, don't you think?'

'But surely they can't all be coming because of that?'

'You're right. I couldn't hear from that far away, and I've still got a pulse. And that's the thing, the noise is just the trigger, David. It's the chain reactions you really need to worry about. You must have seen it? The dead do whatever the ones around them are doing. So, because there's not a lot else happening in London right now, the reactions to what's going on here are disproportionate. The effects of what Piotr's doing will eventually ripple out for miles and miles; there could be no end to it. It might take time, but the dead have got nothing better to do. See, Dominic and Piotr are thinking they can make a bit of noise, then go quiet for a bit, and everything returns to the status quo, but they're wrong. That might have been true once, but we're long past that stage now, and the implications are massive. I didn't fully realise the extent until this last week. With nothing else to distract them, now so many of them have been triggered, I think the dead will just keep on coming.'

'My god...'

'So that's why I needed to talk to you, and that's why you've got to make them understand what's happening. Because if you don't stop them, David, we're all fucked. We need a complete and absolute lockdown. As close to total silence as we can get for as long as possible.'

David was numb, struggling to comprehend the extent of the threat the endless herd below now posed. He knew without doubt that Taylor was right because he could see it: the way the corpses were constantly moving forward, the way that every individual cadaver, no matter how diseased or decayed, reacted to the reactions of those around them, and the way the furthest forward continued to gravitate towards the fighting around Thomas More Street, oblivious to the futility of their actions. Ripples and waves of movement were visible throughout the decaying masses, all of them inexhaustibly trudging towards the Tower of London.

'I'll go and talk to them,' he said. 'I'll make them understand. I'll bring them up here and show them myself if I have to.'

He turned around, but Taylor had already gone.

36

The pre-disaster clock had been all but forgotten by most people, daily routines consigned to the rubbish dump of history. Seasonal variations, however, were harder to ignore. Daylight hours in London in November evaporated fast, the darkness gnawing away at both ends of the day. The light was fading rapidly now and would be gone completely within the hour. Dealing with the dead in daylight was dangerous enough; usually the first stretching shadows of twilight was the signal to pack up for the night and get back under cover until morning, but today was an exception. Relocating the contents of a perfectly preserved supermarket was too important a job to leave until tomorrow.

They'd fortified their access points then cleared more space around the entrance to the building, using heavy machinery to grind a way through the seething corpses packed tight along much of Thomas More Street. Two trucks had been driven slowly forward in unison, crawling parallel along the flesh-filled channel. Brave (or stupid, it was hard to tell) volunteers had been strapped to them and were leaning into the crowds, plucking out troublesome thrashing corpses by their shoulders and hurling them to the dogs. And the ferocity of some of the fighters really was dog-like. With food at stake, they'd displayed a newfound desire to rip to pieces whatever undead scraps were thrown their way. One of the harnessed pair snatched a body from the crowd that was so decayed it was almost hollow and threw it back into the pack like a dried-out branch. It landed at the feet of a woman who plucked its remaining limbs from its torso with unnecessary glee.

Maybe it was the relief of knowing that the tide had finally turned in their favour, and that when today's work was done, they'd eat well? Or perhaps it was thought of all the things they'd take from the shelves of this supermarket that the others had chosen to leave behind at Surrey Quays... the booze, the junk food, the tooth-rotting, additive-packed, addictive rubbish? Maybe it was just the fact that they were on top for once? It felt cathartic to finally make things as unbearable for the dead as the dead had made the last few months for the living.

Whatever the incentive, it was working.

Now that the trucks had retaken enough ground and Thomas More Street had been blocked again, the supermarket was freely accessible, and people had poured inside. Some of the fighters who'd secured the street were sent in first to clear the few lethargic undead that had been trapped inside the store, wandering up and down the aisles for months. The violence outside had provided them with a long overdue distraction, and they'd conveniently grouped around the checkouts, almost as if they were waiting for the break-in. They offered little resistance and were quickly dealt with.

Scores more volunteers arrived from the base to support the clear-out operation. Chapman was ordered to keep the street blockade secure while Paul Duggan was to coordinate the supermarket clearance. Even Paul had been overcome by the sudden proliferation of treats all around. He'd forgotten his position and helped himself, rediscovering so many tastes and flavours he thought he'd forgotten. He knew they could afford to relax; unlike the carefully orchestrated clearance operation over on the south bank, all they needed to do here was haul the stuff a few hundred metres along empty streets back to base. The only instruction Paul had been given was to leave nothing behind.

Since leaving Taylor, David Shires had been looking for Piotr and Dominic, but they'd both disappeared. Part of him was glad he hadn't yet found them. They were belligerent, Piotr in particular, and he didn't think for a second that they'd listen to anything he said. Hell, if he dragged the pair of them to the high vantage point and showed them what Taylor had showed him, the fuckers would still deny there was a problem.

There wasn't time to mess around. He found Marianne and Lynette and told them what he'd learnt, then left them to spread the word and start doing whatever they could to get the population of the base ready and safe. Heading to the front had to be his priority; this was the place where disaster would either be triggered or averted. Christ. As he ran along St Katharine's Way, the noise ahead seemed unbearably loud. He knew it was likely a trick of the all-consuming quiet of everywhere else, but Taylor was right – that was the very reason it needed to be silenced. The constant soundtrack of shouts and crashes, the audible excitement, made his skin prickle with nerves.

David was confused. Rather than the semi-coordinated, violent street clearance he expected to find, he instead met a steady stream of folks going the other way, arms loaded with food and other supplies. When he reached Thomas More Street, he saw Chapman in the crowd and ran over to him. 'What the hell's going on?' he demanded, having to shout to make himself heard over the din.

Chapman pointed the tip of his machete into the encroaching gloom. The headlights of several vehicles were being used for illumination, but the lit-up snatches of movement were distorted and hard to make out. 'Buried treasure,' he said.

David didn't understand. 'What?'

'There's a branch of Waitrose. Can't believe we didn't know about it. Piotr says we're to clear it before we get back to shifting the dead, so get your head out of your ass and go do something useful to help.'

'Where is Piotr?'

'Back at base somewhere.'

'What about Dominic?'

'You think he's going to be out here? Don't be soft. He's still traumatised from going to Surrey Quays.'

'I need to talk to them.'

'What's the problem? I'm in charge here. Talk to me.'

David shook his head. 'You don't understand. All this has got to stop right now. It's not safe.'

'You only just worked that out? Being alive isn't safe these days. Now stop talking and go fight. Do something useful, for fuck's sake.'

David felt isolated and prone. He didn't have his armour on, wasn't carrying his weapon... he was the lone voice of reason, unheard amid everyone else's madness. And the increasing racket coming from inside the supermarket was compounding his anxiety, his helplessness. He looked around, desperate, trying to find anything or anyone familiar in the shadows to cling to and orientate himself, because right now it felt as if the whole world was spiralling out of control around him. Was he really the only one who could see it? The supermarket was a hive of activity, whilst defending the barricades had been left to a handful. It was as if they'd forgotten that it was caution and quiet that had kept them from being overrun by the dead, as if everything they'd endured had been forgotten in a heartbeat. So much was on the verge of being thrown away for the sake of a few more mouthfuls of food... was this stupidity or desperation?

Chapman was dragged away, leaving David standing alone in the middle of the mayhem. Richard pulled him over to one side. 'Dave? What's up with you, man?'

'Everything's wrong...' he started to say, struggling to find the words to convey the enormity of what he knew. 'This needs to stop, Rich. We need to get everyone back to the Tower...'

But Richard wasn't listening either. He handed David a spare blade he'd been carrying. 'We need your help, mate. They're really acting up. Look at this.'

He dragged David over to the trucks blocking the street just ahead of the supermarket entrance, pausing to put a boot through the skull of a glistening creature that had dragged itself out from under one of the vehicles, slug-like. David saw that while the foetid tide was being held back for now, the dead here were furiously animated. He'd never seen them riled like this before, not even at the height of the recent battles in Wapping and along the docks. They were thrashing around with a renewed energy, a desperate desire to break free and attack. They'd formed a solid wall of flesh, loose limbs whipping around like a monster's tentacles, decayed heads scanning tirelessly from side to side as the creatures fought for release. David watched one of them, a particularly aggressive and grotesque-looking creature, writhe so violently that it wrenched its torso from its pelvis and broke free. Without a flicker of concern, not a moment of hesitation, it dropped heavily into the gap between the two trucks and began pulling itself forward, bony fingers clawing at the tarmac. David ended its misery with the knife Richard had given him, and the kill helped him to focus. He pinned Richard against the nearest wall. 'You need to listen to me. There are more of them than we think... tens of thousands... hundreds of thousands...'

'What are you on about?'

'We don't have time. We need to get everyone out of here now.'

Richard either didn't hear him or didn't care. He pushed David out of the way and bludgeoned another slick strip of a cadaver that had squirmed free. David looked around and when he saw Paul Duggan standing near the entrance to Waitrose, swigging from a bottle of wine, he ran across the street to intercept him.

The noise around the supermarket was too much. They were an overconfident crowd, buoyed by a rediscovered sense of purpose and a desire to fill their bellies. It sounded more like a party than a massacre. There were whoops of excitement and delight, cheers and laughter, glass being smashed... Stupid, arrogant fuckers. They couldn't see that the dead were feeding off their energy. They were driving the hordes absolutely fucking wild.

'You need to calm them down,' David said.

'Who?'

'That lot in there, they're out of control. Tell them to shut up. You can feed your face and get pissed when we're back under cover.'

Paul looked to the heavens. 'For fuck's sake, Shires, you're always frigging moaning. Just quit.'

David gestured towards the trucks blocking the road, the voracity of the corpses' reactions now visible even from this distance. They strained for release, hundreds more pushing and shoving from behind. 'Look at them!'

'What's the problem? They're not going anywhere. It's all under control. You do your job and I'll do mine. Remind me what your job is exactly?'

'But, Paul, can't you see what's happening here? You need to tell this lot to—'

'Don't tell me what I need to do.'

'How many people are in that supermarket? There's hardly anyone left out here...'

'Then stop whinging and start helping. Fuck's sake...'

'Don't be such an idiot. You're risking everything.'

Paul snapped. He came at David, forcing him back against a hedge at the side of the road. There were bodies on the other side, more than he expected, and closer too. David could feel their bony fingers clawing at the vegetation, trying to find a way through to him. Oblivious to the danger, Paul leant in closer, breath stinking of booze. 'You're a frigging troublemaker, Shires. I'm tempted to get rid of you myself. No one's going to notice one more corpse in all this lot. Do me a favour and just do what you're told.' He took another swig from his bottle then staggered back towards Waitrose.

'Fucking moron,' David said under his breath, and he went after him again. Ruth had been watching between kills. Sensing trouble, she pushed through the scrum and headed him off.

'Have you got a death wish, Dave?'

He shook his head. 'Things are worse than we thought, Ruth. We need to make them understand...'

'You're not making any sense,' she said, and she was about to speak again when she was distracted by another surge from the dead hordes being held back by the trucks.

'You have to listen to me,' David said, marginally more composed. 'I was talking to Taylor and—'

At the mention of that name, she turned on him.

'Taylor? What the fuck? The same Taylor who shot two blokes in the back, right in front of me? The same Taylor that blew holes in our defences and almost got us all killed?'

'We can argue about what he did and why he did it later. Right now, you just need to listen.'

She could barely contain her fury. 'No, you listen to me. If you believe a word that comes out of that evil bastard's mouth, if it even was him, then that makes you no better than any of these rotting fuckers out here.'

'Please, Ruth, there are thousands more bodies than we realised and they're all converging on this point. Piotr thinks we're going to be able to hold them back, but there are too many.'

'So what? Bring it on, I say. Those fucking things have taken everything I had, everything that mattered, even Vicky. I'll happily stay out here all night and cut down every fucking last one of them. The more I can kill, the better. And if you're not going to help, then fuck off and get out of my way.'

37

Dominic was standing on the roof of 1, St Katharine's Way, looking out across the docks. After many weeks of enforced silence, the amount of noise he could hear tonight was unsettling, but he also knew that it was necessary. One final push.

'All under control,' Piotr said, startling him. Dominic spun around, clutching his chest.

'Jesus Christ, Piotr, you should know better than to creep on me like that.'

Piotr ignored him. 'Paul's getting a lot of decent stuff away from the supermarket. I've got Chapman down there too, keeping an eye on things.'

'Good. And Mihai knows what to do with everything?'

'Yep, I told him. Again, all under control.'

'Excellent. How's Harjinder doing?'

'He has the other end of Thomas More Street covered, but all the activity is around the supermarket.'

'I'll be happier when this is all done.'

'I know. Won't be long.'

'I'm worried how much we're antagonising the dead.'

Piotr shook his head. 'They're dead, Dom. You can't antagonise them. Anyway, what does it matter? We've got rid of thousands of them already this last couple of weeks. All we need is just—'

'I need to talk to you, Dominic.'

Lynette's voice silenced Piotr and took both him and Dominic by surprise. 'What are you doing up here?' Dominic asked.

'There's something you need to know. It's important.'

He walked over to her. 'What?'

She hesitated. Looked at Piotr. 'Can you give us a minute?'

'There's nothing you can't say to me that I wouldn't be

comfortable with Piotr hearing. Now, what is it? What's wrong?'

She'd been trying to think of the best way of breaking the news to him, but every option felt as bad as all the others, so she just said it. 'Taylor's back.'

Piotr laughed. Dominic didn't.

'Taylor's dead,' Piotr said.

Lynette shook her head and looked to the heavens. 'Oh, come on... stop treating us all like idiots. Everyone knows you've been lying about him from the start. He's not dead. You don't even know who he is. You told us he killed Ash, then you picked a fight with him; he blew holes in the walls that were keeping us safe, and you still expect us to believe *you* got the better of *him*?'

'And you didn't think to raise these concerns before?' Dominic said, unimpressed.

'There was no point. We let you carry on with your little charade just to keep the peace, but you can't even do that, can you? All we needed to do was shut up and stay quiet, and we'd have been okay. But you two seem to have a need to keep showing everyone how big and brave and brilliant you both are. None of that matters anymore. Just drop the act and be honest, for once.'

'She's finally cracked,' Piotr said, talking about Lynette as if she wasn't there. 'I told you she was losing the plot. Fucking crazy woman.'

Lynette stood her ground. 'In the circumstances, we could all be forgiven for going a little mad. Fact is, Piotr, I'm completely sane, though some days I wish I wasn't. It would make all of this a lot easier to deal with.'

Dominic wasn't interested in the insults and chatter. 'So, tell me, Lynette, what did the great man Taylor have to say for himself? If it even was Taylor, of course.'

'David spoke to him, not me.'

'And?'

'And he said you're going to get us all killed. He said you've forced the dead into too small a space. There's a pressure point at Thomas More Street, that's why we've had so many problems there. He says if you keep pushing, the floodgates are going to open.'

'And what do you think?'

'I think you should listen to him.'

'But do you think he's right? I mean, what have you observed when you've been out there, Lynette?'

She faltered. Wrong-footed. 'You know that I haven't been—'

'You've been hiding in here like the useless bloody mouse you are,' he screamed at her, his voice so loud that she visibly recoiled. 'I've had a gutful of you, you sycophantic little worm. You and Marianne and all your bloody council pals, you talk and you talk, but none of you actually do anything worthwhile. It's down to people like Piotr here to keep us safe.'

'*Keep us safe?* He's the one who's putting us all at risk. And you've only left this place once, Dom. You're hardly a man of action yourself.'

'Do you have any idea how much damage you could do with this kind of talk? Christ, the people here are scared enough, they don't need you and David Shires whipping them up with this kind of toxic bullshit. You know we're coming to the end of the work we've been doing around the docks, so just keep your mouth shut a little longer and let us finish what we've started.'

Lynette looked from face to face. 'You know, Dominic, I'm not sure what you're more scared of, the dead or Piotr.'

'Now you're just being ridiculous.'

'Am I?'

'Yes. You don't know what you're talking about.'

'Well, maybe if you were more transparent and honest with the council and let us properly debate suggestions instead of riding roughshod over what anyone else does or says.'

'The council is perfectly democratic.'

'Bollocks. You hold little meetings in secret, and your lap dog here does whatever he wants, never mind what anyone else thinks.'

'Told you, she's fucking crazy,' Piotr said, laughing.

'There's nothing democratic about the way you work, Dominic,' Lynette said, railing at him now. 'You're quick to tell everyone you're not in charge, but you absolutely are. You two call the shots, and it needs to stop.'

Dominic shook his head. 'I've had enough of this crap, Lynette.'

'It's not crap. You're playing with everyone's lives.'

He grabbed her by the collar. 'You're right about that, I suppose,' he said, and he shoved her off the roof.

38

Ruth had been drawn back into the fighting. It was impossible to escape its clutches down here on the frontline; the constant attacks, the adrenalin rush, the retribution, the release of her pent-up anger and frustration... She scrambled to catch hold of another snaking cadaver that had wormed past those fighters battling up ahead of her, and she shoved her blade up through its chin and into what was left of its brain with zeal. All around her, people slaughtered corpse after corpse after corpse, so many that the street was becoming impassable. She was incensed that David had claimed to have spoken to Taylor; so what if there were millions of monsters queuing up for execution here? She felt ready to fight all winter if that was what it took. At moments like this, she wondered if the threat the undead hordes presented had even been over exaggerated. David had seemed frigging terrified just now, but things often appeared worse from a distance. Down here, deep in the blood and grime where each slash of the blade made a difference, the threat felt marginally more controlled, almost manageable.

She was aware of Sanjay fighting nearby. He too seemed to be consumed by the moment, focused. David was close too, still trying to make himself heard between kills but being largely ignored. Distracted momentarily, Ruth slipped and lost her footing in a puddle of vinegary entrails. The ground between her and the two parked trucks blocking the street was awash with gore, the piles of body parts so deep that it was hard to get back up again. Exhausted, she started shifting some of the chunks of rancid meat out of the way, glad of the chance to catch her breath. Someone had started a bonfire near to the supermarket entrance and she dumped several sloppy loads into the flames. Loud cheers and a roar of excitement came from inside the crowded building. What were they doing in there – looting or partying?

Returning to the trucks, Ruth grabbed the emaciated wrist of another flesh-stripped cadaver, then jumped out of the way when one of the blocking vehicles shunted back, almost hitting her. She looked up, ready to berate the driver, but there was no one behind the wheel, hadn't been for ages.

It couldn't have happened.

It was a trick of the increasingly poor light, it had to be. But there were fresh track marks in the stale blood covering the street.

She was confused and went to look closer, keen to understand, and when she crouched down near to the back of the truck, it jumped back again. It didn't make sense... the only thing anywhere near the stationary vehicle was the dead. David put a hand on her shoulder and beckoned for her to follow him. 'We need to go, Ruth.'

The truck juddered again. The treads of its tyres were packed with decay, preventing any traction to stop the vehicle sliding through the crimson puddles.

'But that's not possible,' she said. 'How can a few hundred dead bodies shift a truck?'

'I tried to tell you, it's not a few hundred. There are hundreds of thousands of them, and they're all focused at this point.' All around them, people rushed forward to try and beat back the corpses. Ruth grabbed her weapon, ready to fight, but David dragged her in the opposite direction. 'It's too late for that. We need to get away.'

The truck juddered back the best part of another metre, momentum now on the side of the dead as they surged in response to the increased number of people trying to fight back. A firebomb was thrown over the crowd and it smashed against a wall near the blockade, briefly illuminating a mass of frantic undead movement on the other side, and energising them still further. There was an impossible number of them, packed in tight, all pushing this way.

David shoved Ruth towards St Katharine's Way. 'Run!' he yelled, and he turned back to look for Richard, Sanjay, and anyone else who would listen.

Nearer to Waitrose, Chapman had a better view of the sudden reactions of the reeking crowd, and he was finally beginning to appreciate the extent of the danger. The backhoe loader was a little further back, Kevin still waiting behind the controls. Chapman hammered on the cab window. 'Make sure that road stays sealed.'

Kevin started the engine and raced forward, struggling to make sense of the chaos he was hurtling towards. Being unsighted wasn't unusual these days, and to be honest it didn't matter; all he needed to do was keep hitting corpses and trust that anyone on his side had managed to get out of the way in time. He was not impressed at having to work again, though. He'd thought he was done for the day and had been daydreaming about getting back and devouring a decent meal followed by a bottle of something snaffled from the supermarket. Jeez, that was quite the find. He wondered how many more little treasure troves like that they would uncover among all the wreckage?

Kevin was preoccupied with trivialities, lulled into a false sense of security by the gains of the last couple of days and the fact that, in the cab of this machine, he still felt invincible, disconnected from the madness everyone else had to deal with hands-on. Through the mass of criss-crossing figures ahead, he saw how one of the blocking trucks had been shifted, and he drove straight at it to shove it back into position, figuring that if he hit it at an angle and knocked it sideways, that would do the trick. The quicker he got this done, the sooner he'd be back at base with food in his belly and, fingers crossed, a beer in his hand. He couldn't bloody wait.

He dropped the digger bucket and punched it into the back of the truck, then lifted it up and tried to manoeuvre it as he'd planned. But by shifting the rear end of the truck, he opened a slender gap at the front, and the dead poured through. They spilled into the empty space like a landslide, so many of them advancing at once that some were forced up and over the backhoe loader, scuttling above Kevin, trapping him in his cab. He tried to free the bucket from the truck, but it was snagged in the crumpled bodywork of the wreck, and all he did was make a bad situation immeasurably worse, making the narrow gap wider. He panicked, accelerated back, and rotated the loader a quarter turn in the road. *Shit!* Now he was wedged in place, not going anywhere. Desperate, he shunted the powerful vehicle forward again and brought down a section of wall opposite, releasing another captive wave of undead figures.

He had to get out.

Kevin scrambled at the latch, but the second the door opened he was neck-deep in cold flesh. There were corpses surrounding him, all over him. He tried to fight his way free, but there were too many. They grabbed at him, pulled him back, and trod him down into the tarmac. He called for help but was silenced mid-scream, drowned in decay.

Even though Taylor had tried to warn David of the imminent danger, there were aspects of the creatures' collective behaviour that he too had underestimated. When the base around the Monument and the Tower of London had first been established, the dead had flocked here in huge numbers and never left. Whenever Piotr ordered people to push the corpses back, those that had been destroyed were replaced by even more. When Taylor had blown holes in the group's defences to seal them in, unprecedented numbers of corpses had rushed forward to fill those spaces, and countless more had filled the gaps those had left behind. This last week, when the group fought to reclaim The Highway and the area around St Katharine's docks, tens of thousands more dead bodies had advanced. Their numbers only ever increased, never reduced, and everything the group of survivors did, no matter how carefully planned and executed, only caused more of the dead to gravitate here.

The unwavering persistence of the undead masses now gave

them a wholly unexpected advantage. The creatures' slavish responses to movement and noise had caused them to form huge herds. Their individual ambivalence, both to their surroundings and their own deteriorating physical condition, allowed those herds to ceaselessly seep, surge, and flow like rivers formed from some foul, semi-solid liquid. Around this part of London, drawn here in ever greater numbers, they'd steadily occupied every spare scrap of available space. In the area between Thomas More Street and Vaughan Way, a place Piotr had assumed remained relatively clear, dead flesh had oozed into every nook and cranny. And the undead never turned back. Like an endless game of *follow-my-leader*, there were always too many bodies following for any one corpse to ever retreat.

They never, ever stopped. Never paused, never rested.

Over the preceding days, weeks, and months they'd clogged footpaths and public spaces. They'd crammed into alleyways and cut-throughs and had wedged themselves into the entrances of buildings, spilling in through every open window and door. They'd seeped into loading bays, plazas, and carparks, filling them to capacity. Now there were tens of thousands of them hidden from sight right across this small patch of land, mashed up against each other in the shadows, unable to move, just waiting for release.

Just a few metres back from the part of Thomas More Street where the fiercest battles raged tonight was the entrance to an underground carpark. It wasn't a particularly large carpark, only a couple of levels down, and perhaps that was why it had proved to be such a useful cocoon for the many bodies that had flowed inside. They'd been trapped until tonight, but now the succession of mistakes that had been made aboveground had released the pressure and facilitated their release. Able to move at last, lines of corpses now began staggering up the slope, escaping over the rubble of the collapsed wall, sweeping aside the few overstretched fighters who still fought to hold them back. Watching from a distance, Chapman knew the game was up. He signalled the retreat.

Those people who continued to strip the supermarket shelves were oblivious to the danger. When Paul Duggan looked out and saw the stampede back to base, he panicked. Disorientated, and with his reactions dulled by the copious amounts of alcohol he'd helped himself to, he ordered another attack. Improvised firebombs were hurled into the seething masses. Great arcs of flame burned through the sky overhead, fully illuminating the retreat of the living alongside the relentless advance of the dead.

Where the bombs struck the undead hordes, the flames took hold with vicious speed. Those creatures that had been underground were tinder dry. The fire ripped through them, leaping from corpse to corpse, eating its way back along the unruly queue that, even now, still stretched all the way back into the carpark and belowground. Countless cadavers converged on the bright light from all directions, more fuel for the already out of control fire.

Paul couldn't process everything that had happened, couldn't understand how things had gone so wrong, so fast. Even when the vehicles they'd used to block the road caught light and started to burn, he still didn't move. Chapman shoved him in the small of the back. 'Get everybody back to base,' he shouted. 'Find Piotr and tell him what's happened. Make sure Harjinder keeps the other end of this road secure and get ready to block the docks once we're all back safe.'

Most people hadn't waited to be told. David Shires was one of the last few remaining, keen to make sure everyone he gave a damn about was safe before he himself retreated. He was about to leave when he stopped, certain that he could hear a voice behind him, someone shouting for help. In the light from the increasingly intense flames, he saw Richard. He was trapped, stuck between the beached backhoe loader and the partially collapsed wall through which a torrent of unsteady bodies continued to pour. David could see him trying to clamber over the bulk of the loader to get to safety. Burning corpses staggered past on either side of him, tripping through the chaos, oblivious to the flames that consumed them. Cowering from the heat and light, David ran over to try and help his friend across the gap just as the fuel tank of the backhoe loader exploded, hurling him back across the street.

39

Sam, Vicky, and the others crowded into Eric's cluttered flat on the north side of the building to try to get a better view. The place was a pigsty, the carpet covered with rubbish. 'Your friends, eh?' he said as he showed them through. The three of them stepped out onto the balcony, bracing themselves against the cruel autumn wind.

'What have they done?' Vicky said.

'We don't know for sure it was them,' Sam said. 'It could have been anything.'

'Oh, come on, Sam, you're supposed to be the realist. You know as well as I do, there's nothing else over there.'

There was a pall of dirty black smoke climbing up from the general vicinity of the Monument and the Tower of London, its belly lit up by the flames blossoming below. They couldn't make out details from this distance, but Vicky didn't need to. She'd already seen enough. 'I need to go back.'

'And do what exactly?' Sam asked.

'I can't just sit over here and abandon them.'

'You don't really have a lot of choice.'

'You're such a bastard.'

'He is,' Eric agreed, 'but I think he's probably right. You go over there, what you gonna do?'

'More than I can do from here.'

'Yeah, but seriously, what difference will you make? Do you have a fire engine? A big hose? Even a bottle of water? You gonna put out a fire with buckets of water from the river?'

He waited for Vicky to argue back, but she couldn't. They stood together in silence and stared into the darkness. Another burst of flame appeared, incandescent against the endless grey of the rest of dead London. From here it was impossible to gauge the size of the blaze.

'But I can't just leave them... Selena's over there. And David, and Marianne, and Ruth... The only people left in the world that I give a damn about are stuck in that place,' she said, fighting to hold back tears.

'It might burn itself out,' Eric said, sounding more hopeful than anything.

Joanne had followed them into the flat. 'I doubt that very much,' she said. 'Me and Shanice have been watching Canary Wharf disappearing over the last week or so. There's nothing to stop fires anymore. Unless we get torrential rains, they just keep burning.'

'That's why I have to go back,' Vicky said.

'Yeah, we get that, but how? And again, why?'

'But they might not even know about it.'

'Seriously? We all heard the explosions, didn't we? They woke Shanice up. Doreen's half-deaf, and even she heard them. Eric's right, you can't put out the fire yourself. If the few hundred people you say are over there can't deal with it, what difference will one more person make?'

'It's hard,' Sam said. 'I get that, I really do. I'm not as selfish as you think. I've had more than a few sleepless nights over here, beating myself up because I abandoned you lot.'

'But it wasn't your fault.'

'No, and this isn't your fault. Or your responsibility.'

'Listen to Sam,' Joanne said. 'You said they've got a decent boat now, so they'll get away by river if things get difficult. You're not going to help anyone by putting yourself in danger. We just need to keep an eye on what happens.'

'And how do you propose we do that?'

'We can watch them,' Eric said. He clocked Vicky's blank expression and explained further. 'When we first set up here, I used to go down to the river. Look.'

He leant out over the balcony and pointed across the road.

Vicky could just about make out an overgrown running track that backed onto a swathe of grassland. 'What exactly am I looking at?'

'That park goes all the way up to the river, and there's never many bodies there. I think I probably used to watch you.'

'What?'

'Not you personally, your group. Back at the very start, before I found Brian and the others, I could see things happening on your side of the river... It helped me to know I wasn't the only person left alive. You were making a lot of noise over there, and everything else was really quiet.'

'You're telling me you just shut yourself away and didn't try to make contact?'

'The bridges were already blocked. Your people had already stopped me crossing over.'

'Eric told us about your group,' Joanne explained, 'but we couldn't let you know where we were without letting millions of dead people know as well. He's got a house set up down there and everything.'

'A house?' Vicky asked, confused.

'They make me sound like some kind of pervert, but I'm not. I was just keeping an eye on things for a while, that's all. Just keeping my options open.'

Vicky wasn't interested in the whys and wherefores. 'You've still got this place?'

'Yes. If the fire over the water gets too bad, we can go that way and keep a look out.'

Vicky thought for a moment.

'Is it far?'

'A kilometre and a half, maybe. Fifteen minutes' walk tops.'

'I'm going.'

'What, now?'

'Yes, now. I want to be ready, just in case. It doesn't feel right just sitting here while they're struggling.'

'I think you're wasting your time,' Sam said.

'It's like Eric said, it made him feel better knowing there were people on the other side of the water. I just want them to know that there's someone here if – *when* – things go belly-up.'

Eric thought for a moment. 'Get your stuff together. I'll take you.'

'I don't have any stuff. Take me now.'

'This is stupid,' Sam protested.

'Maybe, but there are a lot of decent people over there. I couldn't live with myself if any of them got hurt when I could have helped.'

'How many times do I have to say the same thing? It's not your responsibility.'

'No, but it is my conscience. Come on, Eric.' She paused and turned to face Sam again. 'You coming?'

'No,' he told her, and he went back to bed.

40

The breach bell had been tolling continually since the explosion on Thomas More Street. Over the weeks, the sound of the bell had often been met with indifference from some folks and ignored completely by others. Some didn't care, some just couldn't see the point of leaving the perceived safety of their squalid hotel rooms or apartments. Not tonight, though. This was different, and they all knew it. Almost everyone had made their way here now, and people were out rounding up the stragglers. Georgie was at the foot of the wooden steps leading up to the entrance to the White Tower, ticking off names as people arrived, checking them in. Built by William the Conqueror almost a thousand years ago, she could only begin to imagine the things that the walls of this place had seen in the millennium since, but she knew beyond any doubt that nothing in history could compare to the horror of what was happening tonight.

Lisa ushered a gaggle of terrified-looking people through the entrance to the Tower near the river and herded them towards Georgie. 'That's the last of the folks from the hotel. How many are still missing?'

She double-checked the clipboard she was holding. 'I can't be certain. I don't know how many are still out with Harjinder... I think it may be as many as seventy, maybe more than that. Most of them were out fighting.'

'Shit.'

The scale of their potential losses was sobering.

The daylight was almost completely gone now, but the sky to the east glowed a brooding orange as the unchecked fire continued spreading. The lawn in front of the White Tower was crowded with people who didn't yet want to shut themselves away inside the shadow-filled building. Marianne struggled to get through them. 'Any sign of David?'

Georgie shook her head. 'Sorry, Marianne. He's not made it back yet.'

'Lynette?'

'Nope. Haven't seen her either.'

Marianne looked more shaken with each response but forced herself to keep asking. 'What about Ruth?'

'She's still out with Paul, I think,' Lisa said. 'Richard was with them, and Sanjay. They're trying to block the way back from the dock, stop the dead getting any closer.'

'Liz and Orla?'

'Both inside, trying to get things organised,' Georgie told her.

'Good.' Marianne turned back to Lisa and took her arm. 'We need to make sure everything gets moved into the Tower, just in case. All the supplies we can lay our hands on. Every scrap of food.'

'I think Mihai's already onto it.'

'I know, but Mihai's half-soaked. Will you go and make sure it's done right, love? If what Taylor told David is true, we might be stuck in here for a long time.'

'Okay.'

'Now where the hell's Dominic? Has anyone seen him?'

'I'm here,' Dominic said, coming down the steps from the White Tower, eyes wide and terrified.

'Now's not the time for hiding, Dom.'

'I wasn't, I was just...'

Marianne wasn't interested. 'Round everybody up and do what you can to keep them calm. The last thing we need around here is folks panicking and causing even more of a ruckus. Put your usual spin on things. Tell them everything's fine, even though we all know it isn't.'

'But I was going to—'

She'd had enough. 'Just do what you're fucking well told for once,' she yelled at him, and he meekly disappeared back inside.

Piotr was in his cherry picker at the junction of Thomas More Street and East Smithfield, his elevated position allowing him to see along much of the length of Thomas More Street. The dead were continuing to gravitate south, still jostling to get closer to the supermarket end of the street, drawn towards the fires raging around the burnt-out vehicles, which were in turn being fuelled by more of their number that had already got too close and had gone up in flames themselves.

To Piotr, none of it mattered. It was inconsequential. This was useless land, dead land, and they didn't need a single square metre more of it. And the more corpses that were reduced to ash, the better.

He lowered the basket to speak to Harjinder and his troops.

'They've had enough time to get out of the way down there. You know what to do. Light those fuckers up. Burn the fucking lot of them.'

And the crowd of fighters who'd been holding this end of Thomas More Street with Harjinder obliged without hesitation. They'd harvested empty bottles from all the drinking last night and filled them with fuel from the tanker. They lit scores of makeshift munitions and hurled them deep into the empty heart of the undead masses.

41

Those people who still had enough of a backbone to stand and fight had been forced to retreat as far along St Katharine's Way as the drawbridge at the lock, in the shadow of the hotel. This place had been an Achilles heel for them previously, a restrictive pinch point where the dead had grouped dangerously close to where many of the survivors had taken shelter. Just a couple of days earlier the group had driven through and cleared this area. Now they prayed they'd be able to get it blocked up again in time.

Easier said than done.

In retaking this stretch, the group had stripped it bare. There was hardly anything left to help block the bridge. 'Can we put it through? Make a hole in it?' someone suggested. Ruth, standing mid-way across, stomped her boot down hard on the metalwork.

'Not a chance.'

She looked around for inspiration, but the darkness had erased all form and familiarity, leaving them as good as blind. And maybe that was for the best, because she didn't want to see what was coming. She could already hear it, though, and that was enough to allow her mind to fill in the blanks. The dead were steadily advancing, a lethargic yet unstoppable deluge of decay. Though many of the creatures had been preoccupied by the fires now raging around Thomas More Street, by virtue of their sheer numbers there were thousands of others that had been shoved and jostled and shunted away in all other available directions. An enormous crowd of them had broken away, channelled along the lines of the streets, and it was this vast column of death that was now rolling back along St Katharine's Docks. The fires were behind them now, no longer a distraction, and their collective attention had instead been captured by the fighters' retreat and by the constant tolling of the breach bell in the distance.

Ruth looked back, convinced she could see movement but unsure whether the first cadavers had made it this far or if it was just a phantom of the night. Didn't matter. That they'd reach this point was inevitable. She leant against the railings of the bridge and tried to understand how it had come to this, how the situation had deteriorated so quickly. Had all the pressure really been focused on this specific area as David and, apparently, Taylor, had said? With her eyes screwed shut, she tried to block out the noise of the chaos unfolding all around: the fires burning, the panic here at the docks, the others scrambling for safety. She focused on the washing of the water under the bridge.

Wait. The water. That was it.

'Get stuff from the boats to block the bridge. Get as much junk up here as you can and put it in their way.'

It felt like a shitty plan, but it was all they had. People began to move, criss-crossing with each other in the shadows, feeling their way down steps towards the launches then scavenging from unfamiliar boats, equally blind. After a couple of minutes, some had found lights to help, but it was too little, too late. By the time they'd got enough stuff across the bridge to build a rudimentary barrier, the enemy was already upon them.

Ruth was well used to witnessing the dead in all their putrid glory now. Sights that would have been unbearable before the end of everything had become so commonplace as to be easily dismissed. The grotesque had become the norm, not the exception. But even still, what she was witnessing now – or, rather, the implication of the fraction of the whole that she could see in the limited light – was absolutely fucking terrifying. It didn't look like a crowd of corpses that was advancing towards them, it was more a single horrific *thing*. She'd witnessed similar behaviour before, but never anything on this scale. An unending slew of flesh was crawling along the roads around the docks towards them, absorbing anything that lay in its path. Some of the dead, more through luck than judgement, made it all the way to the bridge, but many, many more of them simply sloughed off the side of the dock and into the water where they thrashed around in the murk. It made no difference; more than enough of them remained on dry land. Casualties were irrelevant when they had endless numbers in their ranks.

Those that had made it onto the bridge were undeterred by the hastily improvised obstruction Ruth and the others had thrown up across their path. The dead had an impetus now, a collective drive, and they just kept going. When the first few fell, those behind simply walked over them, trampling their remains and, by default, creating a ramp of putrefying flesh to get them over the top of the pathetic barrier. Their nonchalance was horrifying, their ambivalence absolute. Short of tackling each one of the hundreds and hundreds of thousands individually, Ruth knew they had no chance of halting their onward march.

She was standing a little way back from the bridge, watching an impossible number of corpses lurch, slip, and stagger towards her, when she heard them moving along the other side of the water too. They were steadily seeping along all the roads and pathways that connected St Katharine's Docks with the Tower of London and the rest of the base, coming at them from every available angle. 'We need to go,' Sanjay said.

When Ruth turned around, she realised they were the only ones left still trying to mount a defence. Everyone else was long gone.

42

He had fleeting memories of moving and being moved – of stumbling and tripping, of dragging and being dragged – but he didn't know where he was until he came around fully. David awoke slumped against a door in the hallway of a decent-sized apartment.

'You're still here then,' Chapman said. 'I'll tell you something, mate, you might not have eaten much over the last few months, but you're still a fucking weight to carry.'

'Thanks. Where are we?'

'Safe... for now.'

'What happened?'

'Major league fuck up. Easier just to show you.'

He helped David get to his feet and took him over to a window. They were in a luxury high-rise between the banks of the Thames and what was left of the docks. David looked down into the seething streets below, but he couldn't make sense of anything he was seeing, couldn't orientate with anything he knew. There were fires raging, one huge blaze and countless other smaller blooms. The flickering lights illuminated teeming undead movement wherever he looked. It was hard to make out precise details. 'What exactly am I looking at?'

Chapman tapped the glass. 'That big fire you can see is what's left of Waitrose, I think. We got distracted. Too many people in the supermarket, not enough manning the defences.'

David's eyes were becoming accustomed to the gloom. He craned his neck to try to look back towards the hotel and the rest of the compound, but other buildings blocked his view. 'It's more than that,' he said. 'I talked to Taylor.'

'What, *the* Taylor?'

'You don't sound surprised.'

'To be honest, I'm not. I went out to his gaff, you know. Nicely fortified, it was. Some crazy woman locked away on her last legs. Well, leg, anyway. It was all pretty well organised. He never struck me as the kind of bloke who'd accidentally blow himself up like Piotr claimed. So, what was he like? The big action hero we all assumed? That's if it really was him, of course.'

'No reason to think it wasn't. Like you, I never believed Piotr's story about his death. He finds Taylor's body, helps himself to all the munitions the guy's carrying, then creeps into Fenchurch Street station and plants a bomb to help me and my lot out? Bit far-fetched if you ask me. Also, it's probably not a good idea to go around pretending you're public enemy number one unless you actually *are* public enemy number one.'

'So what did he say?'

'He showed me that pretty much the entire dead population of London is on its way to our doorstep.'

'We knew that already.'

'Yeah, but we didn't realise how many there were, and how great the pressure had got. I tried to warn you, but you silly fuckers wouldn't listen. And now you've let the whole lot of them in.'

'I was just following orders.'

'Seriously? That's a lame excuse.'

It was, and Chapman knew it.

David continued to stare at the fires burning along Thomas More Street. Even from this distance he could see the flames leaping from corpse to corpse where the heat was at its most intense. But even further out, it was spreading like a bush fire; bodies that were already burning were colliding with countless others. Dried out skin, ragged clothes, straw-like hair, noxious gases produced by decay... the dead had proved to be remarkably combustible.

'The others will be safe in the Tower, right?' Chapman asked.

'*Safer*, I expect, but I don't reckon anywhere's completely safe tonight. I don't fancy our chances up here, to be honest. I think we should get out before it's too late.'

Chapman peered down into the street immediately outside the building in which they'd taken shelter. It was packed tight with dead flesh, more fuel for the fire. 'I've got news for you, mate, I think it's too late already.'

43

Eric and Vicky crept across overgrown parkland together. It was more like a jungle now than the urban oasis it had once been. Vicky had seen more greenery in London over the last couple of days than she ever remembered seeing before. Had it always been there, or was it just an illusion? Was the land being steadily reclaimed by nature? Whatever the reason, she couldn't help thinking she'd initially chosen the wrong side of the River Thames to try and survive on. The south bank had proved far more habitable.

It didn't take long to reach the river. Eric's was a terraced house literally on the banks of the Thames, midway along a row of twelve. Vicky climbed up to the first-floor entrance and paused to catch her breath. She couldn't start to imagine how much the relatively modest townhouse might have fetched in the pre-apocalypse world. Property prices in London had always seemed to her like a terrible joke. Christ, she'd had to stretch well beyond her means to keep her modest place in Luton. Today, though, the position of this house unquestionably made it worth the investment.

Eric pulled the curtains to block out the night before switching on a couple of battery-powered lamps. The house was worse than his flat. It was like a teenager's bedroom with gadgets, piles of comic books, and junk food wrappers everywhere. Boxes and boxes of looted stuff had been stacked against the walls, making the rooms feel like narrow corridors. 'Do you never tidy up after yourself?' Vicky asked, tripped through discarded crap.

'No point cleaning,' he said with a grin. 'My mother used to tell me all the time to clean up, but she's in Canada and I can't hear her nagging from here. If this place gets too bad, I'll move in next door.'

He took her through to a room at the back of the house, where glass double doors opened out onto a balcony overlooking the water. It had taken them less than an hour to get here from John Kennedy House, and in that time, the situation on the north bank looked like it had deteriorated dramatically. A wide swathe of the city was on fire. Vicky helped herself to a pair of binoculars that had been hung over the back of a gamer's chair and tried to make sense of the madness.

She couldn't see as far as the Tower of London, but the distinctive outline of Tower Bridge spanning the river offered some perspective. The blaze appeared to still be confined to the docks to the east of the Tower, and she scanned what little of the chaos she could make out, looking for clues and signs of life but finding none.

'I shouldn't have brought you here,' Eric said. 'It's not helping.'

'It's not making me feel any worse, if that's any consolation. At least here we're on the river. There's a slim chance they'll see me if they come this way.'

'Hard as it must be to accept, I think that's the best you can do for now. Like we said back with the others just now, even if you could get over there, you couldn't do anything.'

Vicky knew he was right. She stood on the balcony and watched the fiery tumult on the other side of the Thames, thinking about Ruth and Selena and the others, wishing there was something she could do to help them.

44

In terms of its construction and defences, there was nowhere safer in this part of London than the White Tower. The heavily fortified castle keep had originally been designed as a place of last resort when the Tower had come under siege, and that seemed chillingly appropriate tonight. It was testament to the enduring strength of the building that it remained in relatively good condition, though few of the people now sheltering within its walls held out much hope of it remaining strong 'til morning. It wasn't the fire that was going to overrun this ancient fort, it was the dead. No one had ever had to defend the Tower from an army like this. An army with soldiers that didn't fear injury and didn't feel pain. An army with soldiers that never tired and never stopped.

People had returned from the docks with news of the relentless advance, and that had galvanised the rest of the group. The breach bell had been silenced, and now the group worked together to shift absolutely everything of value into the White Tower. Around thirty volunteers were working under Mihai's supervision to transport the remaining food supplies from the Tower Place stores to St John's Chapel, a semi-circular projection on the south-east corner of the White Tower. Gary, still hobbling on his injured ankle, feeling less than useful, was concerned when he saw the volume of food that had so far been shifted. 'Is this it?'

Mihai took exception. 'What do you want me to do, Gary? Conjure up some more from thin air?' He stormed out of the chapel. Gary went to follow him, barely matching half his speed, and crashed into Orla who was coming the other way.

'Take it easy,' Orla said. 'What's up with you?'

'Have you seen the stores? There's got to be more food than

that.'

'Just be thankful we've got anything.'

'You don't understand... I'm sure we brought more than this back from Surrey Quays, and that's without counting anything we managed to salvage from Waitrose tonight.'

'Go and see if Marianne knows what's going on. I've got more important things to worry about right now, Gary.'

'Like what?'

'Like the fact we're still missing more than forty people.'

'Who?'

'David, Lynette, Richard, Chapman, Ruth, Sanjay, Allison, Shaun, Kevin, Amit... the list goes on. Go and speak to Holly if you want all their names. Alternatively, do something to help.'

Orla didn't have time for his bullshit. She left him to find someone else to moan at while she continued looking for those who hadn't yet made it back to base.

She walked around the rooms of the White Tower for what felt like the hundredth time, trying to make out faces in the miserable light from various lamps and torches. Georgie had moved to inside the building now. 'Any news?' Orla asked.

'Jan and Shaun came back a few minutes ago. Piotr's still got about twenty people with him, apparently.'

'Doing what, for fuck's sake? Toasting fucking marshmallows on the fire?'

'I don't know, Orla. Don't shout at me, please.'

'You're right. I'm sorry. Anyone else back?'

'Liz is looking after a few people with burns. A couple of them are pretty bad, by all accounts. Marianne's trying to find out who's hurt so I can tick them off.'

'Dr Ahmad not doing anything to help?'

'He's being about as cooperative as usual. He was with Stan and Damien just now.'

Selena burst into the building, breathless. 'Ruth and Sanjay are back.'

Orla ran outside to meet them. They were immediately

recognisable despite the drifting smoke, an odd couple. Ruth towered over Sanjay, and she was carrying a body in her arms. 'Oh, shit,' Orla said, desperate to know who they'd brought back.

Ruth stopped a short distance away and gently laid the person on the lawn. Orla could tell by her movements that whomever it was, they were dead. Despite the frantic chaos of the moment, she was respectful and silent, didn't allow herself to be rushed. She looked around for something to cover the body. Orla handed her a blanket from a pile of clothing that hadn't yet been taken indoors and saw that it was Lynette.

'Oh, Jesus, what happened?' Orla asked, barely able to form the words. 'Lyn never went anywhere near the fighting, how did she...?'

'We found her in the road in front of the hotel,' Sanjay explained, because Ruth too was struggling to contain her emotion.

'What the hell happened?'

'Hate to say this, but it looks like she jumped.'

'She never,' Selena said, and they all turned to look at her. She had tears streaming down her face and she was backing away from the body, hands covering her mouth. Orla reached out for her.

'Come here, love. I know it's awful, but these are terrible times and—'

'She never killed herself,' Selena said again, pushing Orla away. 'I know she didn't.'

'It's hard, but we just have to accept that sometimes things get too much for people and the only way forward they can see is to—'

'She. Didn't. Kill. Herself.'

'I've had enough of this shit,' Ruth said, and she started to walk away.

'They pushed her off.'

Ruth stopped. Turned around.

'What?'

'I seen her go up there. I asked her where she was going. She weren't on her own on that roof. Piotr and Dominic was already up there.'

The dead army had continued to inch around the perimeter of the dock, trickling around corners and slipping down pathways, edging ever closer. The tall buildings that surrounded the water sheltered this mass of corpses from the brightness of the fires around Thomas More Street and, without the distraction of the light, they simply kept moving forward, dragging themselves closer to the living, their interest piqued by the panicked noises and chaotic movement coming from around the Tower of London. In massive numbers they wrapped themselves all the way around the hotel, cutting it off from everything else. If there was anyone left alive inside there now, it was too late; they were fucked.

There were well-trod public footpaths here under the raised section of road on the approach to Tower Bridge, pathways which led straight along the edge of the Thames to the front of the Tower itself, but railings and steps and other well-placed obstructions conspired to direct the monstrous hordes along other, clearer routes. For the moment, through luck more than anything, this kept them away from the entrance to the Tower. Every action has an equal and opposite reaction, and because one route was blocked, they were forced along another. Without even a whisper of complaint, the first of thousands of them followed the gentle curve of the road to the right and began dragging themselves up the steady incline along St Katharine's Way. Had Sanjay and Ruth not discovered Lynette's body a few minutes earlier, she'd likely have never been found. The place where she'd fallen was already becoming steadily overwhelmed by death.

Piotr's troops continued to guard the blockades where Thomas More Street and Vaughan Way met East Smithfield, largely unaware of what was happening elsewhere. They held their ground, because from where they were standing, it looked like progress was still being made. From here, this small, dark corner of a single unlit street, it was impossible to even begin to appreciate the implications of the actions that had been taken just a few hundred metres away.

The pressure at the northern junctions of Thomas More Street and Vaughan Way with East Smithfield had been reduced by the impact of the activity further south. There, fires continued to burn through apparently limitless supplies of fuel, consuming petrol and diesel left in the tanks of abandoned cars, the contents of every building, trees, hedgerows, and other vegetation, the crap the group had stacked up in great mounds against the barricades to defend the perimeter of their precious scrap of land, and the dead themselves.

The dancing light continued to draw many more of them out of the shadows from wider afield. In the patch of land sandwiched between Thomas More Street and Vaughan Way, an office block was well alight, and as the flames licked and climbed upwards, consuming floor after floor, so the tall building became a beacon. The blaze was ever more visible, its impact on the advancing crowds proportional to its height.

There was a surreal order to the way the undead masses approached the fire, a stoicism that gave a false impression of control and intent. They made barely a sound as they edged ever nearer, all but invisible in the unending gloom. Like a glutenous, sticky sludge, they found a way over or around every obstruction with what appeared to be a dogged determination, but which, in reality, was anything but. With no other competing distractions of any scale in what remained of dead London, every single cadaver that caught even a fleeting glimpse of the hellfire now taking hold of Wapping began moving towards it instinctively. Even with their ruined eyes, many of the dead could see the burning building from a distance, and those that couldn't see it wearily followed those that could. Every time another vehicle caught fire because of the heat, every time part of a barricade or part of a building collapsed because of fire damage, more were drawn forward.

The undead masses steadily and silently filled both Thomas More Street and Vaughan Way from end to end. Those people mounting a defence on East Smithfield had been expecting a full-on attack, not this silent, incessant advance. Now, unseen by Harjinder and the other fighters, the dead butted up against the blockades, and as the fire ate through the corpses, so the barriers too began to burn. Discarded furniture, numerous vehicles, other scraps and odds and ends that had been used to fill the gaps... all manner of flammable materials caught light.

In the end there was no dramatic explosion, and a distinct lack of histrionics that might have given Piotr and his fighters some warning. Instead, the defences at the end of Vaughan Way simply gave way and collapsed as if they'd had enough. The dead – some burning, others that had so far escaped the blaze – began dragging themselves over the wreckage.

Harjinder saw them first, though initially he wasn't sure what he was looking at. It was all but impossible to make out the details of the shapeless mass coming along East Smithfield towards him. He didn't understand what it was until it was almost too late. He lit a torch and walked a little closer, then made a frantic retreat when he saw their grotesque, glistening faces glaring at him. 'They've broken through!' he screamed.

'Light the fuckers up!' Piotr yelled, and around him people began lighting the fuses of petrol bombs and hurling them as far as they could into the approaching crowd. The first couple of bottles landed short, illuminating scores more of the hideous undead.

'There are too many of them, boss,' Harj said, and Piotr knew he was right. There were hundreds of them in the street already, and thousands would inevitably be following behind.

More bombs were thrown, setting light to hundreds at a time. 'We need more fuel,' someone said, but Piotr knew it wouldn't make a scrap of difference.

'Block the road,' he ordered.

'What with? There's nothing left here, Piotr. It's all back at base.'

'Then we block them nearer to the Tower. Fall back. Now!'

They did as they were ordered, but it was already clear they would find no quarter. There was no stopping the dead now.

45

Piotr and his troops sprinted back towards the Tower. He abandoned plans to put a new barrier across Tower Hill to channel the dead north and south, but it was too late. The area around the ancient monument was devoid of life but teeming with death. Piotr realised they were trapped between two divisions of the same undead army – those that had followed them from East Smithfield, and thousands more that had continued to drag themselves along St Katharine's Way – and they were destined to collide. He knew that this entire are would, before long, be crawling with decay. By morning, they wouldn't be able to move for dead flesh.

He ran towards Tower Place, skirting around the perimeter of the Tower, which remained clearly defined. Metal railings around the site provided a first line of defence. If the dead breached them, as he thought they inevitably would, then the dried-up moat – between ten and twenty metres of grassland for the most part – would buy the survivors inside the ancient castle a little more time. The ramparts would hold up the dead advance still further, but in such extraordinary numbers, Piotr didn't think it impossible that they'd eventually get over the top. He'd seen more improbable things happen since the world had ended.

He couldn't see any movement around Tower Place, undead or otherwise, and so turned south to get to the main entrance to the Tower, adjacent to the Thames. He raced past the remains of the ticket office and visitor centre at speed. They'd repurposed those relatively recently built buildings early on and put them to good use, but it seemed inevitable now that they'd be lost before morning. It spoke volumes that the Tower itself would be the last building standing. They'd chosen wisely, coming here. In this place, Piotr thought, people still had half a chance.

In the time he'd been away fighting, the entrances to the Tower grounds had been blocked with vehicles. Here at the Byward Tower gateway, adjacent to the river, Alfonso Morterero sat behind the wheel of a Transit van, watching out for stragglers. Piotr gestured for him to get out of the way, and Alfonso immediately obliged. The light may have been low and the situation fraught, but there was no mistaking living people. Their conscious, coordinated actions were in stark contrast to the stilted, staccato movements of the dead.

Piotr followed the rest of his people up towards the White Tower. He was at the foot of the steps when someone jumped out of the darkness and grabbed him. In a heartbeat he'd drawn his knife and had it pressed against his attacker's throat. Then he relaxed.

Dominic Grove.

'What the fuck are you doing? I almost killed you, you fucking idiot. I thought you were a corpse.'

'As good as,' Dominic said, and he pulled Piotr back into the shadows where he'd been hiding. 'They found Lynette.'

'And? She killed herself. So what?'

'It's not that simple. Selena knows we were up there with her. She's worked out what happened.'

'And they haven't strung you up yet?'

'I overheard them talking, then made a run for it. They think I'm still in there.'

'Doesn't make any difference now.'

'They'll lynch me.'

'Only if they see you.'

'I can't spend all night out here. What happens after that? Do you not understand me? They know what I did.'

'I understand perfectly, but like I said, it doesn't matter. Things have moved on. The dead are everywhere. We can't stop them now. It's time.'

*

Orla intercepted Piotr when he entered the White Tower. 'You're back, thank Christ. Let Georgie know you're here and—'

'No time for that,' he told her. 'The dead have broken through the barriers to the east. We can't hold them back.'

She'd long known it was inevitable, but his confirmation still came as a body blow. 'What do we do?'

'Stay here and dig in like we agreed. This place is safe.'

'But for how long?'

'All winter, I hope. You know the walls of this tower are four metres thick in places? They won't get inside.'

'Forgive me, Piotr, but I'm sick of hearing you telling me how the dead aren't going to get in here or through there... they always get through.'

'If you have a better place to go hide, be my guest.'

Harjinder reappeared, with another group of exhausted-looking fighters following. 'Ready, Piotr.'

He turned to leave again and walked straight into Ruth. 'What are you doing, Piotr?'

'We're going to make sure everyone stays safe in here, try and keep the dead away from the door for a little longer.'

'How?'

'A diversion. Give them something else to focus on.'

'All you've done so far is make them focus on *us*. I can't believe I ever listened to you.'

'Now's not the time. We can argue about this later.'

'You do know that Taylor's back, don't you?'

'So I hear. Someone calling themselves Taylor, anyway.'

'Whoever they are, they've got a better grasp of what's happening here than you. You caused all of this, Piotr, you and Dominic. This is all your fault.'

'So, call a fucking council meeting and have a fucking debate about it.'

'You bastard.'

'You think you could have done things better? Remember, you're the one who fucked things up with Taylor in the first place.

Now get out of my way, I've still got work to do.'

He shoved her away. She collided with Marianne, and they both ended up on the deck. Ruth got up quickly, but before she could get anywhere near Piotr, he was gone again.

The night was rocked by another enormous explosion. Crowds rushed out of the White Tower to see where it was and what had happened, fearing the worst. Sanjay pushed his way through to try and get a better view. He assumed the blast had been around the area where all the fighting had taken place today, because there were fires still raging there and anything could have exploded in amongst the deserted buildings. But when he looked around, he saw fire billowing into the sky to the north of the Tower, up near the train tracks and the ruins of Fenchurch Street station. He raced after Orla, who was already running towards the north battlements of the Tower to get a better vantage point. Well-worn steps, used by endless numbers of sightseeing tourists over many decades, led up to the ramparts. Sanjay followed her along the top of the outer wall.

The half-full fuel tanker they'd recovered from the petrol station at the end of The Highway had exploded. Oily black smoke and bulging bursts of flame belched from the remains of its metal carcase.

'How the hell did that happen?' Orla asked, struggling to make sense of what she was seeing. 'There's no other fires over that way.'

'It's Piotr,' Ruth said, breathless. She'd followed them out onto the battlements.

'But why?'

'A distraction. He said he was going to do something to keep the dead away from the door.'

Sanjay leant over the wall and pointed out towards Tower Hill. 'Looks like it's working. Look at the crowds.'

The view from up here was limited by tall trees and other parts of the Tower's outer defences, but through the gaps they could see that hundreds of corpses were drifting towards the remains of the tanker.

Orla was confused. 'But that doesn't make sense... all that's going to do is bring even more of them this way.'

'He's panicked,' Ruth said. 'He's all talk, no trousers. It just makes him feel better blowing shit up. Yeah, it'll give the dead something to focus on for a little while, but it won't last. All he's done is speed things up and waste what's left of our fuel supply. Fucker.'

They watched the fire eating through the migrating crowd. Already flames were licking against the sides of the closest buildings around where the tanker had exploded, and fire was dripping from the branches of burning trees. Although their view was limited, there remained a hypnotic beauty in the way so many corpses gravitated towards the inferno, an instinctive migration. For a couple of seconds, Sanjay began to wonder if the destruction of the tanker might have been a stroke of genius, if it might prove to be enough to keep the dead away from the Tower long enough for the fire to eat through the entire crowd.

The sound of an engine.

It wasn't particularly loud, but it was clearly audible over the uneasy calm of everything else.

'Fuck,' Orla said as realisation dawned. 'It wasn't the dead he was trying to distract. It was us.'

She turned and ran back down the steps to ground level, then sprinted past the White Tower down to the Byward Tower. She hammered on the side of the van blocking the entrance for Alfonso to shift it, but he didn't react. She tried to squeeze down the side of the vehicle, but it had been left at an awkward angle and she couldn't get through. She realised the driver's seat was empty. She stretched and managed to reach the handle, but the door was locked, and the key was gone.

Sanjay was right behind her now. 'What's going on?'

Ruth had worked it out too. 'Middle drawbridge,' she shouted, and she followed the outer wall of the Tower to the next entrance along. This time, they were able to shift the car that had been left blocking the way.

The three of them rushed along the cobbled pathway that separated the Tower from the Thames, but they were never going to make it, and all they could do was watch, helpless, as the Thames Clipper left its dock at Tower Pier. They stared at the vessel as it sailed past them, packed with people and supplies.

46

Vicky had drifted off to sleep in the gamer's chair but woke with a start when Eric shook her shoulder. 'What's wrong?'

'Perhaps trouble for your friends, I think. A big explosion. It woke me up.'

She rushed to the balcony and looked out over a scene of apocalyptic mayhem on the north bank. A full quarter of Wapping was on fire now. Eric had the binoculars and was looking towards Tower Bridge. She snatched them off him when she saw lights on the water. The Thames Clipper was setting sail.

'You think they're leaving?' he asked.

'Well someone definitely is.'

'Coming back for more stuff?'

'Not in the middle of the night while half the city burns.'

'We should send them a signal,' he said, and he disappeared off to another room. Vicky could hear him scrambling around elsewhere, turfing through the junk he'd hoarded. He returned a few seconds later, his arms full of fireworks. 'I had matches somewhere...'

He was distracting her. She pulled the curtains across behind her to shut him out and focused on the clipper as it raced along the water. She kept the binoculars trained on the boat as it approached.

Eric blundered out onto the balcony, still chuntering about his bloody fireworks. 'Leave it, for Christ's sake,' she snapped.

'Don't you want to let them know you're here?'

'There's no point. I've already seen enough.'

'I don't understand...'

This was absolutely not another food run. From what she could see, the clipper was rammed, filled with people and equipment.

Faces were hard to make out from a distance, but Piotr and Dominic were easy to spot.

'There are no other boats, and I can't see anyone else on the pier. Either they're abandoning the rest of them, or they're dead already.'

'Who's missing?' Marianne demanded when they told her what they'd seen.

'Don't shout at me, Marianne,' Georgie protested, 'it's not my fault. I've had to go round everybody again to make sure. Some have only just come back, others have gone...'

'Just bloody tell me!'

She wiped away tears of frustration and fear and tried to focus on her paperwork. The words were swirling in the miserably weak light from her shitty torch. 'Here, I made a list.'

Marianne scanned the names. 'I don't believe David's bailed on us, nor Richard. As for the rest of them, it reads like a who's who of arseholes. Piotr, Dominic...'

'Never trust a fucking politician,' Gary pointlessly said.

'Mihai, Dr Ahmad, Chapman, Stan, Damien... bunch of fuckers. And Allison! Jesus Christ, I thought better of her.'

'They probably held a knife to her throat,' Orla said, jumping to the kid's defence.

'You make it sound like a shitty movie.'

'Have you looked outside recently? There are dead people walking the streets, London's on fire, and half the cast's been stranded. I'd have paid good money to watch something like this back in the day.'

'I tried to tell you most of the food hadn't made it over here,' Gary said. He was seething. 'You didn't bloody listen to me. They're absolute cunts, the lot of them. How long do you think they'd been planning this? It wasn't a spur of the moment decision, I can tell you that much.'

'So, what now?' Marianne asked, looking at the faces gathered around her.

'You make it sound like we still have options,' Orla said. 'Way I see it, we're stuck. The only thing we can do is try and sit this out, see if we can make it through the winter.'

Gary shook his head. 'What, with hundreds of thousands of dead bodies outside, most of our supplies stolen, and the streets burning around us?'

'Yes,' Ruth said, agreeing with Orla. 'There's no alternative.'

'This building can take it,' Georgie said. 'I'm just not sure if we can. Not all of us, anyway.'

'Three hundred people,' Marianne said. 'Christ, we'll be at each other's throats within a couple of weeks, trapped here. Never mind the dead outside, the living inside will be a bigger problem.'

'Just stop arguing!' Selena yelled, silencing all the bickering. 'What's the matter with you lot? No point complaining about how shit things are, we've just got to get on with it. Kath's dead, Lynette's dead, Sam's gone, Vicky's gone, David's gone... I'm running out of people to lose.'

'Where are we going?'

No answer. Allison asked again.

'Will someone just tell me where we're going. When are we going to stop so I can go back for the others?'

'We're not going back,' Piotr told her. 'Just count yourself lucky you're still alive. If we had someone else who knew how to drive this thing, you wouldn't be here.'

'We have to go back... I'll turn the boat around if I have to and—'

'And I'll throw you over the side if you do. You got us away, that's all we needed you for. Stop cooperating and you're history, understand?'

Allison wiped her eyes and concentrated on the water ahead.

'Go easy on her,' Dominic said. He moved closer and put his hand on Allison's shoulder. She recoiled from his touch. 'You're a sensible girl, Allison, I know you are. I know you won't do anything stupid. You've been offered a real opportunity here, we all have, so don't blow it.'

She wanted to fight back. She wanted to argue or change course or even crash the bloody boat and send them all to the bottom of the river, her included. But she didn't. She forced herself to try and stay focused and not take risks. She knew that being seen to cooperate meant she'd have a chance of returning to the Tower later, though she feared what she'd find if she ever made it back.

Dominic left the bridge and walked the length of the clipper to speak to Mihai. 'Are we good?' he asked.

'Pretty good,' Mihai said. 'We've got enough stuff to keep us going for a decent time. We'll run out of fuel before we run out of food.'

Dominic was impressed. 'I know it's not an ideal situation, and we've all had to make some difficult choices that don't sit well, but you've done a great job here, Mihai. The way you got everything organised at short notice, and how you got it all stashed away down here without arousing suspicion or causing panic... we're all indebted to you.'

Mihai was embarrassed, not used to such praise. 'I can't take all the credit,' he said. 'I had help. Tony's been great.'

At the stern of the boat, Tony stopped work and looked up. He'd been repacking a pile of supplies that had come loose since they'd been on the water. He winked at Mihai and Dominic. 'Pleasure, boss,' he said. 'All too happy to help. You never know what's out there these days, do you?'

47

The argument raging in John Kennedy House was loud enough to attract the dead. Sam was pacing the room. 'We've been through this already. There's no way of going back, and there's no point.'

Vicky despaired. 'No point? There are three hundred people over there, Sam. Is that your definition of no point? Jesus Christ, there might not even be another three hundred people left alive in the bloody country.'

'I get that, I really do, but from where I'm standing it looks impossible.'

'From where you're standing? Yeah, that just about sums you up, Sam. It's all about you and what you're thinking. You don't give a shit about anybody else.'

'If that was true, I'd have left you and Selena in Trafalgar Square to die all those weeks ago. My point is not that you shouldn't help the folks over there, it's that you physically can't. Even if you managed to get back, the only difference you'd make is that there'd be three hundred and one people at risk instead of three hundred.'

'I don't accept that.'

'And now it's all about *your* perspective. Jesus, after what you told me about your health, I think you're mad to want even be thinking about going back.'

Vicky was incensed. 'How dare you? That's got nothing to do with you. If anything, it gives me more of a reason to try and help. I've got less to lose than the people stuck over there.'

'All the more reason not to just throw everything away.'

'You really don't get it, do you, you self-obsessed little gobshite.'

'*I'm* a gobshite?'

Brian entered the flat. 'What the hell's going on? You woke me up.'

'Sorry to interrupt your beauty sleep, Brian, but there are people dying out there,' Vicky said.

'Vicky's friends are in trouble,' Eric explained, filling in the blanks. 'She wants to help.'

'Understandable. I heard the boom.'

'And I'm just trying to get it through to her that there's no way of helping, and probably no point,' Sam said. 'They're surrounded by creeping undead, and half of north London will have been razed to the ground by morning. There's no way.'

'But I can't just sit here and do nothing,' Vicky said. They were going around in circles. She slumped onto the sofa and held her head in her hands.

Brian sat down next to her. 'I take it there's nowhere safe for them to go on the north bank?'

'They're in the Tower of London.'

'I doubt there's anywhere safer. Couldn't say whether it would be safe enough though.'

'I've been through all the other options I can think of. They're pretty much surrounded. The only way they can travel is this way, but the bridges are blocked, and it looks like they've lost their only decent boat. Unless you're about to tell me that you've got a fleet of ships moored on the river that you're able to skipper, I don't know what they're going to do.'

'Nope, afraid not,' Brian said, and he folded his arms and sat back. 'But there are other ways of getting across the Thames.'

'There are other bridges, sure,' Sam said, 'but how do you get to them once you're across? They're surrounded, victims of their own success. They've done such a good job of keeping the dead out, that they've backed themselves into a corner. We'd struggle to get to them, and they can't get out.'

'That was one of your reasons for not signing up, I recall.'

'Absolutely, and that's proved to be a justified concern.'

'There's no need to be so bloody smug about it,' Vicky snapped, unimpressed. She went to leave the room, but Brian stopped her.

'There is another way,' he said. 'I wasn't talking about other bridges.'

'He has a helicopter on the roof.' Eric laughed at his own joke. No one else did.

'Ever heard of the Thames Tunnel?'

Vicky shook her head. 'I've heard it all now. You want us to dig under the Thames and get them out that way?'

Brian ignored her cynicism. 'Do you know anything about the history of this area? The Thames Tunnel was the first tunnel in the world to be constructed under a navigable river, as I recall. If I remember correctly, Marc Brunel started the work, before handing over to his son, Isambard Kingdom Brunel. You've heard of him, surely?'

'Of course,' Sam said, indignant.

'So, the tunnel took the best part of twenty years to complete, and it was something of a tourist attraction by all accounts. It was initially a pedestrian route, but eventually became a railway tunnel.'

'Get to the point,' Vicky said.'

Brian continued at his own pace. 'I went down into the tunnel once, must have been more than ten years ago now. They let the public have access while they were doing repair work.'

She began to realise the implications. 'You're saying it's still open?'

'Very much so. Until everything ground to a halt a few months ago, the London overground railway ran through it.'

'And we could walk it?'

'Like I said, it was originally designed for pedestrian use. Can't imagine it'll be very pleasant down there but hey, is there anywhere that's not pretty grim these days?'

'How do we get to it?'

'It's right here. That's why I mentioned it. Canada Water station is your best bet. Half a mile from here.'

'And where does it come out on the other bank?'

'Wapping.'

Sam remained unconvinced. 'You need to think about this sensibly, Vic.'

'I'll bring them back the same way. There's more than enough space around here.'

'We don't want any trouble,' Brian said, sounding nervous.

'No one does. I'll keep them out of your way. Look, we were never the ones who wanted to wage a war against the dead, that was jerks like Piotr. Now that him and Dominic are out of the way, all we need to do is shut up, keep our heads down, and stay safe for a couple of months longer.'

Sam stared at her. 'I'll come with you.'

Vicky was confused. 'What, after all the shit you've just been giving me? I don't need your help.'

'I think you need whatever help you can get.'

'How do I know you won't change your mind again once we get over there?'

'I won't, I promise. Thing is, you were talking about risking your neck for nothing before, but this is different. If what Brian said is right, now you're going to risk your neck for *something*. You have a viable plan in mind. For the record, I still think it's a bad idea, but there are good people over there who look like they've been screwed over. Dave, Sanjay, that little bastard Omar... I'm sure I'll end up regretting this, but I'll give it a shot.'

It was still dark when four of them set out for Canada Water station. To Sam and Vicky's surprise, both Eric and Joanne volunteered to make the trip too. She'd had to fight to get to Surrey Quays early days, and Joanne admitted to having struggled with the guilt of living in relative comfort since then when there had clearly been so much suffering on the north bank. A there-and-bank trip to help the folks on the other side of the river felt like the very least she could do. Eric, on the other hand... well, he just wanted a little adventure. After all, his holiday fortnight hadn't been all he'd expected and he wasn't one to sit around on his hands. 'I had really set my heart on seeing the sights around the Tower, might not have another chance,' he told Vicky. He'd drawn up a wish-list before leaving Quebec. Big Ben, St Pauls, the London Eye, the Shard... all the usual tourist traps. The Tower of London was on the list too. 'Might as well start there,' he'd said.

Many of the dead on this side of the river continued to be distracted by the fires in the distance, reducing the number of them left milling around the immediate neighbourhood. The dark provided more cover than expected, and though the group reached Canada Water station with ease, they agreed to take a chance and stay aboveground further through to Rotherhithe, limiting the distance they'd be below the surface. They travelled light, though Eric had a rucksack twice the size of the anyone else's. He had food, a first aid kit, extra clothes, his fireworks to cause distractions if needs be... 'Don't be asking me to carry any of that for you because it's getting heavy,' Sam warned.

'I haven't been in as many fights as you three,' Eric told him. 'I didn't know what I should bring.'

'You do know we're walking into a warzone, right?' Joanne said. 'This isn't a bloody sightseeing trip.'

They were relieved when they reached the station at Rotherhithe. It was reassuringly small, and Joanne knew it well. 'What's the layout?' Vicky asked as the four of them crouched behind a car on the opposite side of the road, scoping it out.

'Pretty straightforward. One line, stairs down onto the platform,' she whispered. 'Then nothing but black until we get to the other side of the river.'

'Are there going to be dead people down there?' Eric asked. His phrasing made him sound naïve, almost child-like. He had a kitchen knife gripped tight in his sweaty hand.

'Without doubt,' Sam said. 'Shouldn't be too many, though. I'm sure some will have wandered down onto the tracks, but not in huge numbers. That is, not unless there's been a derailment, a train trapped down there or something like that.'

Vicky remembered the hell she'd faced in Fenchurch Street station and wondered if they were about to walk into something equally horrific. She kept her mouth shut. No sense frightening the others unnecessarily. It wasn't like they had any choice.

Amongst the treasure trove of junk Eric had brought with him were a few useful items. The head torches he handed around were a blessing. Although their lights would make it harder for them to stay out of sight underground, the fact they'd be able to see what they were facing down there, hands free, made it a risk worth taking. They switched them on once they'd slipped into the ruins of the station and were out of view.

The quiet inside the building was welcome – no noise likely meant no wandering bodies. The interior was damp and the smell of smoke that permeated everything outside was noticeably absent here. Weeds had sprouted through cracks, and Vicky thought that in time it would likely become completely overgrown, perhaps impassable. The same would also be true of the tunnel under the river they were about to try and walk through... was it watertight, or had it already been similarly damaged? In his impromptu history lesson, Brian had said the tunnel was two hundred years old, but without anyone maintaining it, how long before it fell into disrepair?

They moved in a line through the small ticket hall and down a stationary escalator to a mezzanine level where a lone corpse was trapped. It staggered back and forth in a scrap of space between a vending machine and some discarded cleaning equipment, appearing visibly exhausted yet moving unceasingly. Assuming they were the first people to come through here, it was likely this lone cadaver had been traversing the same metre of space all day, every day, for months since it had died. Vicky put her crowbar through its skull.

Joanne leant over the side of the staircase, the light from her torch reaching all the way down to the platform. She paused, waiting to see if the bright circle drew any unwelcome figures out from long-held hiding places then carried on once she was satisfied the platform was empty.

Sam climbed down onto the tracks and scanned the walls until he found a direction marker. 'Looks the same both ways,' he said. 'Don't want to end up walking back towards Canada Water by mistake.' The dark beyond the reach of their torches was so complete he felt it might swallow them up and never spit them out again.

The main tunnel split into two smaller tunnels, one set of tracks in each. That the four of them had already found themselves with half the space they expected added to their claustrophobic unease. The atmosphere was different again this deep, musty and stale, and sound echoed endlessly, noises appearing to run away along the tunnel in both directions, no matter how slight. It was impossible to stay quiet. Vicky sipped her cough medicine, fearing the effect of a coughing fit down here. She was getting near the bottom of the bottle. Sam walked alongside her. 'What are we walking into, Vic?' he whispered.

'Christ alone knows.'

'You said parts of Wapping have been cleared?'

'Yes, but not down by the river. To be honest, it's all academic. I reckon the dead are going to be everywhere by now.'

49

The hotel the group had come to loathe was on the verge of collapse. It had been burning all night, and its lower levels were now so badly damaged that the building was struggling to support its own weight. It groaned and shook. Windows shattered and showered the dead below with shards of glass. A lump of masonry sheered away from one corner of the building and hit the deck, crushing several of them. Others collided with the concrete block then shuffled around and carried on, oblivious. In the street below, a vast column of burning bodies now stretched along the full length of St Katharine's Way, efficiently transferring the fire from the hotel to other nearby buildings.

When he heard the building collapse, Sanjay returned to the battlements to assess the damage. It had been hours since any of them had been outside, and it was hard to make sense of the view. The sun hadn't yet started to rise, and the ever-changing light from the flames made every detail that much harder to discern. Familiar landmarks had been erased, either obscured by smoke or destroyed by fire, and lines of well-established trees had been reduced to rows of blackened stumps. He could see patterns of movement where there had been empty spaces before; eddies and flows where huge herds of corpses had filled the base, continually staggering forward for as long as they could until they caught fire and were charred then blackened and finally reduced to ash.

From his limited vantage point, Sanjay was only aware of a fraction of the problem now facing the group. With the rest of the north bank all but completely silent, the aftereffects of the chaos here could be seen and heard for miles in every direction. The Tower of London was completely cut off.

Until now, the barriers to the west and north of the Tower had held strong. Massive accumulations of meaty sludge had formed in the shadows of the group's blockades nearest the Monument to the Great Fire of London, but the sheer number of corpses allowed an uneasy status quo to be maintained; those already trapped here, compressed and compacted in place over weeks and months, had prevented more from getting close. But the unexpected bursts of light and thunderous noise had changed all that. Many more were on their way, clambering over the liquifying remains of those that had come before, threatening to scale the barriers.

For months, the section of raised railway line between Fenchurch Street Station and Limehouse had been enough to prevent any large-scale incursion, but many small-scale problems were combining to expose major weaknesses. Smouldering cadavers had become trapped under the arches below the tracks and had continued to burn, setting light to the vehicles and piles of rubbish that had been wedged into the gaps there months earlier. There was no malice or intent, no design to the actions of the undead, but in these confined spaces, fuelled by the dry wind whipping through the arches, the fires burned like blast furnaces. Cars and trucks were reduced to shells, and enough of the packing around them was destroyed to allow unfettered access to slothful waves of corpses. In places, the severity of the fire damage caused sections of the two-hundred-year-old structure supporting the railway line to collapse.

From Sanjay's position they appeared to be surrounded by a curtain of flames on all sides but the river now. However, it was the situation over to the east that remained most dangerous of all. There was hardly anything left to hold back the tides. It had become a sort of pilgrimage as millions of the dead converged on the very last remnants of the living.

In contrast to Sanjay's limited perspective from the Tower, the penthouse apartment where David and Chapman had holed up afforded them a spectacular view that clearly showed the scale and speed of north London's demise. Below them, they watched the phantasmic glow of the fires, the continuous flow of the dead, and the end of whatever safety they had once perceived David rested his head against the window and watched. 'Not a bad place to spend your final hours, I suppose,' Chapman said.

'Final hours? You're giving up that easy, are you?'

'Couple of weeks ago I wouldn't, but I'm not so sure now. I'm worn out, mate. Feels like the harder I try, the less I succeed.'

'You're just sore because you're stuck up here with me while your mates did a runner in the boat you helped bring back.'

'We don't know for sure it was Dominic and Piotr we saw. We only saw the boat for a couple of seconds, and we're so high up here that—'

'Oh, come on, don't be soft. Who else do you think it was? It had to be them. There are very few people here with the kind of shitty, selfish qualities it takes to run out on everybody like that. You can bet they've taken most of the food with them, too.'

'Yeah, I know,' Chapman admitted.

'Ever get the feeling you've been had? They're so fucking arrogant,' David continued. 'They both took immediately to being dictators, telling everybody what to do and bigging up their great masterplans, but they were the first to run for the hills when it didn't work out, fuck everyone else. Fuckers. You backed the wrong horses.'

'Oh, for Christ's sake, shut up. I get it. It's not the first time I've fucked up, and it probably won't be the last.'

David wasn't so sure. 'Given the circumstances, I think it might well be.'

In a bedroom adjacent, David found a clock on the wall that was still working. It was coming up to five. 'I'm trying to work out when the sun will come up. Going to be another couple of hours yet.'

'Don't forget to add another hour on. The clocks used to go back at the end of October, remember. Why, are you planning on going somewhere?'

'Yep.'

'Where?'

'Anywhere.'

'You're not going to wait it out up here?'

'If it comes down to a choice between going back out there or sitting up here at the top of this building waiting to be burned alive, I'll take my chances outside. I'm going to try and get back to the Tower. That's where the rest of them will be.'

'If any of them are still alive.'

50

'We live in a world full of frigging zombies,' Joanne grumbled, 'but it's still the dark that scares me more than anything.'

They'd quickly reached the point where neither the beginning nor the end of the tunnel under the Thames was visible. Cut adrift, down here they were detached from absolutely anything that could anchor them in time and space. It was disorientating. Frightening. They hadn't been walking long, but it already felt endless.

Joanne had been right to be afraid.

The train tracks, already difficult to walk along, were frequently covered in rippling carpets of vermin. They regularly saw skeletons that had been stripped of meat, gnawed clean. The whiteness of bone was stark against the muck and murk of everything else.

'It's always what you can't see that scares you most,' Vicky agreed. She was walking alone up ahead of the others, and Sam wondered whether she was talking about the state of the world or the state of her health. The cruelty of her cancer trumped everything else. It had affected him more than he'd told her. *Imagine*, he thought, *surviving this far but knowing all the effort you put in counts for nothing. Imagine living through this knowing it doesn't matter how hard you fight, because your body's tearing itself apart from the inside out.* He wouldn't wish a fate like that on his worst enemy.

Vicky stopped suddenly. The others bunched up close behind her.

Bodies.

'Where the hell are they coming from all of a sudden?' Sam

said. The first few undead had just staggered into the limited range of their torches. Christ, they looked more terrifying than ever down here, given their claustrophobic surroundings and the creatures' nightmarish appearance, shadowed in the stark light. They looked as horrific as ever, but down here they'd been protected, and there was something about their expressions that was recognisably sentient: just as monstrous, but undoubtably still human. It was ghastly, far more terrible than the vacant, clearly dead beings aboveground. They frequently tripped on the tracks, and whilst that might have made them seem less of a threat, the unpredictability of their movements only increased Sam's unease.

'Kill them, he said.'

Eric sounded nervous. 'What, all of them?'

He turned on him fast. 'Yes, kill all of them.'

Weapons raised, the four of them waded into the oncoming crowd and began hacking, slicing, and stabbing. Bringing up the rear, Eric was as unsure as he'd expected to be. He hadn't been in a position like this before, and his arms and legs felt heavy, almost like he was mired in a nightmare, unable to move. Vicky, Sam, and Joanne were dealing with most of the corpses before they got anywhere near him, but several slipped past.

Now or never.

He braced himself and started to hack at the wave of death coming towards him, expecting the dead to attack him with strength and energy. It surprised him how little resistance they offered, how easily they went down. He was already soaked with his sweat and their stale blood and other discharges, and the sounds and the smell turned his stomach. He could think of a thousand reasons why he wanted to stop... but he didn't. He'd taken the easy option for too long, hiding away in John Kennedy House and watching the rest of the world suffer. It was time for him to make some effort.

A handful of kills and Eric found a rhythm and certainty to his actions, a confidence the likes of which he hadn't felt in a long time.

They must have got rid of more than a hundred of the damn things between them. Time and distance had become even more indistinct as they'd fought their way along the line. It was a massive relief when the bodies dried up. 'I'm exhausted,' Eric said. Vicky didn't have the heart to tell him that what they'd just battled through was likely a mere fraction of what they'd be facing when they got back up to the surface. 'Where did they all come from?'

'There's something up ahead,' Sam said. 'Looks like a train.'

'Crashed?' Vicky asked.

'Not sure,' he said.

'It could be that we're at the station,' Joanne said.

'Already?'

'Yes. These trains were pretty long.'

Vicky wasn't convinced. 'So, where's the platform? Shouldn't we be able to see the way out by now?'

'Not necessarily. The platforms at Wapping are shorter than the trains. Sounds crazy, I know, but if you wanted to get off here, you had to be in one of the first four carriages.'

'You sound like Brian,' Eric said.

'No, I sound like someone who got caught out a couple of times and ended up where they didn't want to be. I think this is just the back end of the train. We should be okay. We just need to carry on along the tracks.'

Eric shone his torch up at the windows of the train's rear carriage, then stumbled back with surprise when a remarkably well-preserved cadaver slammed against it. One attracted another, then another until the glass the entire length of the carriage was packed with dead faces, leaden hands slapping against the windows. Eric was on his backside on the tracks. 'What the fuck, man?'

Vicky helped him up. 'You have to understand, this isn't going to be like Surrey Quays. The bodies over here have been riled up. They're not the placid, easily tricked fuckers that you're used to.

Understand?'

'I get it, I really do. But also, I don't get it. If they're all still stuck on this train, where did the things we were just fighting come from?'

'Good question,' Joanne said, and she went on ahead. She returned less than a minute later. 'There's a problem. There's a section of track at the end of the platform that's open and doesn't have a roof.'

'So?'

'So, the outside has got inside. Look.'

They followed her along the side of the train, then stopped again.

'What the hell is this?' Eric asked, trying to make sense of an enormous mound of chaos piled up in front of them. It was impossible to work out exactly what had happened on the surface and when, but the implications for them getting out of the tunnel were clear. A garbage truck had dropped onto the track and landed on its roof, crushing part of the front of the train. Much of the truck was barely visible because, over the weeks and months following the crash, detritus from the outside world had fallen through the gap and landed on top. A mountain of accumulated debris now prevented them from going any further along the tunnel. Lumps of masonry, crushed vehicles, more corpses than they could count... the pile-up (pile-down?) had occurred in such a way as to completely block the track and any access to the platform. It had formed a dividing wall that almost reached the roof of the tunnel.

'So that's where they came from,' Eric said, still preoccupied with the dead. 'They fell down here.'

'How the hell are we going to get past this?' Sam asked.

'Up and over?' Vicky suggested. 'Looks like there's a bit of a gap up top.'

He started to climb, but the rubble and wreckage immediately began shifting under his weight and he jumped down before he caused a landslide. He tried to look for another route but was distracted by the head and one arm of a corpse. It reached out for him, despite its torso and legs having been crushed paper-thin under an enormous block of concrete. The dead at the lower levels of the pile had been squashed to a pulp, but those that had fallen later had fared somewhat better. The nearer to the roof, the more active they appeared. Up towards the summit of the heap, jaws continued to grind, tongues still lolled, fingers twitched, eyes followed movement... it was the single most disgusting thing Sam had ever seen. A mountain of gore. He half expected it to get up and come at him like something out of a video game boss level.

'We could wait and see if the light improves and try and dig our way out,' Joanne suggested.

'We can't afford to wait,' Vicky said. 'There'll be nothing left up there if we leave it much longer.'

'Just go through the train,' Eric said. 'All that junk is covering the track, but the other side of the train is clear. We can use it to get through to the platform, can't we?'

He was right. Sam looked up at the carriage he was level with. 'Give me a bunk up.'

'With your dodgy leg?' Vicky said. 'No, I'll do it.'

Eric leant back against the train and cupped his hands. The doors of the overground train were smooth with little to grip on to, but Vicky was able to shove her crowbar between the two sides of the sliding door and get a hold. She forced them apart, grunting with effort to make the gap big enough, then squeezed her head and shoulders through. She ignored the first few dead passengers that were already showing an interest, pulled herself up, and pushed the doors apart.

'Keep out of the way, Vic,' Sam shouted from down on the track, and she did as he said, switching off her light and curling up into a ball on the train, tucking herself under a seat. He called the corpses to attention, whistling and hammering on the side of the train. Vicky remained completely still as bodies began streaming past her to get closer to the noise. Oblivious to the drop, they fell heavily onto the track, landing with thud after thud after wet thud, splitting open like sacks of rotten fruit.

And they kept coming.

Sam couldn't work out why there were so many of the damn things in this specific carriage. It hadn't looked particularly crowded from the outside. And then he remembered: *overground, not underground.* He cursed himself for not paying more attention to Brian. He'd told them the trains here were on the overground line, not the Tube. And unlike the iconic compartmentalised trains that used to criss-cross beneath the capital, the inside of the train here at Wapping station was continuous and labyrinthine, like the innards of a worm.

Between them, Eric, Sam, and Joanne dragged the fallen corpses out of the way, slicing or smashing the heads of those that continued moving after they'd hit the deck. They had little weight to them now, just movement and ferocity. This second sudden flurry of violence made Sam feel unexpectedly nervous. *We've not even got onto the north bank yet...* He didn't feel match fit. If he was honest, he didn't feel fit at all.

Eric was struggling too. He kicked out at one corpse that had snagged his ankle. He caught it square in the face but then tripped over the rails as he tried to shake it off. He booted it repeatedly until it finally let go and stopped fighting. 'Fucking things... horrible fucking things...' But all his whining did was make more of them scuttle towards him like broken spiders.

They'd stopped falling from the train now, all passengers finally disembarking almost three months after their final journeys had begun. Aware that the movement around her had stopped at last, Vicky picked herself up. 'That's it, I think,' she shouted down to the others, and she switched her torch back on.

There was one more corpse left on the train with her.

It wasn't moving; was it stuck? Trapped on something, clothing caught in an automatic door, something like that? For half a second, she wondered if it might be someone from the Monument base who'd come down here to see what all the noise was about. She knew how ridiculous an idea that was, but what was the alternative? Confused, she walked towards the figure. It was a woman, similar height and build to her, and there was no question, from the extent of her decay, that she'd been dead for as long as all the others. And yet, she didn't react like most of them did. She remained almost completely still, swaying slightly but not yet attacking. Vicky was confused more than concerned. She'd seen others hesitating in a similar way before, but this woman was the most self-restrained of all. She'd been cocooned from the rest of the world here on the train. In the same way her body had been protected from the ravages of the endless battles and crushes outside, had her brain, too, suffered less damage? Had she simply stopped functioning, or was she actually demonstrating a modicum of control? Vicky took another step towards the dead woman, and she swore the corpse visibly reacted. It was slight, and it might have been nothing more than a clumsy twitch or spasm, but Vicky was sure she'd shuffled back a step.

Sam put his hand on Vicky's shoulder and scared the shit out of her. 'Fuck's sake,' she cursed, turning on him. 'What the hell are you doing?'

'I could ask you the same question.'

She gestured towards the dead woman. 'Have you seen anything like this before?'

'I have, as it happens.'

'And?'

'And she'll click into gear in a second and go for you. Watch.'

He walked right up to the corpse, his light burning brightly into what was left of her face. Appearing almost on a time delay, she lifted her clouded eyes to look at him, waited for a moment as if she was considering her limited options, then attacked. He was ready for it. He caught her by the throat, stabbed her through the temple, then dropped her onto the nearest seat, her head resting against the window as if she'd fallen asleep on the morning commute.

Sam helped Joanne and Eric up from the tracks. All aboard,

they moved through a couple more carriages until they reached one that was level with the platform. Vicky prised open the doors and they emerged into relative calm. The momentary space and quiet was welcome. 'We all good?'

Eric looked traumatised. He was panting, soaked with sweat, and covered in more blood and gore than the rest of them combined. His eyes were wide, his face muck-spattered. 'I look the part now, yes?'

'You do. You sure you're okay?'

'I'm good.'

'The exit's clear, thank Christ,' Joanne said. The way out had escaped the cave-in that had blocked the tracks. She led them along the platform to the foot of a staircase.

Sam was surprised to see how high it climbed, well beyond the reach of their torches. He tapped the blade of his knife against the metal handrail and listened for any response. The clanging noise echoed up and down, but there was little reaction they could hear. He was about to start climbing but Eric held him back.

'It's going to be bad up top, isn't it?'

'I'm not gonna lie to you, Eric, it's going to be fucking awful.'

'What do we do when we get out there?'

'It's not the kind of thing you can plan for, mate. Just take your time and don't do anything stupid.'

'What, like leaving a perfectly comfortable and safe flat and walking into a place filled with zombies and fire?'

Sam laughed. 'Yeah, exactly that. Just remember, less is more out there. You want to blend in, not stick out.'

'I've been thinking,' Joanne said, 'we should try and stick to the river as best we can. We might even be able to keep off the streets altogether if the tide's in our favour.'

'Makes sense,' Vicky agreed. 'If there is anyone left alive they'll likely be holed-up in the Tower, and that's right on the Thames.'

Sam nodded. 'Okay. So, if we get split up for any reason, just stay as close to the water as you can and keep moving west.'

'Got it,' Eric said.

'And be careful. Remember we need to come back the same way, hopefully with another couple hundred folks. Don't do anything that's going to lead the dead back here, otherwise we'll never get back to the tunnel.'

51

The world they emerged into was unrecognisable. Whatever they'd imagined it would be like aboveground, the hellish reality they found was infinitely worse. They paused inside the entrance to Wapping station, reluctant to leave the shelter of the dilapidated building. Hordes of cadavers packed the street outside, filing along in unspoken unison, shoulder to slouched shoulder. They'd never seen the dead on the move in such numbers as this before.

'I'll go and have a look. See what our options are,' Sam said.

He'd anticipated breaking into a decent height building to get a better view of the area, but as soon as he'd slipped outside he realised that wasn't going to happen. The sheer volume of putrid flesh clogging Wapping High Street was such that he was immediately trapped, pinned against the outside wall of the station. Sam had spent more time in amongst the dead than most, but the amount of movement out here today made his legs weaken. Though the sun hadn't yet risen, and the smoke hid as much as the flames illuminated, he could see enough to appreciate that this was a storm surge of death. He knew that, as soon as he stepped out into the flow, he'd be swept away, unable to get back.

Vicky pulled him back into the station. 'I did think you were being a bit optimistic, talking about "options," plural. Keep going or turn back, those are our only choices.'

'As bad as you thought?' Eric asked.

'Worse,' Sam replied.

'So do we turn back?'

'Is that what you want?'

'No, I want to keep going. But if it's so bad out there, are we going to make it?'

'I don't know.'

'We have to try though?'

'Yep, we have to try,' Vicky said. 'We've come this far. Getting people to the tunnel is the only way I can see of getting them out of danger.'

'How far is it?'

'The Tower's about a mile and a half along the river,' Joanne said.

Vicky was ready to move. Sam stopped her. 'Listen, once we get out there, we're committed. We keep going at all costs. Stop and they'll notice you're different, and if they turn on you, you're screwed.'

'I know the area. I'll go up front,' Joanne said.

'Thanks. Keep your torches switched on. It's the only way we'll be able to see each other.'

'I'll stay as close to the left side of the road as I can,' Joanne said. 'That'll give us the best chance of getting down to the riverbank.'

And before she could talk herself out of it, she slipped out of the shadows and was swallowed up by the madness. Eric hesitated. With brittle legs and atrophied muscles, the clumsiness of the cadavers meant their pace changed constantly, impossible to predict. They didn't move in straight lines, rather they ambled, guided by the frontages of buildings on either side of the road and kept in check by each other. He looked back for reassurance and Vicky leant forward and whispered, 'Don't overthink it, just let yourself go.'

And he did. Knocked off balance, he collided with an abandoned car, the rebound keeping him upright. He looked up; he'd lost sight of Joanne already.

Vicky was appalled by the total devastation all around her. This had been a respectable, desirable neighbourhood where even the pokiest flats had cost as much as the largest houses in other parts of the country. Today, it was an uninhabitable, germ-infested ruin.

Dirty smoke hung in the air like fog, a ground-level thunderstorm. Above the crowds, the belly of the rolling clouds was illuminated by the fires they were moving towards. Vicky might have thought this was the apocalypse, had she not already lived through that, last September. But was this the next stage? The beginning of the end of the end? Part of her wished she'd never come out here, that she'd stayed at Surrey Quays, but it was pointless dwelling on that now. She couldn't do anything but keep going because the dead were pushing against her from all sides. It was sobering to think that there were likely many, many more behind her than ahead. The way so many of them willingly marched towards the inferno around the Tower of London made this endless procession feel almost Biblical. It was a cliché, but it truly felt as if they were marching towards the gates of Hell.

The dead were preoccupied with the maelstrom up ahead, and though the pinprick lights from their torches made it easier for the four of them to keep track of each other, here at the back, Sam was struggling to keep everyone in view. He'd spot Joanne, only to lose sight of Vicky, only to then find Vicky again but lose track of Eric. And now he'd lost all three of them. All he could see from his position was the backs of hundreds of heads, all indistinguishable from one another. He'd told the others to blend in and they'd done exactly as he'd said.

At the beginning of this nightmare, Sam had made a habit of walking among the dead and studying their behaviours, but the dumb, slothful creatures he'd walked alongside back then were nothing like the vile, unpredictable, wretched things that surrounded him today. A short distance ahead, one of them became snagged on the wing mirror of a parked car, the protrusion wedged in its hollow chest cavity. The grotesque figures immediately behind lashed out in anger, tearing chunks of rotten flesh from the cadaver in their way. There used to be a passive listlessness about the dead, but it had been replaced with unbridled aggression. Stuck behind the hold-up, Sam cursed himself. He was boxed in but couldn't risk doing anything that might mark him out as different. Christ, he'd been quick to lecture the others, but this was harder than he'd imagined. He already felt like he'd been out here forever, but he'd hardly moved any distance from the station. For fuck's sake, did they seriously expect they'd be able to do anything useful here? Five minutes in and he'd already fucked up. He'd lost sight of the rest of them, no sign of their torches anywhere. It was beginning to look like their well-intentioned rescue mission would end up a poorly conceived mass suicide attempt.

The dead shuffled forward again. Finally free to move, Sam dropped his head and went with the flow. He'd just managed to get up speed when a hand grabbed his arm and yanked him away to the left. It was the others, waiting for him in a side alley. 'You're going to have to do better than that,' Vicky hissed at him. 'Focus!'

He shook his head, angry for letting himself become distracted. He thought he'd seen it all over the last few months, but this place was something else. He didn't see how they could possibly come through it.

'What now?' Eric asked.

Joanne gestured down the alleyway. 'River's down here. We can climb down onto the banks, see how far we can get.'

They followed her towards the water. A short flight of steps led down onto the muddy riverbank, the tide having only recently gone out. The mud sucked at their feet, but the danger presented by the water and the unpredictable tide was insignificant in comparison to what they'd just escaped up on the streets. They were still far enough away not to be able to make out any level of detail, but they'd already seen enough. Every building they could see near to the Tower was ablaze. As they watched, the heart of the city crumbled further into ash, and all around them, the dead continued their tireless advance towards the firestorm.

52

The apartment building was rapidly filling with smoke. The horseshoe-shaped block next door had gone up in flames with sobering speed a short time earlier. David and Chapman had still been readying themselves to head back out onto the death-filled streets when an explosion had reduced half of the neighbouring block to rubble, forcing their hand. Their building had been damaged in the blast and was beginning to burn, the flames devouring the contents of individual apartments with an unstoppable voracity. St Katharine's Docks was crumbling around them.

David held on to the back of Chapman's belt as they descended into the smoke-filled gloom. They'd taken a fire escape at the far end of the building, Chapman feeling his way along with one hand, his machete gripped tight in the other. Both men had covered their faces with strips of cloth soaked with the last dribbles of water from bottles they'd found in the upstairs flat. It was the only protection they had. That the coverings limited their vision didn't matter; they couldn't see anything anyway. On the lower levels of the building, the smoke had become thick, impenetrable, a poisonous black wall. When he couldn't go any further down, Chapman felt his way along for a door and kicked it open. The two men fell out into the open, gasping into their face coverings, doing all they could not to cough. For now, the dead were distracted, but it remained unnaturally quiet outside and they knew that the noise would give away their location in a heartbeat.

The Thames Path – a wide pedestrian footway that wound along the banks of this side of the river – was filled with death, like everywhere else. Chapman had hoped it would be quieter, a way of bypassing the bulk of the corpses that filled St Katharine's Way and other roads, but it looked even more congested, if anything. Every route back towards the Tower appeared equally impassable. There was simply no way through that wasn't obstructed by fire, rubble, or thousands of dead Londoners.

As if to make a point about the precariousness of their situation, an apartment on the top floor of the building directly ahead of them exploded outward. Rubble and broken glass showered the ground below, crushing and slicing those corpses caught underneath. Even after all he'd seen and done, Chapman was still caught out by the bizarre behaviours of the dead: the danger was less of a concern than the distraction. The sudden noise and movement caused a surge towards the unsound building.

'We don't belong in this world anymore,' Chapman said.

'Yes, we do,' David said, removing his mouth covering to speak, then immediately putting it back again, gasping for filtered air.

'So, what now?'

'Head for the river. There are boats down here. I saw them from the apartment. We'll head up towards the Tower first... see if anyone's left alive. If not, we sail away into the sunrise together.'

'Sounds shit.'

'I know. You and me, stuck on a boat together. It doesn't sound at all good, does it?'

They began to move, going against the flow of dead pedestrians, dissolving into the shadows and edging around buildings to minimise the chance of being noticed, moderating their speed. Chapman struggled not to quicken his pace as they quick-stepped around more fallen debris. It felt like it would barely take a breeze to bring any of these buildings crashing down on top of them.

They were at the junction with Wapping High Street, and though the number of corpses coming towards them was undiminished, for once this stretch of road was not lined with the kind of endless towering buildings they'd become used to. It gave them more options. Here, there was open space, a patch of parkland, and at the diagonally opposite corner of the park, an elevated, sloping footbridge that stretched out over the water to reach moorings in the Thames. The sky was finally beginning to lighten, and the drifting smoke shifted, allowing them to see all manner of craft on the water. Pleasure boats, a few little dinghies, rowing boats, narrowboats that would have looked more at home on canals; the water was full of possibilities.

'Go for it,' David said, nudging Chapman forward.

There was no time to debate. The two men slipped through a gap in the railings and raced across the long grass to reach the jetty. Surely they'd be able to get at least one of those boats moving? David had a little experience, and he'd heard that Allison had shown Chapman the basics... Christ, how difficult could it be?

There was a tall, open gate across the end of the walkway. When Chapman reached it and looked back, he saw that David was only halfway across. A sizeable number of corpses had peeled away from the main mass and were now lurching after them across the park. They were pouring through the numerous gaps in the low boundary wall designed to encourage the public to spend time here in pre-apocalypse days. More of them stumbled over a patch of debris where a vehicle had veered off the road, crashed through walls and railings, then dropped into the river. The wreck was long gone, but the damage it had caused allowed even more corpses to flood through. David thought he was about to be intercepted and swallowed up, but he reached the walkway just ahead of the nearest cadavers. Chapman slammed the gate as soon as he was through, then shut it on the latch and secured it with length of chain.

'All this shite going on and they still won't give up on us,' David said. 'It's the second Great Fire of London, for Christ's sake. You'd think they'd find that more interesting than two old blokes running for their lives.'

Chapman was offended. 'Old blokes? Fuck you, mate, I'm not

old. Anyway, it doesn't matter, they can't get to us now.'

And he was right. The gate held strong. The dead didn't have either the capacity or coordination to remove the chain.

Chapman went down to check the boats. David remained where he was, panting hard, protected by wrought iron railings taller than he was. This was the first time he could remember being able to face the dead head-on without concern. It might only have been a few hundred that had followed them into the park, but it felt like thousands. He stared into the nearest of the hideously decayed pack of faces that stared back at him. 'Beat you,' he said.

Enraged by his voice, the deluge pushed closer still. David stood his ground and watched as they crushed each other in their desperation to get to him. Many were smashed up against the gate whilst more lost their footing and were sent tumbling down either side of the high footbridge, falling heavily onto the muddy banks of the Thames below. They couldn't get anywhere near either of the two men.

'Are you going to come down and do something useful, or do I have to do all the work here?' Chapman shouted, unimpressed.

53

The tide was high. Some sections of the riverbank were well exposed, while other parts remained underwater. And when Vicky and the others were able to keep moving forward, the glue-like mud sucked their boots down, not wanting to let go. Finally, the sun was beginning to make its presence known. Vicky willed it to stay low a little longer still. The thought of dawn finally arriving made her feel exposed. It made her feel like time was running out.

The dead were everywhere, even down here where they struggled with the conditions as much as the living. Already unsteady, any wash of water swept them out of the way and out of existence. And those that showed a little more persistence frequently became bogged down in the glutenous mud. They were left stranded, sinking knee deep, only able to flail wildly at the group as they went past, waving their arms like the branches of trees in a storm. Vicky, Sam, Joanne, and Eric dealt with them with a tired indifference, barely even conscious of what they were doing.

They reached a cobbled slipway down to the water, overgrown with algae and weeds. Joanne stopped. From the bottom of the slope, she could see back up towards Wapping High Street where the roads were still congested with an unimaginable volume of death on the hoof. 'We're about halfway,' she said.

Eric was gasping for breath. 'We have all that to go again? Jeez. I thought we were almost there.'

The end of their journey loomed ahead like something out of a dark fantasy novel, the evil kingdom in the near distance. Vicky could see what was left of the buildings around the docks behind the squalid hotel, flames reflected in many windows. Fire was ripping through everything still standing now, the light a vivid contrast with the monochrome emptiness of the rest of the world.

'It's like someone's pressed the reset button,' Sam said. The others looked confused, and he explained. 'That fire's going to wipe everything out. There will be nothing left. If it keeps burning, everything's going to disappear. All of London, gone. All that history...'

'It's sad,' Joanne said.

'I know,' he agreed. 'Stupid, isn't it? Millions of people are dead, and yet in some ways this feels worse.'

'What are the chances of anyone being left alive up there?'

'Doesn't matter. We keep going,' Vicky said, no room for negotiation. 'You're right, it might be futile, but while there's the slightest chance, we have to try.'

She started to walk but Eric called her back. 'Wait.'

'You're not talking me out of this. You stop here if you want, but I'm keeping going.'

'It's not that... listen.'

They'd been carefully quiet anyway, but the small group became quieter still, holding their collective breath and wishing the river would stop flowing alongside them for a second.

'I don't hear anything,' Sam said.

'Shh...'

Vicky braced herself, because whatever Eric had heard, it was inevitably going to be more bad news.

The wind. The water. The fire. The shuffling dead.

'You're imagining things, Eric,' Joanne said.

'Shut up and listen!' he yelled, uncharacteristically aggressive.

And they did. And then they heard it. Faint at first, distant, washing in and out on the tide... once they'd locked onto the noise, everything else seemed to fade.

'Sounds like a boat,' Sam said. 'Is that an outboard? Reckon Dominic's had a guilt trip and turned back?'

'It's got to be something to do with the Tower,' Vicky said, and though she tried to move faster, the mud continued to slow her down. Was it the idea of finding survivors that was making her race, or the fear of being left behind? The way life had been treating her recently, she was worried that they'd make it to the Tower of London just in time to see the last of the group disappear, sailing away to safety while the four of them were left to burn.

They walked under a building on stilts that stuck out over the water – something to do with the river police, Joanne recalled – then pressed themselves against the retaining wall where the river swelled and the land all but disappeared for a few metres. The engine noise built and faded continually, swirling around them. That gave Sam a little reassurance. Whoever it was, they weren't leaving just yet.

When the four of them emerged from the shadows of the supported building, they were forced to stop again. This time, they couldn't see a way forward. The riverbank up ahead was a congested mass of dead flesh, no obvious way through. Hundreds of corpses. 'What the fuck?' Sam said.

'What the hell are they all doing down here?' Vicky asked.

'It has to be something to do with the boat, don't you think?' Eric suggested. The outboard was noisier again now, buzzing around like a disproportionately loud fly.

'But that noise isn't loud enough to attract this many of them, is it?' Joanne asked, confused. She had a point. The riverbank ahead was flooded with corpses, as if a rancid wave had broken over the side of the street above.

Sam cautiously edged closer to the nearest cadavers. From this new perspective, he could see a little further. 'There's a jetty, I think. Maybe that's what's got them excited?'

'Is it safe to keep going?' Vicky asked.

'Impossible to tell.'

He could see more bodies dropping down from street level, like a leaking tap dripping putrid jelly. From here, though, he couldn't see why. In the end, it was irrelevant; the only question that needed to be answered was could he and the others get through?

It was looking increasingly unlikely. There were masses of corpses being swept off by the river, thrashing so much that the water seemed to boil, but their numbers were such that despite scores being washed away, hundreds more remained. The first wave of them had become stuck in the mud and trodden down, and now a raft-like layer of bone had been formed across the shingle and sand. It gave those that followed behind some unexpected traction. It allowed them to keep advancing. More of them kept tumbling down.

'They're reacting to each other,' Eric said. 'It's what we saw back at Surrey Quays, remember? It's how we kept them out of our way. They can't see the fires, but they can see what the dead fucks next to them are doing.'

'You're right,' Sam said. 'They're reacting to each other and to that bloody boat.'

'Not quite,' Vicky said, grabbing her crowbar. 'It might have been the noise of the boat that triggered this, but it's us they're interested in now.'

She was right. Irrespective of what had caused them to be here, the entire dead gathering was now focused on her, Sam, Eric, and Joanne.

'We have to keep going forward,' Joanne said, and Eric turned around and saw that there were corpses behind them now too. Back along the riverbank in the direction from which they'd just come, another horde had begun crowding along the mud. He could see them tripping down the old slipway they'd passed moments earlier. For now, most of them were being slowed down by the claggy mud, but it would only be a matter of time before the remains of the bodies that had already gone down began to provide stability to those that followed.

The bubble of space between the group of four and the advancing dead on either side was rapidly disappearing.

Vicky was furious with herself. 'And to think, we seriously thought we'd be able to bring three hundred people back this way and lead them to safety. We couldn't even keep ourselves safe.

We're a bunch of fucking amateurs. I'm sorry I dragged the three of you into this.'

'Don't talk bollocks,' Sam said. 'We'll worry about how we're going to get the others back later. For now, just fight.'

Joanne marched towards the advancing dead and began cutting them down. It was a token gesture, wouldn't even make a dent in their numbers, but it made her feel fractionally better to be doing something. Vicky followed her lead. Sam glanced back and saw that Eric was leaning against the retaining wall, fishing for something in his rucksack.

'What the hell are you doing, man? You need to help. We don't have time to stop for a fucking picnic.'

'Not food,' Eric said, unfazed. 'Something to distract them.'

He rummaged deeper and pulled out a handful of fireworks.

'You and your bloody fireworks. You're not going to rest until you've set them off, are you?'

Eric ignored him and continued to rummage through his bag. 'Shit,' he shouted, loud enough to excite some of the nearest dead and make them move faster towards him. 'Lost my damn matches.'

'Here,' Vicky said, and she threw him her lighter. 'Just make sure I get that back, okay?'

'Okay.'

The dead were closing in. Until now the focus had been on the block of rotting bastards dragging themselves downriver from the west, but the number advancing from the other direction was increasing rapidly. Eric saw corpses spilling down the slipway in unstoppable numbers now, an avalanche of flesh. Even if they weren't capable of posing a threat individually, there was already enough of them here to make any thought of escape back along the riverbank a virtual impossibility. A festering bank of putrefaction was forming that would stop anything getting through.

Sam turned around to see what was happening, then ducked for cover when a firework screeched past his face and shot out over the river. Its high-pitched whistle rose above all other noise as it climbed into the air.

Then silence.

Then a star-shaped burst of green light, followed by a belly-shaking boom. The noise echoed along the Thames, and for a moment, everything seemed to stop. Some of the dead began wading into the water, chasing the noise, others lifted their withered faces to the heavens. But as soon as the echo had faded and the light had died, it was forgotten and forward they marched. Business as usual.

'Do it again,' Sam screamed at Eric, and he obliged. Hands shaking with nerves, he fired another rocket into the air.

Joanne punched her gloved fist into the face of a distracted cadaver, then threw the listless corpse into a group of others, knocking five more down like skittles. Determined to take advantage of the split-second reprieve, she grabbed another one by the arm and swung it around, sending others flying. And in the momentary gap where the dead had just been, she saw a small motorboat racing along the Thames towards them.

'Again, Eric,' she yelled, and a couple of seconds later a third rocket raced up into the air. The whoosh, the roar, the vacuum-like pause, then the detonation. She watched the boat race straight past. 'And again,' she screamed. 'There are too many bodies. They can't see us!'. The volume of her voice made a glut of corpses surge towards her from all angles.

Eric set off another firework. 'Only one left,' he shouted to anyone who could hear.

Sam hacked down as many of the spindly figures as he could, both to try and protect Eric and also to clear a space so they could be seen from the water. He could hear the boat turning around, but feared they'd come past just as fast and would miss them again. Through momentary gaps between random bobbing heads, he caught a glimpse of the motorboat coming back, but he doubted whoever was onboard would be able to see him. He'd lost sight of Vicky and Joanne himself, all of them covered in as much mud and discharge as the corpses, making them all but indistinguishable from the mob that surrounded them. At least the boat was moving a little slower this time, its skipper taking time to navigate the rubbish-strewn water.

'Now, mate,' Sam yelled over to Eric. 'Give it your best shot.'

But as Eric lit the final rocket, corpses collided with him from both sides at once, knocking him to the ground. A dead man dropped on top of him, and the tip of the burning firework wedged into his exposed rib cage. Sam saw what had happened and tried to fight his way through, and though Eric himself did what he could to get the burning firework out and get back to his feet, he'd sunk to his knees in the mud and was unable to stand. The corpse clawed at the flames bursting from its chest and all Eric could do was grab the creature, twist it around and hold its flailing arms behind it as the fuse continue to burn.

The firework exploded like a bomb, destroying the corpse. Sam ducked away from the blast, then scrambled over to help Eric but stopped when he saw what was left of his friend on the ground. Eric had been killed in the blast – a fate as kind as it could have been – and all that remained of the monster he'd been grappling with were burning chunks. There must already have been more than twenty corpses between him and what was left of his friend, all of them closing in on the flames.

'There!' David said, pointing at a position roughly two-thirds along the massive scrum of corpses that stretched along this section of the riverbank. The failed firework had exploded, and now many of the dead were ablaze, burning cadavers staggering aimlessly. On the outermost edge of the confusion, he could see someone fighting, though he couldn't tell who. 'There's someone still out there. Get in close so we can help.'

Chapman did as David said, pointing the bow of the boat directly at the skirmish then racing towards it at full speed. The hull scraped on the shingle shore, wedging into the mud. David jumped out and looked for the woman he thought he'd seen, but all he could see now was more corpses. Almost in unison, they turned and came towards the boat, the engine noise now the focus of their collective ire.

'Bad fucking idea,' Chapman said, panicking. 'We're gonna end up stuck. Get back in...'

But David didn't have a chance. The woman he'd glimpsed fighting burst through the advancing corpses, shoved the boat back, then leapt in. David scrambled back in after her. 'Who the hell are—?' he started to say, but two more people jumped into the boat before he could finish his question. 'Vicky? *Sam?*'

Vicky ignored David and spoke directly to Chapman. 'Go!'

54

Introductions and explanations were handled in the few minutes they were on the water, but all conversations ended abruptly when they reached the Tower of London. The sun was almost fully risen now, and the absolute horror of what was left of the world was in full view. 'Of all the awful things I've seen,' Vicky said with tears running down her dirt-streaked cheeks, 'I don't think anything hurts as much as this.'

The dank hotel where they'd lived in squalor had all but disappeared, reduced to a mound of rubble. On the other side of the Tower, the waterfront apartment building where the group had originally based themselves was still standing but was now just a blackened skeletal frame. Behind it, Tower Place had been similarly ravaged. There were no trees anymore, just lines of stunted charcoal nubs. Everywhere they looked, the ground was covered with the charred remains of an incalculable number of bodies. And more were still coming. Even now, great hordes of them continued to stagger through the maelstrom, congregating at this point.

So much of the area had been destroyed that it was hard to believe it was the same place. The surroundings were all but unrecognisable. But it was what had happened to the Tower itself that shocked them most of all.

1, St Katharine's Way, the building Dominic had used as a lookout and where he'd taken the council less than twenty-four hours earlier to share his great plans, had collapsed onto the raised section of road directly below. With Tower Bridge Approach compromised, the dead had been able to crowd around the outer wall of the Tower itself. Vast accumulations of trampled flesh, rubble, and smoking debris had allowed them to breach the

Tower's defences. Battlements that had held back enemy attacks for centuries had been overcome with relative ease by the undead army. Even now they could be seen staggering along the ramparts, milling listlessly, frequently falling into the grounds of the Tower. Smoke was rising from various parts of the estate, many bodies still burning, keeping the flames alive.

'The whole place will fill up, and there's not a bloody thing we can do to stop it,' Sam said.

'We have to try,' Chapman said, and he steered the boat towards the jetty at Tower Pier.

'Don't,' David said. 'It's too much of a risk. Look.'

The dead were already reacting to the noise of the boat and were staggering down the walkway towards the river. Chapman switched off the engine, and the silence that replaced its noise was deafening.

This was a desolate, lifeless place that belonged to the undead.

'We should just go,' Joanne said. 'Head back to Surrey Quays while we still can. There's nothing worth staying here for. Coming here was a waste of time. A waste of life...'

'We had to try,' Vicky said. '*I* had to try.' Struggling to contain her emotions, she reached into her pocket for a cigarette. The packet was wet, but a couple near the centre had survived intact. She patted her pockets. 'Fuck it. Eric had my frigging lighter.'

'Ironic, eh?' David said. 'The whole of London's burning, and you can't get a light. Probably for the best, Vic. Bad for your health.'

She threw the cigarettes into the river. 'Bollocks.'

'Who's Eric, anyway?' he asked.

'He was an absolute nightmare,' Joanne said. 'He did my head in. He was infuriating to live with, but he saved us just now.'

'We can go back. If there's a chance that he's still alive then maybe we could—'

Sam was shaking his head. 'There's no point. He's gone.'

'But if—'

'There's no point,' he said again, more forceful. 'I saw what was left of him. Awful way to go.'

Other than the rippling of the water against the hull of the boat and the popping and crackling sounds of the fires, the world had become almost completely silent. Vicky stared across the water at what was left of the Tower of London. 'Christ, if the dead can overrun a place like that, what chance did we ever have?'

Chapman agreed. 'Doesn't matter how hard we try, how hard we fight, it won't make any difference. We're the minority, and quickly becoming extinct. It's their world now.'

'Wait, look,' David said, and he pointed towards an area of the battlements where they'd begun to move with more speed, more intent. 'Something's got them riled.'

'Wish I'd thought to hold on to Eric's binoculars,' Vicky said, trying to make sense of what was happening. 'Should have traded him for my lighter.'

A flash of movement caught Joanne's eye. 'Look. What's that?' She put a hand on Vicky's shoulder and pointed up at the building beyond the battlements. There was someone standing on the roof of the White Tower.

'There's someone still alive in there,' David said, struggling to see who it was.

'Poor fuckers,' Joanne said. 'They're trapped, whoever they are. I don't reckon we're ever going to be able to get them out.'

'We're going to have to,' Vicky said. 'I made a promise to her.'

Through the decay and the waste, through the smoke and the flames and the heat haze, through the rubble and the ruins, she could now see who it was on the roof of the White Tower. Her red hoodie gave her away. She was waving their arms furiously at the boat.

'Bloody hell, *is that Selena?*' Sam asked.

Someone else showed up on the roof. 'And Ruth!' Chapman said. More people appeared behind them.

'We need to find a way of getting in and getting them out of there,' David said. 'I can't believe they made it. This is amazing, eh Vic?'

But Vicky didn't answer. She was too busy working out her next steps.

Get into the Tower.

Get the others out, however many were left alive.

Get them out of London.

Get to Ledsey Cross.

THE STORY CONCLUDES
THE LONDON TRILOGY: BOOK III

autumn
EXODUS

ABOUT THE AUTHOR

David Moody first released Hater in 2006 and, without an agent, sold the film rights for the novel to Mark Johnson (producer, Breaking Bad) and Guillermo Del Toro (director, The Shape of Water, Pan's Labyrinth). Moody's seminal zombie novel Autumn was made into an (admittedly terrible) movie starring Dexter Fletcher and David Carradine. He has an unhealthy fascination with the end of the world and likes to write books about ordinary folks going through absolute hell. With the publication of new Autumn and Hater stories, Moody has furthered his reputation as a writer of suspense-laced SF/horror, and "farther out" genre books of all description.

Find out more about his work at:

www.davidmoody.net
facebook.com/davidmoodyauthor
instagram.com/davidmoodyauthor
twitter.com/davidjmoody

"Moody is as imaginative as Barker, as compulsory as King, and as addictive as Palahniuk." —*Scream the Horror Magazine*

"Moody has the power to make the most mundane and ordinary characters interesting and believable, and is reminiscent of Stephen King at his finest." —*Shadowlocked*

"British horror at its absolute best." —*Starburst*

"As demonstrated throughout his previous novels, readers should crown Moody king of the zombie horror novel" —*Booklist*

If you are the original purchaser of this book, or if you received this book as a gift, you can download a complementary eBook version by visiting:

www.infectedbooks.co.uk/ebooks

and completing the necessary information (terms and conditions apply)